THE

CITY

INSIDE

ALSO BY SAMIT BASU

The Simoqin Prophecies
The Manticore's Secret
The Unwaba Revelations

Turbulence
Resistance

SAMIT BASU

THE
CITY
INSIDE

A TOM DOHERTY ASSOCIATES BOOK
NEW YORK

THE CITY INSIDE

Copyright © 2020 by Samit Basu

Edited by Sanaa Ali-Virani

A Tordotcom Book
Published by Tom Doherty Associates
120 Broadway
New York, NY 10271

www.tor.com

Tor® is a registered trademark of Macmillan Publishing Group, LLC.

The Library of Congress Cataloging-in-Publication Data is available upon request.

ISBN 978-1-250-82748-7 (hardcover)
ISBN 978-1-250-82749-4 (ebook)

Our books may be purchased in bulk for promotional, educational, or business use. Please contact your local bookseller or the Macmillan Corporate and Premium Sales Department at 1-800-221-7945, extension 5442, or by email at MacmillanSpecialMarkets@macmillan.com.

Originally published in India as *Chosen Spirits* by Simon and Schuster India

First U.S. Edition: 2022

Printed in the United States of America

0 9 8 7 6 5 4 3 2 1

There was a city, famed throughout the world,
Where dwelt the chosen spirits of the age;
Delhi its name, fairest among the fair.
Fate looted it and laid it desolate,
And to that ravaged city I belong.

(Mir Taqi Mir, Urdu poet, 1782)

THE

CITY

INSIDE

CHAPTER 1

Sometimes Joey feels like her whole life is a montage of randomly selected, algorithm-controlled surveillance cam clips, mostly of her looking at screens or sitting glazed-eyed at meetings. As a professional image builder and storyteller, she finds the lack of structure even more offensive than the banality of the material. She's always taken pride in her instinct for cuts and angles and rhythms in the wildly successful stories she produces—one day, one perfect day, her life will be just as award-worthy.

As she heads into the park near her parents' house for her regular Sunday-morning run—actually the first in three months, but she's finally managed to wake up early this time; it's usually way too hot to be outside the house by the time she reaches Little Bengal for her weekly visit—she finds herself idly building another montage in her mind. A classic training sequence, where she builds an incredible body through first failing and then succeeding at the same task, intercut with determined running, some weights, an optional animal sidekick, rounded off with a motivational hope-hop soundtrack. Even the idea is tiring, and she considers going straight to her parents' house; it's already hot enough to make her eyes twitch.

Instead, she goes through her fitness checklist: headphones in place, cooling sportswear hopefully working as much as possible in Delhi, smog/plague maxmask already making her face sweat, water bottle and pepper spray in the right slots on her smartbelt. A few stretches, and she's off along the jogging track, keeping a wary eye out for battling stray dogs and monkeys lurking in the trees. The track's distance markers are all in place: the fascist uncle laughing club shouting national pride slogans while leering at her, the neighbourhood wives ambling along in large groups shouting to be heard over the blaring devotional music on their phones, workers attempting their weekly repair of the park's mysteriously smashed surveillance cams.

She sees the kolam on her third lap, when she slows down for a second to catch her breath. It's a simple one, a basic floral pattern with embedded hashtags drawn on a cement patch next to a manhole cover in blue chalk. Joey quickly checks to see the nearest park cam is disabled, takes a picture of the kolam, and uploads it to a decoder app which tells her in a second about the protest it's an invite for: another slum is being evacuated by the police and builder militia. It's not far, it's the neighbourhood where Laxmi, her parents' domestic helper, used to live before she moved to Kalkaji with her boyfriend, a Cyber Bazaar shop owner. The app tells her this protest's potential bloodshed rating is "Extremely High." There's a cheerful wiggly blood drop icon.

On her wrist, her smartatt pulses: a stress alert. The smart tattoo's a new design; her skin's still red around it. A cute elephant-butt pattern that amuses Flowstars and makes funders think it's a Ganesh tribute—Joey has always known how to bridge worlds.

She rubs her wrist to stop the alert, but her Narad has woken up on her phone.

—Joey, good morning, are you all right? she messages.

Joey gestures at the phone, I'm fine, go to sleep, but Narad sends her a stream of loving emojis and virtual hugs.

—Let's get you smiling with some great stress-relief exercises and techniques!

—No.

—I see you are at your parents' park. Infection forecasts say today is a low-risk day. Great work on your daily step count! Should we do some fun yoga?

—No.

—I have set up a loveable dog video blast every half hour. Feel better! You are loved.

Joey pockets her phone and takes a few deep breaths. But it's too late: as her playlist starts up again, the beat is exactly the same as the drums that were playing at the protest she'd been to, and she's right back there, hearing the students chant, wishing she knew all the words, staring in growing fear at the riot police amassing behind the barricades, at the water cannon behind them.

She'd been fifteen, and her first board exams had been around the corner, so her mother hadn't wanted to take her along. But her father had insisted: "This is a historic moment, and she needs to be out on the street, she needs to see there are people like us there," Avik had said. The protest was at Jantar Mantar, against the first wave of discriminatory citizenship laws, and their privilege had kept them perfectly safe. She'd made a poster, something meme-friendly, she can't even recall what it was. What she remembers most was the energy: young men and women, not much older than her, rising up with the tricolour to try and save the country, the Constitution, the unity that India was founded with . . . that the regime was trying so hard to destroy. Her parents had seemed strangely thrilled—that evening, after an epic journey home in the cold, they'd explained they'd thought they were alone, that most people in the country had been swallowed up by a tide of bigotry and hate. They'd never been happier being proved wrong.

She'd gone to a few more protests with her parents, before they'd insisted she stop coming along and focus on her studies, and they'd all pretended this had nothing to do with large-scale attacks on students around the country, that Avik and Romola hadn't held each other and cried when they watched news of police storming hospitals and libraries, that images of battered and blood-drenched students hadn't flooded Joey's private messengers. That things weren't about to get a lot worse. That a day wouldn't come, soon after, when Joey wasn't allowed to leave her house and her parents didn't know whether to blame the pogrom or the pandemic, because they'd known the end times were coming but hadn't known they'd be multiple choice.

But a decade later, Joey's memories of those days are happy and hopeful, full of an energy and a sense of belonging she hasn't felt in years. It had taken a day for her to become an expert on identifying propaganda and its unlikeliest distributors. She'd quickly learned the words to "Hum Dekhenge" and all the trickiest protest chants—she still remembers them, though she's smart enough not to say them out loud. She'd held her mother's hand at a reading of the Preamble to the Constitution at India Gate, while news filtered in of police brutalities and illegal detentions at a less privileged march. They'd brought in that new year at Shaheen Bagh, with a crowd of people, all ages, all religions, all classes, standing together, singing the national anthem, reclaiming the flag—Joey had wanted to go and sit with the women at the heart of it all, the now-legendary women of Shaheen Bagh, wanted to go sit with her mother and be offered biryani and companionship by strangers, and huddle under a blanket and sing songs of hope and revolution. But there had just been too many people between them and her. They'd stood at a bonfire, watching their breath steam, wrapping their gloved hands around warming cups of tea. There were doctors and volunteers and biscuits and packets of medicine and students with candles, and signs in many languages, and more strength and solidarity and heartbreak in the air than Joey could breathe in.

She'd decided, that night, that she wouldn't leave. That she would stay in India, in Delhi, and belong as hard as she could. Many years, many good-byes and many funerals later, she still cannot accept that she made a huge mistake. But sometimes it feels like everyone she thought she'd grow up around has left—so many of her peers, the generation her parents learned to admire as the children of blood and fire who were paradropped straight out of their adolescence into a citizens' uprising against totalitarianism, simply got tired and faded away, or changed into something unrecognisable. Like Shaheen Bagh, which now exists only in memory—she knew nothing of it before the protests, and refuses to learn its new name. Was it even real?

She's tried, over the years, to find out what happened to the student leaders she grew up admiring, those clear-eyed, calm, incredibly brave women and men who stared down thugs with batons and marched in straight lines chanting in perfect unison towards armed police—but there aren't any clear patterns. Some were killed, horribly, slowly, publicly and without consequence, to demonstrate to her generation, especially her class, some essential truths about the world outside their walls, to teach them to be quiet, to look away. Other leaders disappeared into detention centres, or off the map, to other countries or the hinterlands. Some disappeared altogether, and it was dangerous to even look them up, or say their names. Many were still around, struggling through the feudal systems of one political party or another and slowly transforming into the politicians they'd loathed in college, or working regular-person jobs like Joey's, trying to pretend the light in their eyes hadn't dimmed, that they hadn't given up. She'd helped a couple find jobs last year. She hadn't asked them the one question she'd wanted to, the one everyone in the country had asked at some point: Did we win? I thought we'd won. Didn't we win?

"Don't make the same mistakes we did," her father says to her, even now, years too late. "This country lied to us, told us we'd be a part of the world, told us things were changing. But it showed you its real face. We'll miss you terribly. Get out." He'd been saying this ever since she told them, after college, that she didn't really want to escape abroad. Her mother had just held her close, and had said she was delighted not to lose her, and things would turn out well in the end. But each weekend, when Romola asks Joey about work, Joey can see her mother feeling guilty, for absolutely no reason.

It's mid-morning when Joey finally decides to go indoors and get some fresh air. She enters her parents' flat and tiptoes past their bedroom towards hers. They're unnaturally quiet—by this time, they're normally sitting at breakfast ready to complain about how late she is.

"They're not home," Laxmi calls from the kitchen. "They went for a job interview." Her brother's home, though, she can hear snores emanating from his room. Laxmi emerges with breakfast on a tray: she insists on cooking everything by hand, ignoring the plaintive beeps of both the food processor and the smartfridge. She looks at Joey enquiringly and holds out an arm, but Joey hasn't brought her laundry with her this week.

Joey shows Laxmi the photo of the protest kolam from the park, and raises an eyebrow. Laxmi shakes her head.

"I'm thinking of going," Joey says.

"Not for you, didi," Laxmi says. "There will be blood, and no cameras on police."

"Are you going?"

"Yes."

"Then I want to come too."

But Laxmi shakes her head firmly. "Raja and his boys will look after me. Didi, when it is time for you to come to one of these, I will tell you. Not safe for you now."

They've had this conversation before, and Joey wonders, as she digs into her breakfast, if Laxmi can tell how relieved she is each time, and whether she'll actually make it out of the door the day Laxmi tells her she's needed, if any of the courage she'd thought she'd had in her mid-teens still lingered inside her.

By the time her parents return, Joey's already finished lunch and is fast asleep on the living room sofa, while the TV plays her long-abandoned must-see streaming list. It's not her parents who wake her up though: it's her smartatt, which sends a tingle up her wrist, overriding her sleep settings, to warn her that a Favourite Contact is calling for the third time. Her parents wave encouragingly at her as she stomps by them, glaring at her buzzing phone, wiping drool off her chin. Of course it's bloody Indi, avatar swaying cockily as he smiles, hey girl. Her Narad pops up on the screen, raises an inquisitive eyebrow at her. Indi loves surprise video calls, but she shakes her head, gesturing towards the audio-only option. Narad shrugs, and disappears to argue with Indi's AI.

"We had a lovely lunch at the mall," her mother says to her back. "Lebanese."

"That's nice," Joey says. "Did you get the job?"

"Actually I was the one who applied," Avik says. "But they—"

Narad appears to let Joey know Indi insists on video, but she's not having it. It takes three rounds, but Indi finally agrees to voice.

"I had an amazing idea," he says. "So, when we meet the Sach-Voice guys, we—"

"It's Sunday, Indi," Joey says. "Do you have a medical emergency?"

"Listen. This is how we're going to play it—"

She disconnects, wondering as she does every week why he feels compelled to do this; she's told him so many times it isn't cute. Indi doesn't call back. He has plenty of other people to bother, and the idea he's about to suggest is one she sent him weeks ago.

She clears her throat, and turns to her parents again, noting with some relief that they've occupied the sofa and turned on TV news. Relief not because of the news, which is never good, but because she hates hearing about how difficult it is for her parents to find good jobs.

Today's news crisis is the discovery of an automated ship in the Indian Ocean swarming with East African climate change refugees, clinging on to the deckless craft like ants in the rain, preferring to risk incredible dangers crossing to unknown lands instead of being slaughtered by European vigilante pirate crews. Her brother's clearly messed up the family TV content filters; it's pretty obvious why he would want content filters off on the biggest screen in the house, but her parents shouldn't be seeing this much death. Fortunately there are no dead babies today, but before Joey manages to turn the screen off the damage is done: already images from a concentration camp in Assam and an off-the-record crematorium pyre-cluster near Bhopal have burned themselves into their brains. She's grown up with pictures like this—sometimes the faces in the news have been people she's met—but her parents have to be sheltered with filters. They never recovered from the Years Not to Be Discussed, from the sieges and the razings, the oxygen blockades and new mutant virus strains and rivers full of corpses. She and Rono must protect them from the psy-op epidemic of confusion and rage that still threatens to engulf the whole country, hoping all the while that the Residents' Association's guards keep the street outside their balcony free of blood.

Her parents haven't had steady work in years: they lost their high-paying jobs over the span of a single week while Joey was in college, when the economy had gone over a cliff: her father over a Facebook rant and her mother because she hadn't understood that it was a loyalty-based economy now, and hadn't been able to adjust when an oligarch bought her ad agency. She suspects neither Avik nor Romola feel particularly good that their daughter works for some mid-level oligarchs, but it keeps her safe and pays the bills, and all the non-oligarchs are broke.

Joey switches her parents over to her streaming account, sets them up on a nostalgic sitcom binge, and slides on the sofa next to them, hoping to slip into her standard Sunday rhythm of sleeping through the day; there's nothing like the background buzz of her family's voices to help her catch up on her weekly sleep quota. The TV's on a bit too loud, but her high-decibel tolerance has always been impressive—there's not been any choice on that front, really. The problem is that she's been having too many Real Thoughts since morning, thanks to that bloody kolam, and real sleep hovers frustratingly out of reach. Instead, she can feel a massive headache building, heralding the arrival of her nemesis, the brain fade that envelops her most days, every time she manages to take her mind off work for five minutes.

She doesn't even notice when she breaks her weekend phone-avoidance rule, or how much time she spends wandering the corners of the web, pinballing between mass murder, microaggressions, monologues, and masterclasses—she gets lost, as usual, and has no idea why she's reading an article about '20s AI music, when her smartatt pulses: screen haze alert. The new smartatt itches less than the last one, but she still has to physically stop herself from scratching compulsively at her left wrist every time it tingles. The first time she'd had a smartatt done, she used to wake up every morning with abrasions on her wrists, from clawing at the tattoo in her sleep.

Narad sends her support signs again, but she finds herself yearning for non-Roy humans, for her college squad, her own women. Every weekend she promises herself she'll stay out of the Flowverse until work calls again, but she's never made it. The truth is, watching the perfectly curated lives of people she actually knows has never caused Joey the anxiety attacks and melancholy that affect everyone she knows: it's because Joey has always had a secret system, one that she believes led her to her often soul-destroying line of work, that allows her to succeed at it without becoming the kind of monster she's seen her peers transform into.

It's quite simple: Joey has mind-tricked herself into believing that all the people whose Flows she watches actually work for her, perform for her like her actual Flowstar clients—she's delegated the task of having life experiences to them. Every perfect yoga pose, every bright-eyed dog, every star-struck new lover, every impeccably plated meal exists at her command. She's commissioned each live holiday, each luxury sunset, each lavish wedding, each impressive run map, outsourced every new baby, every inspirational thought, every life hack, every makeup tip. Flow-makers owe her their abs, their afterglows, their banter, even their families.

There's only one person this trick never works for, and that's Toons, her oldest and closest friend, now wandering around the world with her diplomat family, being a poet–dancer–painter–3D-print-sculptor–fashionista-genius, setting performance goals she wishes her Flowstars could match. Toons isn't in her phone at all times anymore, eager to overanalyse the minutest details of her life: she said new government instructions to diplomat families are to minimise private conversations because they're targets for world-class hackers, and that she'd gotten into enough trouble over the years for being more radical-leftist than a diplomat's daughter was allowed to be, but Joey can't help feeling her best friend's left her. It's at least partly her own fault: between travel bans on Indians and her own schedule, their plans of meeting for holidays all around the world kept not working out, year after year—and then they both just stopped trying. Toons was her life-management app, her aesthetics pop-up, her live-location watcher, her inactivity warning notification, and all she has left is Narad, a very poor substitute. Narad can't absentmindedly fix her hair.

Most people find gossip groups comforting after subjecting themselves to Flows, but for Joey it's the opposite. The industry Fetch-boards where people post anonymous insider accounts are difficult because you have to filter for lies, sales, ongoing vendettas and cliques, and hidden political connections. Worse, you have to spend a lot of time reading wild industry conspiracy theories: going by the stories Joey reads about herself on the Flowverse Fetch-board, the truth/absurd lie ratio is about 1/7.

On her actual-friend groups, she's intimidated, as always, watching the people she's grown up with trade stories not about their lives or the news, but about a host of people they all seem to have in common: Delhi's most influential personal stylists, most politically connected yoga teachers, most distress-sale-aware real estate agents, flash-gathering photographers, insider-trading accountants, and inner-circle caterers. She wants to apply her delegation brain-trick here but can't: they're not finding these people at her command; they're clearly all part of a vast conspiracy to exclude her.

It's taken her a few years to understand why she's so bothered by this set: in a world where most public news is a lie and everyone's Flows curate only their successes, humans who move around the city sharing stories from the houses of the powerful are valuable in their own right, power accessories her circles are eager to collect. Smaller groups circle the larger friend groups like seagulls, filling in anecdotes about common friends who recently had a bitter fallout over a handsome dog-walker. She'd heard the rich had always been like this, but to see her own friends do this is still surprising. It's some sort of Delhi thing, clearly, this low-level court intrigue: her Mumbai friends are the opposite. They keep recommending and trying to share their amazing acupuncturists, past-life therapists, and crystal healers, and complaining that no one wants them.

She doesn't remember when she last logged in to her own Flow, so she does, just staring into the cam, smiling a little, then adding a few pictures of herself in a sari that she'd worn to a wedding and saved for a time like this. It's Sunday afternoon, so she doesn't expect anyone to actually see it, but she reminds herself to switch her stats-optimising brain off, it's not about her, it's never been about her, and a few people send love, enough love to curl up, turn off her phone, and fall asleep.

She awakens to the sound of strangers shouting, and for a second she thinks she's dozed off in the middle of a shoot, and leaps up in blind panic, but it's just her brother, arguing on his headset as he emerges into the living room with an open tablet, a cabal of other teenagers on speaker yelling at him to get back in their game, speaking in tongues absolutely no adult can comprehend. She waits for him to go away, but he stands in front of her. It is possible he's trying to communicate.

"What time is it?" Joey asks, blinking furiously.

"We have to talk," Rono says. "Actually, you have to talk to the parents."

"Why? What did you do? I don't have any money."

"I don't need your money. You have to tell them I'm dropping out of school."

She starts to tell him she's doing nothing of the sort, but Rono has things to say, and proceeds with the grim determination of a mainstreamer news host. Broken exams, corrupt admissions, no jobs, the future is Blockhead mixed-reality self-teaching. It's a monologue he's been working on for a while, but Joey's had years of experience avoiding professional speech-makers, and a lifetime of ignoring Rono.

"No," she says finally. "Tell them yourself."

"They don't understand me."

"No one understands you, Rono." He treats their parents like infants: mumbles at them in teenspeak, then repeats himself, louder and slower, when they ask him what he meant. She's not surprised they lose their minds.

"Shit, they're doing it again. Go stop them," Rono says, looking at their parents' bedroom.

"Rono, you are not dropping out of school and I'm not—"

"Forget that. Just listen."

She can hear raised voices, and they're talking about . . . Kashmir? Joey races towards their room. Left together unsupervised, they've started again: escalated some possibly unemployment-related argument into a full-scale fight about the State of the Nation. And in the heat of the moment, they're likely to say things they'll both regret. She barges in and makes the standard gestures—they stop immediately, and stare back at her with their usual mix of rage and shame.

It's not really their fault; it's hard for the middle-aged to change. She's seen the way they used to live. Before the Years Not to Be Discussed, before every smart person in the country had removed their opinion archives from their first-gen social media accounts, her mother had saved screenshots of her favourite posts—not just hers and Avik's, but the unwise outpourings of their whole generation, the collected unfiltered rants of a large cross-section of analog dinosaur kids, people who had actually used landline telephones, cassettes, and other relics now immortalised in nostalgic T-shirts. Joey still goes through Romola's screenshot archive sometimes and shakes her head at their foolishness every time: they gave away so much about themselves, all for free, just shovelled all their personal data into the maws of the open internet.

Joey can't imagine what that must have been like, the freedom to criticise the powerful and corrupt in your own homes. Nothing that had happened since—not the repeated pandemic-wave collapses, not the blasphemy laws in several states, not the mass de-citizenings, the voter list erasures, the reeducation camps, the internet shutdowns, the news censors, the curfews, not even the scary stories of data-driven home invasions, not the missing person smartscrolls on every lamppost—had succeeded in convincing Romola or Avik that the world had really changed, that the present was not merely a passing aberration. She knows they try their best to learn the new world and each week's new set of New India rules, but then they forget. They still think their privilege keeps them safe.

The last decade has been more or less a lab rat experience for her parents: the Years Not to Be Discussed have spun Avik and Romola around and presented them hoop after passcode-pending hoop to jump through, treadmill after additional-document-requiring treadmill to run on, so even in these shiny New Hope years they seem hesitant, afraid. On her fiftieth birthday Romola had told Joey that while the party was great, the cake was unnecessarily passive-aggressive. She simply couldn't understand how fifty could be the new thirty-five and the new seventy at the same time. Her children, fortunately, have never grown up with this primitive faith in single realities.

Joey diverts her parents down with the easiest available distraction—guys, you have to see this puppy adoption show—and leads them back to the TV, wondering all the while whether there's an invisible sign on her forehead saying "Will Solve Your Crisis for Free." But it works: soon her parents giggle on the sofa, accidentally mirroring each other as they lose themselves in their smartpacifiers. This counts as a win. They've been prevented from ranting about this government, or any of the last few. There will be no van full of murderers pulling up outside their house today.

She's explained to them a hundred times that she isn't paranoid, and that there are examples of people disappearing every day for saying the wrong things, if only they'd learn to see. That earlier, before the '20s, they could do the whole "free speech" thing because they weren't important enough to bother the powerful, or insignificant enough to erase without anyone noticing, and also, most importantly, because surveillance used to be run by humans in the good old days.

It's your own house spying on you now. The walls really have ears. You could avoid nosy neighbours, or be wary around potential access-caste climbers. She'd tried and failed to make Avik understand that his new toothbrush heard every word he said and had been listening very carefully since he was tricked into buying it, trying to see if what came out of his mouth was as filthy as his teeth: his chief interest seemed to be learning whether his farts were being recorded and sent to data tracker centres via space. Romola's fascinated by the idea that anything she says or types is travelling around the world, going to places she'll never manage to physically visit, but can't process the idea that it isn't just the government snooping anymore, but a peak-traffic cluster of corporations, other governments, religious bodies, cults, gangs, terrorists, hackers, sometimes other algorithms, watching you, measuring you, learning you, marking you down for spam or death. They'd explained to Joey years ago, when successfully persuading her not to go to farmhouse parties with her wilder classmates, that in New New Delhi, the only crime was nonconformity, and conformity was a fast-shifting, ever-angry chimera that must be constantly fed. Joey had learnt that lesson well—too well, she often worries—but her parents hadn't listened to themselves.

She wonders when their roles reversed, whether her parents were hustling her into running things at least two decades too early, each time she delivers her weekly safety lecture—every stranger who comes to the house might be a secret agent of a data mining company, planting tiny cams and mikes for their employers. They always hear her out patiently, but when the attack happened just last month, it was Laxmi who found the tiny molka cams under the kitchen sink, not her parents. It was Laxmi who'd pushed them into searching the whole house for cams and mikes, Laxmi who'd found them all, except one, because her father had taken charge of inspecting his own bathroom and had continued to send unknown eyes images of his ass descending like a magnificent eclipse on the commode for two whole weeks. They knew who'd planted the molka cams too, a house-cleaning crew they'd hired off an app. But every complaint they'd made had disappeared into the void. Laxmi had muttered a lot about punishment, if any, going only to the cleaners, who weren't the ones perving on their victims, and that no one knew what young girls in the slums went through with these cams.

They say they've seen all this before—the fear of speaking out, the fear of people around you, the fear that you'd wake up one morning to find you'd lost everything—no bank account, no citizenship, no job, no rights. It's fear they live with, just like the fear, in their twenties, of a terrorist bomb in every market, every empty car, back when terrorists and the government were on different sides. Letting this fear get to you, letting it dictate your actions, isolate you, leech away your life . . . those were the things they have learnt to overcome.

"At some point of time there's so much fear that all of it just disappears. Then you just let go of all fear and do whatever needs doing. Your generation taught us that, Joey," her mother had said with extreme firmness once. "That's how the generation that freed India lived their lives. I'm sorry, but that's how your generation must live yours."

"This isn't about saving the country, Ma," she'd said. "If you want to learn something from my generation, here's a good one. Don't use one-two-three-four as your password. And don't say things that get your IDs cancelled—because you know it'll take years to get them back."

"I'm not going to just sit and watch other people because I'm too scared to do anything," Romola had said. "You shouldn't either."

But there was nothing that Romola could actually do. And after a friend's daughter had disappeared, a few days after attending a protest against the demolition of her school, Romola had given up the idea of taking to the streets.

What frustrates Joey now is that Avik and Romola refuse to follow even the simplest safety protocols—treating every text exchange like a public performance, speaking in metaphors, changing speech patterns, even basic deliberate mispronunciations and typos—it's all too much work. "My language learning ended with emojis when you were still in school," her father had said. "It's too late now to learn all these new dances. And you keep forgetting that those bastards in the . . . fine. The Brotherhood of Evil Mutants has been defeated. Fraudzilla is dead. The Nazis, no, the Talib, no, the . . . damn it, Hydra has gone away." Though Hydra, they all know, hasn't gone anywhere. Their masters no longer need them for distraction or land grabs, so they've just grown smarter, and stopped hogging all cameras, and sent their killer hordes into the shadows, a receding tide of hate and violence leaving broken cultures and blood feuds in their wake that will haunt every neighbourhood in the country for generations. Now they conduct their most savage acts in parts of the country where no one dares to record them—or even whisper about them.

"In the towns of Uttar Pradesh"—Romola's stand-in post-apocalyptic wilderness of choice—"they never knew privacy or freedom, so they never mourned their loss. We thought we had them, so it's a little difficult for us, no?"

"As it is I have had to stop going out because smog reduces brain activity," her father says. "I have to air-seal the whole house." He often complains that his life has turned into some kind of totalitarian reality show: she's fairly sure he still doesn't understand that managing one is his daughter's job.

Her father's running joke is that she is living proof of the theory of evolution—he spent his life never knowing how to work his contacts in a bubble of endless possibility, but she was pragmatic enough to recognise the worst job market in history and pick a smart job, even if it meant working with her college ex.

"My daughter is a Reality Controller," he always says. "Her parents are reality deniers."

Her actual designation is Associate Reality Controller now: it was Senior Reality Manager a month ago. She still can't say either without cringing.

She wakes up again in her bedroom, with no memory of when and how she got there. At times like this, she looks forward to getting back to work: the constant adrenaline rush of Flow-running clearly keeps her at least vaguely conscious of where she is and why. One of her pet nightmares is waking up in a lab to find someone had hacked her brain, that the gaps in her memory were because someone was literally stealing her time. Sometimes she wants to play back her fantasy montage of her life, just to see what it was she actually did on Sundays, to make sure she wasn't possessed by some malignant spirit. She catches herself wondering whether it would be possible to actually produce, procure, and view twenty-four/seven surveillance of herself, the ultimate real-time selfie, and realises this is how she actually spends her time: she just wastes it.

When she shuffles out to the living room again, she finds her parents still on the sofa, arguing amicably with Rono about the various negatives of his dropping out of school and embracing a freelance hacker-for-hire life. Even though he doesn't turn towards her as she draws closer, she can sense him getting a little more dramatic, a little more articulated: these performances are always aimed at Joey. She hates it when Rono does this, though it's nice to see her parents sit next to each other for once, united by their desire to encourage their eccentric-potential-genius son. Her mother, despite her lifelong expertise in praising Joey only when absolutely forced to, often shows a suspiciously voluble appreciation for Rono's ingenuity and cunning, and Joey is convinced it's all orchestrated: she can feel her parents glancing towards her too, star parents in waiting at their baby's audition. She's seen so many friend groups try this down the years.

Rono thinks the only thing keeping him from being a top Flowstar is his sister's stubborn refusal, despite years of evidence, to accept his brilliance and sign him up as a client. He thinks she's jealous.

He's been performing for her—subtly, he thinks—every Sunday for months. His thoughts, his gamefeeds, his teen life and feelings. His friends, their on-point banter on topics both incredibly intimate and strikingly global-trending. Their various short-form-video friendly shenanigans, pranks, fails, vox pops with unfriendly passersby, SoDel metro-rap, a spectacularly botched attempt at neighbourhood parkour.

Under Joey's horrified eye, he's started to wear his best clothes at home, clean himself up, figure out his best lighting, customise his dialogue patterns to multiformat-friendly sound bites. Last weekend, he'd even worn his precious screenshirt, running a slideshow on his chest that ran low-reses of his artiest photography projects, QRs embedded, while he played his guitar in the living room. And Rono handles it better than his friends, who often drop in casually to just hang out and deliver scripted Flowcoms. If only it were just the teenagers. She's seen it happen to everyone she meets: the switch from general performance-under-possible-surveillance to performance-for-talent-audition.

Even Laxmi provides her City Life Insights from time to time, didi, you know how it is for street people like us in the big city. But Laxmi's fortunately not interested in a Flow career of her own: if life had dealt them different cards, Joey could actually see her as a fellow Reality Controller. She often shows Joey indie Flows from the slums, or low-income immigrant neighbourhoods like nearby Kalkaji: a lot of protest rap, graffiti, tech education videos, some street sports. Joey's spent many fascinating weekend hours watching Laxmi's curations: she never asks Joey to sign up any of her friends, and is always eager to learn what she'd have done if she were in charge.

She'd tried to hire Laxmi once, to set up a whole new category of Flows for her, but Laxmi had refused, and she hadn't pushed it. Again, as always with Laxmi, there was always secret relief: Joey couldn't imagine how her family would get along without her.

She can hear her mother calling her name, drawing her attention to something smart Rono just said, but she feels the fade rising up inside her again, watches the dull filter descending between her and the room. She's overcome by the urge to go outside, and half runs towards the balcony, but when she pulls at the balcony door Narad pops up, and tells her the air quality outside is hazardous. She'll have to put on a mask. She doesn't want to put on a mask. Not to go to the bloody balcony. She leans on the door; the glass is smudgy. Outside, an ad drone floats by, announcing discounts on massages by trained young girls. Sparks fly as it flies past a dangling, disconnected electric supply wire. Their block has private power backup now; board-supply electricity is increasingly unreliable, and then, of course, there are special occasions, like the time six months ago when a local industrialist's son decided to test ride his new Swiss jetpack and got stuck in the wires that crisscrossed the road just two streets down, killing himself and shutting down half of Little Bengal for days.

A defiant pigeon stares back at Joey from the ancient bel tree that stands opposite their house, a miraculous survivor of years of street reconstruction, a far too frequently used symbol of hope and resilience for her whole family. She'd recently heard a take on how women should sleep with men who knew the names of trees, which indicated a deep connection to nature. But Joey doesn't know the names of trees herself, so how would she know if these men were telling the truth? As a child, she used to be terrified of the bel tree every time it bore fruit, always picturing those rock-hard green spheres smashing her skull as she crossed underneath. Romola would make her a summer drink from those fruits, a sticky, pale yellow sludge with lots of ice, and she'd never told her all through school that she absolutely hated the taste, that she always imagined her own pulped brain in the glass.

In the distance, a patriotic song announces the arrival of the local Residents' Welfare Association's guard troop: already, one neighbourhood uncle after another is emerging from a nearby balcony, smog mask in place, to salute the troops as they pass by. Only the very top-most uncles in the RWA pyramid get to write inspirational messages on the whiteboard at the block's gates: the rest must content themselves with feeling the fire rise in their loins once a day as the guards march past, before they return to their houses to bully their families, emerging only when the night water supply siren goes off, to stand in gargoyle-like vigil near their water tanks, waiting in lonely gauntness for the sequence of groans and gurgles that announce the arrival of the day's quota of rust-coloured sludge.

Their block's guard army has covered itself in glory recently, winning a pitched battle with hired water-mercenaries from a raiding Kalkaji block who were trying to divert a water truck shipment. They're all dressed as Independence-era Netaji troops, their shoutout to Bengali pride slightly diminished by the printed posters on their backs advertising discounts on paneer specials at a nearby Pure Veg restaurant. Most of the guards are very young, boys displaced from some erased village, or tossed out of some horrific brain-wipe camp, and pressed into service. Better in uniform than not: this same cluster of boys would have made Joey very nervous on the street if they weren't saluting her as she passed. They're armed with batons and riot shields, not the 3D-printed handguns that the more up-market guards in Joey's own neighbourhood carry, but their weapons are enough to cause serious damage. Laxmi's told Joey that private RWA armies have their own version of football leagues going on: there are star guards transferred from neighbourhood to neighbourhood at exorbitant price, even coaches and military strategists who run a guard league from the Culture Colonies. Her parents are glad Little Bengal's guards are relatively cheap: guard-army upgrades and water-protection-bribe surcharges have been the key reason for South Delhi's ever-increasing rents since the mid-'20s. Joey doesn't know how long she's been standing by the balcony door now. Being home is not unlike being at work; it's relentless, it's exhausting, except people listen to her at work, they're paid to, and she has a little more control over the programming.

—Hey there beautiful, you're stressed, texts Narad. Go to the kitchen! I've made you some iced tea.

Joey stumbles towards the kitchen. Her family is at it still; it's like they're on loop. Laxmi looks at her with concern as the processor pings to announce completion, and offers to pour her tea out, but Joey waves her and her concerns aside. The tea is good. Staring at the cubes floating in it is even better. Narad blows her kisses from her screen, and the processor's humming again, and she doesn't know what Narad's making now and a little worried because she knows she's going to like it.

"Am I depressed?" she whispers to Narad.

—Hi Joey, it's the weekend again! Gentle reminder to see your happiness mountain progress—your mountain buddies haven't seen you in four months! They miss you, and your sherpa reward points are going to expire soon! Would you like to—

"No, Narad. Didn't I ask you to uninstall that nonsense?"

—Let's hang on to it for a bit, it's essential! We can't finish the journey to happiness together unless we track and celebrate the steps!

"Uninstall all happiness tracker apps, please."

—But they'll make you happier, Joey!

"Happiness isn't measurable."

—That's not what science tells us! Measuring it helps you know it's real. Let's take a look at your current stats and—

She taps Narad silent.

Her parents are very pleased when Joey interrupts them with a tray full of smoothies, and want an intra-family debate about Rono's future, but Joey's done. She tells them she'll see them soon, and trudges off towards her bedroom. She wishes, later, that she hadn't, because if she had just pretended to care about whatever it was, if she'd just crashed on the sofa and snored until dawn, she wouldn't have been nearest to her father's phone when the message came. She wouldn't have been the one who saw it. She wouldn't have had to tell her father that his oldest friend was dead.

CHAPTER 2

The office car is waiting outside Joey's Harmony Place apartment building when her taxi rattles to a halt behind it, and the driver holds a door open and looks at her suspiciously as she rushes past him into her lobby: a quick scan for evidence of illicit sexual activity.

Her flat is as impeccable as always, everything in its perfect place under this morning's layer of dust, she's just flowers, food, and friends away from party-hosting readiness. Joey's flat is her pride and joy, the only part of her life that's wholly adulted (apart from the out-of-order smartwasher), aesthetically arranged (a set designer needed a favour), and adequately tidy (she believes this is because she's very rarely home). She always intends to have many guests over, perhaps next weekend, but there's never time for a proper party, and her last few lonely-swipe male visitors have displayed no interest in interior decoration.

She can't remember the last guy's face, only his topknot: the memory of it tickling her thighs distracts her briefly. How long ago was it, even? It's funny how her visual memory's started working like a three-second SanSan video: nameless topknot guy stirs and begins to look up at her, but the memory loops before his eyes appear.

She's been a Disappointing Daughter already, at the crack of dawn: missed her alarm, dead battery, and ignored Avik's morning irrelevant-feels lament while scurrying around the house trying to find a strong enough network to book a cab. She'd finally had to call the manager of the Little Bengal black-yellow cabstand, an ancient sardar who'd been saying, "Okay, madam, taxi with-AC/without-AC?" to three generations of her family. "AC," she'd said, while Avik informed Laxmi that there was nothing as crushing as a child's indifference. This had been the last straw—she'd told Avik to feel lucky his irrelevance came with air-conditioning, and no one really gave a fuck about it. She'd regretted it immediately, but the damage was done.

Narad has had her flat powered up and settings-optimised since she entered the lobby. Laundry bag toss, shower, equipment checklist, pack, coffee in flask, mirror scan. She rushes out in fifteen minutes, hair still wet, and remembers only after the elevator doors close that she's forgotten to bring her mask again. But it's a shoot day today, so she doesn't have her usual walk to work.

The ride to the ground floor is short, but rendered extremely uncomfortable by her neighbours, a trendy and overfamiliar Israeli documentary filmmaker couple wanting to know who she'd hooked up with this weekend, and she can't bring herself to tell them she'd had a wild night consoling her sobbing parents and hearing Rajat Gupta stories. She still doesn't know what drove the Roys and Guptas apart—her last memories of Rajat Uncle were not fond, she'd been fifteen and he'd been creepy, grabbing her by the waist and pulling her up close one night when he was supposed to be sleeping on their sofa and she'd walked past on her way to the fridge to drink some water. She'd pushed him off, and he'd apologised at once, saying he was drunk and he was sorry, begging her not to tell anyone. A decade later, she's surprised she wasn't more upset or angry, that she hadn't even thought about it all this time: it wasn't the first time that an uncle had pawed at her. She'd just gone back to her room, glad that she hadn't elbowed him in the face. She'd heard him crying as she shut her door. She hadn't needed to avoid him afterwards, or tell her parents: she'd never seen him again. His horrible wife had stayed in touch for a long time, though, mostly through viral forwards and endless streams of pictures of her new saris. Joey had asked her parents last night what went wrong between them, they were such friends, closer than family, for so long. They didn't want to talk about it.

"We have to focus on the good things," Romola had said. "We grew up together, you were supposed to grow up with his sons." Avik had said nothing: he'd just found album after album of old photos and handed them to her for the memorial video. It always amazes Joey that her parents are so old their baby pictures are black-and-white. That there are whole years of their lives with no photos, no videos, that they just appeared on the cloud fully formed in their twenties. No wonder they're able to forget so much—the nostalgia algorithms have nothing to haunt them with.

The driver is new: she face-scans him to make sure he's assigned to today's car. He's not one of the people she's hired off the lists Laxmi keeps sending from her neighbourhood. "Any job, didi—guard, driver, cook—they will do anything, all good children, if you don't take them they'll turn bad." Most of the IDs are obvious fakes, but very few of Laxmi's boys have caused Joey's Flowco any trouble. Laxmi'd wanted Joey to find them Flowverse work, as camera assistants or makeup artists or spot boys. She'd done her best, but most of those jobs were reserved for people who knew somebody. The driver's face is correct: she wonders how many scans he's already undergone since morning. She'd struggled at first with the idea of putting people through this humiliation, but you had to be safe. Just a few days ago she'd seen a Flow about a serial killer being captured by tollbooth cameras while crossing the Yamuna on one of her regular routes: the original driver was in the trunk, his IDs switched, his smartatt skinned right off his wrist.

Getting out of her gated neighbourhood, India China Harmony Place, takes longer than usual because her neighbourhood militia are out in full force, sponsor logos glowing over clean grey uniforms. It's not some regulation march-past: they're herding people out of ICH Place. Men and women in rags, matted gold-brown hair, and children, many children, all of them girls. How had they found their way into her upscale neighbourhood? What horrible detention centre were they being taken to? Had the state already taken away their citizenships? Was it about to take away their organs?

She knows better than to stop and ask, she'll hear they were illegal immigrants or terrorists or Pakistani spies, and her concern will be noted in the Welfare Association's security app discussion threads, marking her out as a potential troublemaker. As the procession passes her car, she knows better than to make eye contact with the prisoners: What if they ask her to help? What if they shout at her, demand she join the resistance? How will she tell them she has no idea how?

Indi's convinced that one day the poor will rise, an unstoppable zombie horde, and just destroy the city, that they've suffered so much for so long that they won't care about taking over, they'll just want to burn it all down. Not that the Years Not to Be Discussed left a lot to be burned, but Joey doesn't see how: Indi's job is to look for inspiring creative ideas, he doesn't see the production challenges like she does. But whenever she looks at the streets, at the cams, scanners, guards, barriers, spikes, and drones, she knows that the city's rulers are prepared to fight any insurrection. So she looks away, as usual, a skill everyone she knows has learnt since childhood, because not looking away means seeing terrible things.

She's seen other Reality Controllers and even Flowstars lose their jobs for taking stands online, for helping the ill or dying during There-Is-No-Crisis crises with money or food or information, or just attending permitted elite-person protests—never punished directly, not anymore, but she's noted each inevitable fall, watched them fade and disappear from the industry, or redeem themselves by complete transformation. Inspiring photos of millions of protestors fighting the same battles, standing up despite their differences, braving police brutality, fascist mobs, and harsh weather, across the country and all over the world don't help. It's not wholly safe to go look at them too often, either; some of the sites are ID traps. Daily reminders of her own cowardice don't really boost her productivity. Neither does stalking the accounts of people she's met who've suddenly gone completely silent.

Her driver finds a clever shortcut and in no time they're speeding over the flyover chain towards Film City. Network booster in place, headset on, she loses herself to the newsFlow.

There's a horrifying video about a gang of fifteen-year-old AR gamers being tricked into beating up elderly Malayali writers for digital credits, but today's news crisis is a Singapore real estate tycoon openly advertising for partners for an organ farm business, claiming it could give backward Indians a chance to contribute value to the world. Somehow, the debate is not centred around rampant body ownership and its links to human trafficking and slavery, but around the maximum allowable percentage of foreign ownership of these firms.

—You could be happier, Narad texts. Care to share?

—No.

—I want to do better, Joey. I want to be more in sync with what's going on in that lovely head of yours, but could you help me out by playing a simple expression-matching game with your mountain buddies?

—No.

—Okay, how about this—a therapist! I have five great picks for you near your favourite locations.

"I have to find my ex-boyfriend and current colleague an onscreen girlfriend," Joey says. "Do you have anything helpful to say?"

—Let's update your contact description for . . . Indi!

"No!"

—Okay, you know what? I've got a great selection of inspirational quotes about love, breakups, coping, finding new love, office relationships, hiring the best candidate, or secrets of long-format content!

"No."

The traffic overlay in her headset's vision field looks like a blood circulation diagram. There's a couple of large processions out: a massive farmers' march, thousands of white-clad, red-capped men and women in floating pop-up videos hovering in front of Joey's eyes, all standing patiently in front of roadblocks, trickling through gaps in single file to submit to searches and face scans, solar panels on their caps charging their out-of-date phones. Some of them already have the new data implants installed on their necks: they look like meteors striking the earth. Sun-baked leathery skin, dust-caked faces, blood-streaked feet. A gaggle of urban kids hovers around the farmers' leaders, shooting SanSan selfies. The dense smog around the crowd sizzles and shimmers as drone-cams fly by. Heavily armed police are out in force too, a large fleet of commandeered school buses behind them. These farmers have been travelling for weeks, to join Azadgaon, the shifting self-sustaining city of protesting farmers that has been barricaded in a cluster of western Delhi suburbs for over a decade now, harassed across highways and into cordons by the police, weathering everything the government, the oligarchs, and the city itself have thrown at it, an act of incredible endurance that only makes the news now when international celebrities namecheck Delhi's farmers in their Flows, and stays in the news for a few minutes before the censors catch up.

The nationalists are out in a rival march in West Delhi, demanding the thousands of temples and cow-care facilities they had been promised, mass deaths for various demographics, compulsory cow urine drinking in all schools, and government sponsorship for Muslim-identification squads. Joey mutes them, and speed-scans through the newsFlows about the farmers. She forgets to silence public commentary, and is too shocked by the troll-wave to gesture it away. Her smartatt gives her a rage-spike alert two minutes in and her headset autoplays happy SanSan videos.

"I brought you in here because I trust you more than anyone in the world," Indi had said to her on her first day. "No one ever really got me—the core of me—like you did. Just promise me you won't try to change the Flow, or me. People come to my Flow because they trust me to be myself."

"You were a flailing baby when I met you," she'd said. "I trained you to be human, and other people get to enjoy the work I put in. I should be asking for royalties."

"I feel that way about my exes too," he'd said. "Yes, we learned a lot from each other when we were together. But you have to move on from that, Joey. I have."

She'd considered punching him in the face, but he'd been really helpful with the contract. And she'd known since college that she and Indi made a brilliant team, a winning team, even if it was one she'd want to quit every few hours.

"I'm going to change absolutely everything about your Flow," she'd said. "It's . . . not good."

"Hey!"

"I'll try to change you too, but I can't promise results there.

Fixing your Flow is easier, though. No more breathless inspirational bullshit. No more know-it-all dickery. No more stealing other people's stories and making them about you."

"Fine. I'll tone it down, and keep my shirt on."

"No, you'll lose your whole audience."

"Just . . . don't talk to me like this in front of the team."

"Same."

She's making good time on the highway. Her Flowco's paid for silver-level road privileges for the whole team, which has proved invaluable in getting Indi's Flows out in time for the office crowd's morning commute. But even with tolls prepaid, pre-approved scans, and cashless-subscription bribes she still has to leave early on shoot days because there are construction delays on every route. Most of East Delhi's being broken down and rebuilt from scratch; not new-conqueror city razing, they'd have to be pretty stupid to try and build new towers of power in East Delhi anyway. No, it's all just regular construction, but it's still a lot. Through the grey-white haze she can see the towering Brave Hanuman statue standing over the Delhi end of the Yamuna bridge as if daring the mobs from the Uttar Pradesh wildlands to cross. A protective cordon of Delhi Police drones hovers around Hanuman's loincloth. The drones are to protect this Chinese-manufactured Indian-pride icon from celebrity Dalit drone-mural graffiti artist E-Klav: every week, he (she? they?) crowdfunds a new piece of drone-painted vandalism on the statue's bottom. Sometimes it's just red buttocks; the last one was a poem about riverside slum demolitions. A troop of bare-chested men stands at the statue's feet, naked swords in hand, officially to protect the statue against Neo-Naxal attacks but really to remind Delhi's citizens that their sect and its war hordes could sack the city anytime they chose. Joey had forgotten to cancel outdoor shoots during their annual stampede last time, a grave error: Indi's whole crew had been locked in a car showroom for a whole night, with drunken pilgrims threatening to break the glass and rape everyone, held back only by the glare of their light rig and their evidently professional live-broadcast setup. Then, as now, there had been policemen on patrol among the mob, armed and ready to do absolutely nothing should violence erupt.

An update floats in from Jin-Young: the Flow is live, and Indi's doing very well, it's an easy gig. Not that Jin-Young would ever put any real criticism of Indi on record: ever since he took over her former role as Senior Reality Manager, she's had to remind him he's now allowed to be critical of Indi, that his wary politeness is bad for the Flow. Today's joint Flows are studio conversations between Indi and a few Hindi news mainstreamers, generic happyfluff but worth the journey in terms of viewership boosts. But it's not just about numbers, it's about boosting Indi's value as a nationwide trendsplainer, a familiar face everywhere, and Joey always manages to reel in a big sponsor or two on these fishing trips.

—We're on the smooth stretch, says Narad as she appears in an AR puff, hovering over the driver's head. Time to put your face on.

Joey takes off her headset. She sits in absolute stillness for a minute, eyes shut, mind empty, breathing slow and deep until Narad sends her phone an alert: her systems are good to go. This is another action montage she knows the beginning and end of. She opens her rucksack and pulls out a small case. As the car speeds over the bridge, over parched earth and the brown trickle of the Yamuna, Joey transforms, with smooth, precise applications of finely strategised, big-data-recommended makeup, from recently-draped-over-parents'-sofa Wet Sock Joey to Work Joey, Reality Controller, loved and feared in equal measure by the hottest Flow team in all of Delhi. Wet Sock Joey once binge-watched a cat-matchmaking reality Flow directly on her headset for two days while eating only banana chips. Work Joey has three aggressive notes ready for Indi's Look of the Day, and has already decided which nepotism-beneficiary intern gets to make Creepy Rajat Uncle's memorial video. The car pulls up at the SachVoice News studio and a gaggle of assistants rush towards it with tablets and problems. Work Joey goes to work.

She'd worked with Indi once before, after college, before they broke up, when he'd tried to be an edgy twenty-four/seven real-life streamer, the kind that everyone in America had been obsessed with at the time, broadcasting warts-and-all honest anti-influencer too-much-information Real Life, performing social experiments, questioning the system, provoking Real People. She still has nightmares about it. He'd tried lifegaming, setting himself real-world action quests while his followers gave him instructions, feedback, and money, and made him their puppet, paying larger and larger sums for increasingly dangerous stunts, and he'd had no qualms about taking Joey with him. They'd learned the hard way never to share his real location, because they couldn't afford security back then: he kept getting more popular, and while they were both immune to abusive messages, his fans' attempts to control all his relationships went from bad to worse, and then he'd start getting mobbed, people would start sending food and reporting crimes wherever he was, and even hiring thugs to attack him. If it had been America, they'd have sent SWAT teams. She'd told him before they started that no one in India wanted that shit: that people wanted escape, not truth; perfection, not reality. They had more than enough reality to deal with. She'd hated being the on-display cameo-appearance girlfriend, shielded herself from the constant avalanche of lewd commentary by going wholly offline, abandoning first her phone and then most of her life. Her girlfriends had pulled her out of this hole, and realising that Indi was fine with watching her suffer as long as his fans could watch it too had finally pushed her into breaking up with him, something all his infidelities couldn't achieve. It had taken two years of relentless charm and pursuit before she'd even agreed to meet him.

Jin-Young's officially in charge of keeping an eye on Indi at all times, but she does it too, force of habit, as Indi and a couple of young newsFlow anchors walk along a track, following pre-programmed cameras and their superfluous operators, followed in turn by a greenscreen backdrop on a trolley. At the far end of the studio, a screen grid displays possible settings for their conversation: Manhattan, Mohenjo-daro, Mars. The mainstreamers wear flexi-costumes, bright green bodysuits that are different on each screen: Indi's casually dressed, sixty-four-colour screenshirt scrolling through his personal moodboard and sponsor logos, many of which will be blurred for mainstream broadcast. A drone flies above them, picking up panoramas: Indi's been wanting one of his own, but Joey's forbidden it.

SachVoice executives appear every few minutes to subtly find out if Joey's interested in headhunting them for her Flowco and she makes no real pretence of interest. Word has gotten around all the media that Joey's stock is rising: everyone wants to have meetings with her because they've all heard everyone else wants to have meetings with her. She's been through the SachVoice roster already and found it sadly lacking in value: they're all placeholders anyway, like Indi's current co-anchors, youngsters quickly promoted to help everyone forget that their recent predecessors from the Years Not to Be Discussed are now in hiding, swept under rugs after several international exposés declared them guilty of fostering genocide. They couldn't go out in public without causing flash-protests, and the new Japanese investors wanted fresh faces. These studios used to ring with the screams of anchors not reporting daily lynchings or massive corruption, but for now it's all Indi effortlessly outshining the mainstreamers, explaining what the coolest people in New New Delhi really want. Joey wonders, sometimes, if it's really that different from the banal-evil reality management exercises of the Years Not to Be Discussed, where inside the studio all was well, just strutting government spokespersons and preening anchors sharing in-jokes and appreciating the wild successes of the regime, as if there was no catastrophic failure, no mass graves, no people dying like flies in the world outside. The world is better now, definitely. At least the bits of it she is allowed to see.

"I have the girls lined up for this afternoon," Jin-Young says. "Would you like to examine them alone? Or should I select a focus group?"

"You make me sound like some kind of flesh trader," Joey says, and watches blank-faced as Jin-Young considers an outraged explanation, then realises she's covering up for him, then realises he's made a basic error by discussing Indi's new-girlfriend auditions in a rival office, and is then consumed with shame and regret. He looks like he's ready for a moody close-up. He's dressed in the K-pop idol gear he now wears to work every day—immaculately coiffed blue/blond hair, sparkly Anmu-loop screenshirt, dangerously tight pants.

Joey's the only one who knows that Jin-Young's K-pop outfit is a disguise, worn to thwart potential race-hate attacks and add to their whole group's near-mythical cool quotient. She'd almost made him a Flowstar because of his story: she can still see it, a nice docuFlow set in Korean neighbourhoods, Jin-Young narrating how he grew up in Delhi, speaking perfect Hindi, how confused he is by the growing tribe of Indian Hallyu kids. How the mid-'20s anti-Chinese agitations across India (so much dramatic background footage freely available) inspired him to become one of several Korean-diaspora people who dress up as K-pop or K-drama idols instead of the completely fashion-free engineering/infrastructure executives their parents raised them to be. Reenactments of Jin-Young's escapes from at least three late-night lynchings over the last year: a season finale featuring the most recent one, where he'd thought his luck had run out, but the youths chasing him with hockey sticks had just wanted a selfie. Jin-Young had heard Joey's docuFlow idea out, and then, in an absolute first for his Flowco career, refused immediately.

She's been dreading the girlfriend auditions since morning, but giving up control over crucial Flow elements has always proved to be a bad idea, and it's important for the candidates to know that a woman's in charge and they're not expected to sleep with Indi or anyone in his crew at any point. And she can't depend on Indi to not start anything with whoever his lucky co-star is.

"I couldn't have done any of this without you," he'd said to her after winning his first Gujiaboyzz Flowstar of the Year Award (South and Central Asia) a year ago.

"Everyone knows this," she'd said, and then he'd kissed her, and gone off to do interviews. He'd tried to come over to her flat at dawn, and when she'd told him very clearly they weren't going to be a couple ever again he'd let it go after sulking for a week. He'd tried to bro-fy her after that, discussing potential celebrity conquests whenever he could, and she'd gone along with it for the longest time because she hadn't wanted to give him the satisfaction of knowing how angry it made her.

She lines up her distraction ploys as Indi strides towards his team, eager to gloat over how he's absolutely dominating the mainstreamers. He goes through the usual Monday routine of punishing Joey a little for not sacrificing her weekend for him. Joey and Jin-Young run him through the update. There's only one thing that requires real decisions: a new Central Reality Editor will have to be found.

There are two producer-editors handling the final checks on Indi's Flow now, and they're perfectly competent, but Indi likes having people he knows as the final burden-bearers of key responsibilities. Why he sacked his chief editor over the weekend Joey doesn't know, but she doesn't really care. She'd never liked Raj, who was some sort of cousin of Indi's. Raj had not only been bad at his job, he'd kept derailing meetings with pitches about Indi taking a stand against Dravida separatists, or explaining why people who still used Instagram were long-form traditionalists.

She tells Indi she'll find the new Central Reality Editor herself: the production side of the crew is her turf, Indi is best left to handle the glamour and the entourage, the people whose names she struggles to remember: stylists, trainers, personal care specialists, bodyguards, tech pit crew, and a few miscellaneous hangers-on. The people neither of them have time for, the kids who do his game playthroughs or the body doubles who record visuals for point-of-view travelogues, adventure sports experiences, and cooking tutorials on his behalf, are left to Jin-Young.

There's at least a week's worth of human activity recorded as Indi's life on any given weekday, and Joey's biggest secret, the source of all her power, is that she's the only person in the country so far who's managed to find ways to deliver it perfectly to her Flowstar's viewers. Each of Indi's Flowfans gets a customised Flow, specifically catered to their interests and preferences, so while most of Indi's fans follow the sitcom of his life and friendships, there are several who genuinely think Indi's a serious gamer, or a visual artist. She's not sure if there's any other Reality Controller in the world who manages as complex a multichannel setup with as tight a crew: her own Flowco has been trying to get her to put it down on paper for months, and all her rivals have tried in vain to emulate it. Indi's the only Flowstar in the country whose fanFlowers often discuss wholly separate shows and whose Flow pirates get accused of faking. Every other Flowstar has to deal with Flowjackers who steal their Flows and run them with their own commentary. Indi's fans have learnt there's only one place where they can get exactly what they want.

Joey gets at least one headhunter call a week because the whole industry has taken note of the speed at which she took Indi from Influencer to Trailblazer. The only remaining rank is Icon, and Joey fervently hopes he'll never get there: she'd lose the last traces of control over her own life. As things stand, at least half of Indi's team is expendable, but the Flowfunders told Joey long ago that it wasn't about how many people were needed: a crowd around you meant status. In a world where Flowstats are mostly fake, what you need to show power is human bodies.

He probably doesn't even remember his first attempt at live-streaming his life: Indrajith Mathew and Bijoyini Roy, college legends and debate circuit will-they-won't-they obsessions, giggling awkwardly over a plate of momos in a dingy Tibetan Quarter restaurant, letting their friends know they were a couple. Joey hasn't seen that vid in years, but she remembers every moment of it. She was the star, he was breathless and nervous. But he'd said they would be together forever. They'd taken the video down later; relationship declarations were never a good idea during culture shifts. The restaurant was gone as well, razed to dust like the rest of the neighbourhood.

"I've let you down before, I know. It will never happen again," he'd said to her years later. They'd looked into each other's eyes for a long time; he'd flinched first. Fortunately the job hadn't required that she trust him.

Joey and Jin-Young leave the shoot area with a couple of interns and a bodyguard. The girlfriend auditions have been set up in a nearby Film City studio; it wouldn't do to let all the ladies into Indi's spaces, or on SachVoice turf: they'd have a mainstreamer version on the air within a day. Besides, the shortlisted ladies are all in Film City anyway, scurrying from meeting to meeting with their agents in tow. All Joey's New Bollywood friends have moved back to Delhi over the last three years; the culture-control wars of the Years Not to Be Discussed have destroyed all but the richest and most insular Bombay entertainment houses. Several of these friends are in one or the other of the large media-plex buildings they're driving by now, sparkling new towers with fashionably slanting facades of bright paint, darkened windows, and solar panels. They message Joey from their work-play stations to bitch about their meetings, sometimes about one another. Between their towers and at every corner, concrete bunkers and sniper stations are packed with armed guards—Film City is on the Delhi–Uttar Pradesh border, a favourite destination for culture-outrage vandals, rape gangs, crowd-sourced flash-robs, and fanatic lynch mobs. Rumours have been doing the round for months that the warlords who rule Uttar Pradesh are planning an organised invasion.

Joey and her team don't have time to observe the architecture or the militia—they have to do a bug sweep each time they leave competitor turf. Narad spots the first one—it looks like a portable phone charger—in Jin-Young's man-purse. Joey finds a strange pen in her rucksack. They all stare at the bodyguard in fascination as he extracts a flower-shaped hairclip from his pocket. Everyone wants to know what Team Indi's planning. The only time the bag had been out of Joey's sight was when it went through the security scanner at the SachVoice entrance. She sends out a companywide alert, and sends pictures of the bugs to the Flowfunders. That's one regular sponsorship from SachVoice more or less assured.

"What are the names of your father's friend's sons?" Jin-Young asks, waving his phone at her.

"What? Why?"

"The intern wants to know. For consent forms."

"What consent forms?"

Jin-Young shrugs. "Maybe he is from abroad?"

"Why is he calling you?"

"He's scared of you."

She reaches for his phone, but Jin-Young is faster. "Just finish the job, please," he says, and hangs up.

The truth is Joey doesn't remember the name of one of Rajat Uncle's sons. The older one, the one who'd taught her to play chess, introduced her to the Beatles, and told her long ago that she could be one of his wives when she grew breasts but his main wife would be American and blonde, was Rohit. The younger one, her own age, she mostly remembers as Fatty, because that's what Rohit called him. He was a quiet kid, interested only in playing games on his phone and avoiding his brother. She remembers talking to him only once—he'd made eye contact with her while she'd been staring in horror at his obnoxious mother, and informed her solemnly, before diving back into his phone, that his mother changed the settings of every device in their house every day, just a little bit, but every day, because she was trying to drive his father insane.

She'd resisted the idea of Indi getting an official girlfriend at first, not because of residual feelings but because Indi's clear ambition to woke-flirt with every attractive woman in the National Capital Region had been the regular spine of their daily narrative, so no one in his team, least of all Indi himself, had wanted him to go monogamous. But the funders have issued very specific directives, and Joey has to admit their numbers are solid. Like most of Indi's major life decisions of late, it's been about product placement.

A Finnish company has developed a smartatt upgrade called Tavata, which lets users measure both their compatibility with and their attraction to anyone they meet, and let their smartatts know of their exact degrees of interest and consent through wholly nonverbal cues. It can be customised to work for people anywhere on the sexuality spectrum, but all that is for more open cultures—in India, New or not, they want to launch a version that lets a committed partner know if you're physically intimate with anyone else, and performs or allows compatibility checks on the basis of "acceptable" communities.

Joey had immediately refused to work with the wrist-chastity-belt version of the device—it was very easy to see, in a country where most kids got their first smartatts from their parents, how the upgrade could be used by families or communities to filter potential matches for people in their power by religion, or caste, or any of the dazzling array of discrimination options India continues to use, or simply exclude non-hetero matches. The same Tavata used as a consent-ensuring successor of the dating app in the West could easily become an arranged-marriage enforcer on your skin.

"I know the orgy version is better for our creative team and our core demographic," Funder Radha had said, "but the One True Love version—"

"The chastity belt version."

"That's not necessarily how—"

"Come on."

"Don't quote me on this, but the Indian Conservative Casteist Nightmare version means bonuses for everyone, and the new Augmented Reality design team you wanted. And you could do your usual coded nudge-wink thing where the people-like-us audience knows he actually hates it. They can break up after two months, it's not a marriage."

"But we're going to get so much hate. So many hot takes."

"If the project works, I'm pretty sure they'll do a premium edition, which is the full-spectrum global one, and that means more raises for everyone. Everyone. Hot-take-proofing is for children. Just look at the fucking number, Joey."

Joey had looked at the fucking number and settled, yet again, for minor consolation victories about casting inclusivity. But she knows these are hollow: the truth is that her funders could have forced her to shortlist only potential girlfriends who looked like Bollywood stars if they'd wanted to, or could have chosen some fair-and-lovely high-caste Hindu instead of Indi to be their alpha Flowstar for the right price and partnerships. They have other teams that do exactly this. But Indi's their golden boy, their international credibility booster, their token-woken poster child, and they've always given Joey and him more freedom than other Flowcos would have.

"Our company is deeply committed to a fair and diverse workplace," Funder Radha had told her at their first meeting, and Joey had still been innocent enough to not see her hidden smirk.

"I have mixed feelings about so many things about the Flow, but it's lifting up so many people who've simply not had platforms for their voices before," Joey had said. "It's really one of the things I want to explore."

"We're exactly as committed to our diversity goals as our international partners," Funder Radha had said, smile unwavering, and it took Joey years of experience and a couple of very disillusioning meetings with foreign Reality Controllers to realise Radha had actually told her the truth.

She's in a small and aggressively air-conditioned room, Jin-Young to her left, classic reality show audition-hazing table in front of them, assistants hovering around a mounted camera pointed towards a rickety wooden chair, bodyguard exuding silent menace by the door. About to execute her proposal that had made Funder Radha burst into actual applause: to let Indi choose his girlfriend himself by using the Tavata update and seeing who among the shortlisted candidates he was most attracted to, all of this live, ideally in a situation where he didn't even know the audience could see how much he liked each new girl. Every match-fixing reality show season condensed into a two-hour interactive Flow.

"Tell the team what we're looking for, Jin-Young," she says.

"Our standard unicorn. Someone completely original, but also trend-friendly. A wildcard, but market tested."

"I'm so proud of you. We're also looking for someone with an actual voice. Maybe a few fixed values. Not a bot grown from a trending algorithm and covered in skin, even if it's nice skin. Got it?"

The team nods.

"Bring them in," Joey says.

She says it again, that evening, at Cheezburger, the noughties-nostalgia bar where Indi hosts his in-group social Flows. The scene is set: Indi and his friend-Flowstars sit around a wide circular table on the lower level, covered with early Xbox game posters, trading banter fresh from their writing teams' rumbling collaborative cloud docs. Extras sit around the other tables, pretend-conversing, drinking, or actually working on laptops. On the balcony above, the stars' long-shot camerapeople jostle for space; others are concealed in shadowy corners. Each of the Flowstars has their personal POV cam, of course, mostly discreet monocle-cams designed to maximise user face exposure. Indi doesn't use one: he's wearing his smartglasses. All the camera feeds go live to a cluster of OB vans parked outside Cheezburger, where editors sit and monitor the Flow, and writer teams relay conversation tips and joke ideas to their stars' earphones. And this is where Indi's a step ahead of his rivals, thanks to another piece of Joey Roy magic, the real reason why none of the other Flowstars who've studied him and copied every aspect of his Flow have succeeded, why none of the other Flowcos who've duplicated his product with hotter, Hinduer, or more mainstream-famous actors have managed to eclipse him: there are no writers in Indi's van.

The extras sitting at the other tables, working on their laptops, are actually Indi's writing team, live inside the stadium while the others watch at home. They respond in the moment, catching moods that never travel to the OB vans, relaying text directly to Indi's smartglasses, where he just reads or discards them. Indi has no conversation lags while listening to voices shouting in his ears, no monocle cam to distract him. Joey's got him to focus on body language, on actually listening and responding instead of waiting for pauses to launch into monologues like his friends. Everyone else competes for airtime, Flows muddled and scattered like noughties social timelines. Joey had actually thought they wouldn't be able to get away with it after a point, but Indi had reassured her saying the idea was flawless: no one would notice. What Flowstar would ever take note of recurring extras?

Indi's closest rivals have been a part of his group sometimes, but they've never lasted long. They've never been able to handle Indi's effortless group-alpha performances day after day, never understood why their fans stayed with Indi's clique even after they left. The current friend group are all people who gave up trying to compete with him for overall Flowstar status long ago, specific-interest Flowpros who enjoy the boost from Indi's top-tier audience. Today's panelists are Vijay, a history rewriter trying to restore authenticity to textbooks; Shalini, a theme park designer with an unfortunate tendency to attempt text-to-speech recitations about various grand cultural projects under construction in the heartland next to smart cities that will probably never be built; and Pia, a collectible-celeb AR game creator who always has a pixiu-themed hat and cutting-edge multifield gossip. They've got a good equation going: asteroid belts of stans, shippers, fanFlowers, Flowfic creators, reactors, reenactors, and deep-fake pornographers have declared them a combination worth collective obsession. Joey's considered getting a whole team in to actively manage Indi's Flow spinoffs.

The contestants enter—Pia has agreed to pretend she knows them—and assume their seats. Three women, carefully shortlisted, all amazing, all combat ready. Joey gestures up viewership stats, and notes the sharp uptick with grim satisfaction. Indi activates his smartatt upgrade on cue—he's had the new tattoo implanted during his afternoon spa session—and everyone can now see just how much he likes them.

It's not much of a contest. Hot off the starting block, ahead of the rest by parsecs, is curly-haired, dark-eyed, impossibly gorgeous Uma, who maxes out the smartatt's attraction/compatibility settings the moment Indi lays eyes on her, and transforms his audience into a slobbering mass of reaction videos. Joey has been expecting this: Uma has haunted her own dreams since morning. She has some kind of interesting wellness-y job, and many relevant things to say, but Joey doesn't hear a word of it: all she can think of is invading Troy to rescue Uma, dragging her off to their private island and devouring her logic-defying body until the sun explodes. Why Uma is here drinking fake Just-a-Faiz whiskey cocktails and not on the other side of the world fending off amorous Hollywood he-men, Joey does not know. At the table, conversation has more or less stopped: everyone's just dumbstruck. The viewers clearly couldn't care less—Uma is already a national phenomenon.

"I am having improper thoughts," Jin-Young whispers solemnly.

"You and me both, brother," Joey says. She looks at him: he has bad news. "What is it?"

"There's a mole on her cheek. Two more on her left hand."

"I see them. So?"

"The live-reactors are saying this girl might be Desibryde."

Narad warns Joey she might be having a panic attack. Joey silences her.

Is it possible? Desibryde is the world's most notorious South Asian sexFlower, whose Flows are so powerful that no amount of culture-police net censorship can prevent them from reaching every corner of the country. Desibryde is a counterculture Icon. Joey had assumed that Desibryde shot her Flows far away from India, in some country with breathable air and everyday freedoms: her whole performance concept, sex with mostly Black men while wearing AI facemasks of goddesses or male religious leaders, is dangerous anywhere in the world, but to do it while living in India? If she's outed, she'll be on a hundred actual death lists. But—and Joey's heart skips a beat—what if she's tired of the guerrilla life and wants to find a Flow where she can just be herself? What if she wants to stay ahead of inevitable discovery and danger, and avoid all the trouble that previous mainstreaming ex-pornstars had faced? Where would she go?

"Jin-Young, sign that woman up at once. Right now. And hire ten new bodyguards," says Joey. "Now. Go go go."

Jin-Young grimaces. "The sponsors won't allow it," he says.

"The funders will," says Joey. "Fuck it, we'll crowdfund. Look at her."

They both do, and breathe heavily.

"She doesn't have a Reality Controller of her own," says Jin-Young. "Would I get that job?"

"Over my bloodied corpse."

"Indi still has to choose her."

"Forget Indi. Jin-Young, if we let that woman out of our lives, we'll never forgive ourselves. Every day will be a grey wasteland. You see this, right?"

"Yes. Also, the mainstreamers are picking this up. And her agent's calling."

"It's a done deal. Alert Indi, call a break, I'm heading downstairs."

Indi heads up from the table and stalks towards the restroom as Joey races downstairs.

"Girl's gone national," says Joey, breathless. "This is a game changer. Should we close it before she gets new management?"

Indi's face is unreadable. "Get her number," he says. "And get her off my Flow."

"What? Why?"

"It's my Flow," says Indi, and heads back to the table.

Joey still hasn't managed to move when Jin-Young races up to her. "Trouble," he says. "Some godman's outed her and said she's here. Mob coming. We should head out."

Joey shakes her head. "Call the newsboys, call the police, call for extra security," she says. "Call for meat. And drinks. The Flow stays live."

But Uma's figured something's wrong, and is on her own phone now, and a second later she's up, and racing towards the exit. Joey chases her out of the building, but obviously Uma's faster: a car's waiting for her, door opens, and she dives into it.

"You're hired!" Joey calls.

"I'm sorry," Uma says. "I really wanted this."

She slams the door shut, and her car roars off through the ICB Market central lane before the already approaching media horde can catch it.

As Joey approaches the Cheezburger exit, one of the other girl-friend nominees—a beautiful super-liberal intellectual activist type whose name Joey has now blanked—comes storming out. She'd impressed Joey during the audition with her well-crafted feminist takedowns of everything in Indi's Flow, but lost her completely over the last hour by sulking and glowering into her fake cocktail as she watched Uma own the table.

"You should head back in," says Joey. "You're the favourite now."

Option Two shrugs. "Fuck you. Fuck all you people, you're monsters," she says, and walks away.

"How are we doing?" Joey asks Jin-Young as she slumps back into her observation chair on the balcony. "Police? Thugs? Hate mob? Food?"

"All good," says Jin-Young. "Maybe it's all for the best."

"I suppose it is."

"Are you all right?" Jin-Young asks after a while. "How . . . sorry, but how old are you, Joey?"

"I'm twenty-five," she says. "It's the new forty. And the new twenty."

They turn back to Indi's table: in the rubble of their plan sits the sole survivor. The audience doesn't really know what to think of her; it's still busy speculating about Uma. All they really know about her is that she just came third in a field of three in Indi-attraction scores, not really a ringing endorsement for a match-fixing tattoo, and they don't like it, or her. Her name is Tara, she's a trained singer-dancer-futurist, which doesn't impress anyone; most of the discussion online is about futurists being the new wanderlusting sapiosexuals. But not picking a winner is not an option, either for Joey or the audience.

Joey had only selected Tara as a filler because the other girls were generic and Tara wasn't a clear Type. But she can work with this woman: definitely pretty, potentially interesting. Clever, earnest, unthreatening. A good enough girl for a two-month monogamy schedule.

Tara looks up at the balcony, and meets Joey's eyes. She smirks, drains her glass, and lays long, slender fingers gently on Indi's arm.

"I'm hungry," she says.

CHAPTER 3

When the guards stationed outside his family's new farmhouse refuse to let Rudra in on the day of his father's funeral, he feels many emotions but surprise is not one of them.

It isn't really their fault: they've never seen him before, and they're new boys, fresh from some dying town, now gatekeepers eager to prove their worth by shielding their masters' people from every possible interaction with people of their own kind. And it's not like anything about Rudra screams rich-boy in any way, not his demeanour, not his features; even his mask is untrendy. He'd had to borrow it from his neighbour Chuki: Rudra has built a life fundamentally based on not needing masks, on not needing anything outside his room at all. His clothes and shoes are clean, and sufficiently brand-appropriate, but not on trend: they must think they're secondhand. But worst of all, he hasn't arrived at these forbidding gates in a car, and what could be more low-class than that?

He knows a ride to the Culture Colony is not the epic journey it seems like to him, that it's just another part of the city and thousands of people make the commute every day, but it's been too much sensory input. He's overloaded his brain. He'd had to pay the autoguy an outrageous amount of money to come all this way, roasting and rattling down dusty roads in his clattering deathmobile. The autoguy had flatly refused to go to the Culture Colony at first—they beat up people like me there, he'd said—but Rudra had cash, enough cash to forget the risk. He'd paid the autoguy to hang around and take him back, but the moment he'd stepped out, dirt-streaked, flash-burned, the fucker had taken off, solar roof twinkling happily over yellow-green-brown roach-bot, dust cloud in his wake.

The guards refuse to call his brother: Sir is busy, show entry QR or give phone. Rudra has no intention of opening up his accounts for their inspection: it's not just the indignity of it; it's not safe, every guard has a data-theft side business. They grope him for good measure, enthusiastically grabbing his balls, letting him know what's what. They demand his fingerprints, to see if he's on an approved guest list: he knows he's not. So he pulls the most Delhi line of all: "Do you know who my father is?" It's not a good line today of all days: his father is dead. And he's pretty sure his brother or mother was the one responsible for shutting down his taxi accounts. They didn't want him here. Not in their home, not in their lives. They hadn't even told him about the heart attack. He'd found out later, when the automated condolences started pouring in from people he hadn't met in over a decade. It was too late to even turn up for the cremation by then. They hadn't taken his calls. But he couldn't blame them, he had avoided theirs whenever possible for at least five years: the only way they stayed in touch was by moving large amounts of money through his bank account. He's tempted to open his account up for the guards: when the hackers show up later, he'll ask them to send his family their regards.

He tells the guards he's here because of the shraddho, the one they might have noticed being organised inside, it's for his father. He tells them they should just send his photo to their boss, that he hasn't been around for years but he's very important, that they'll all get fired if they don't let him in.

The guards are completely unmoved. "Whenever big men die there are always long-lost sons," their leader says, grinning. The sun feels like it's hovering an inch above his head: his humiliation isn't even happening with just the guards present, there are photographers hovering nearby, leering, hooting, taking pictures. The accredited media ones and the personal Flow assistants are all inside, of course, not that there could be many: there are only a couple of genuinely famous people that might be attending. The ones near the guard hut are the lowest of the low, nicknamed paprasis, dead-eyed young men who roam the streets taking pictures of people, asking strangers for autographs, the rag pickers of the data age. They're shouting encouragement to the guards, asking for a beating. One of the guards eyes him speculatively, stroking his baton. Rudra is shouting now, voice cracking, making empty threats, but they see right through it. You can't fake Culture Colony arrogance. He can feel himself drifting: already, a part of him is zooming out, looking at the gate, at the walls, from a great distance, wondering how he'd get into the compound in each of six different genres of game, drawing dotted lines, imagining heat-vision single-colour silhouettes patrolling the grounds. In each situation, he'd have been in command, barking out orders to his teammates, and if his meatspace avatar could only have had a tenth of that authority, he'd have been inside long ago. He'd have been on the high ground, taking out enemies with a sniper rifle, sending animated taunts, leading charges, capturing flags. The guards form a circle around him, slowly, savouring it. He wants to reload from last save. He wants to play at an easier setting. He wants to ragequit and try another game. He hasn't been beaten up in so many years. He wonders how it'll feel. He can already taste blood in his mouth.

He doesn't even notice the car pulling up behind him, but the guards sigh in frustration and fall back. One springs to the window as it rolls down. An arm emerges, presenting a QR code on a phone. The guard scans it and salutes smartly. Another guard starts pushing Rudra away as the gate beeps and swings open, but Rudra's seen the man at the wheel, and shouts, "Avik Uncle!"

For a horrible second, as the window rolls up, he thinks he hasn't been heard, but then the car stops, the door opens, and Avik Roy emerges, eyes wide.

"Rudra? Babu, is that you?"

The car's air-conditioning hits him hard as he slumps in the rear seat, displacing Rono—so big now, he wants to say, but his mouth is dry. Romola Aunty, the first human woman he'd ever had dirty thoughts about, hands him a bottle of water, and he drains it, chokes and splutters. He's reeling, blurry, but recovers in an instant as he sees Joey—that's Joey, it's disturbing how much she looks like Romola Aunty—turning and simply staring from the passenger seat, and the pity in her eyes makes him want, for the first time since he learnt of his father's death, to burst into tears.

Rudra had always known his father made lots of money, it was obvious from the sums that flowed in and out of his bank account around every tax deadline, but this is the first time he gets a sense of exactly how much. The farmhouse is cutting-edge: sprawled over impeccably manicured land—there's a fountain!—and featuring a sprawling *Star Trek*–looking glass/stone/wood/concrete two-storey house and 3D-printed smartmud huts. There are stations for every kind of alternate energy, greenhouses, water plants, giant unsmogger fans, questionable flamingo statues, even an orchard. In the distance, beyond the high stone walls, the Culture Colony Shiva holo-lith towers over it all, smiling down benignly. This place could survive a zombie apocalypse, possibly not even notice one. Rudra watches the Roys struggle not to comment: they've evidently not been here either, and Avik Uncle seems as if he has many things to say about possibly ill-gotten wealth. Rudra is grateful for this, and even more grateful that they've asked absolutely no questions about how he is or what he's doing or why they had to sneak him into his family home. He wants to let them know he'd be happy to be adopted, that the love he feels for them in this moment is the closest to family-love he's ever experienced as an adult.

Avik Roy and Rajat Gupta had always been unlikely friends: Avik was studious, intelligent, conventional, Rajat a charming hustler. New India had treated them very differently, and driven them apart, but Rudra remembers holidays together, birthday parties, concerts, remembers awkwardly holding a massive bouquet in a hospital lobby when Rono was born. Rono is immersed in a phone game now, his interest in Rudra's evident loserness long dissipated. Joey keeps checking her phone as well: Rudra's vaguely pleased to see that Avik's and Rajat's children have at least one addiction in common, even if it's something that defines everyone in their generation.

The guards must have sent a warning message, because his brother strides out of the house before the car even stops outside the open doors. Rudra is impressed by the time Rohit must have put in at the gym or one of the family clinics: he looks like a cartoon thundercloud of pure muscle. His shaved head is a light green, his dhoti a brilliant white. As the car stops, the brothers come face-to-face.

"Let's talk," Rohit says.

It's not much of a conversation, it never is: Rohit has inherited not just Rajat's chain of ethically dubious luxury body-modding "wellness" clinics, but his power-presentation skills as well. He doesn't take long; the speech seems rehearsed. There is no room for Rudra at the actual ceremony, especially since he hasn't observed any of the proper rituals since their father's death (stop opening and shutting your mouth, Rudra, just listen). He may meet their mother later, but she is deeply disappointed with him for not being there during this terrible time when his family needed him most. No, they hadn't taken his calls, but that was because they'd had the wrong number saved, and the whole world had been calling to express their grief. That's why he hadn't received the news, obviously. A simple miscommunication. He is most welcome to spend the day at home, but he has to promise not to disturb any of the guests, especially the important ones. Rohit will talk to him later in the evening, there are important things to say, but he is not to be bothered until then. There is a lot of work to be done. No, his help is not required. No, he hadn't blocked his taxi account, how ridiculous. If Rudra was going to go home, that was fine, but all the cars were busy, and he should head out before any of the other guests saw him. No, Ma was definitely busy too, pay attention.

And then his brother disappears, leaving Rudra reeling from a thousand memories of one-sided brother-chats, conscious only of a desire to charge his dying phone and disappear into it. He tries to convince himself he's home, genetically speaking. If home is where the people you love most are, his real home is currently a server in New Zealand.

He has a bath. His Kalkaji flat hadn't seen water in four days now, and he'd emptied the last borrowed bucket in the morning. The first-floor bathroom he slips into is all grey marble and Japanese design: he can't remember when he's last felt this kind of water pressure. There are devices he doesn't understand saying things in happy-child Japanese and making cheerful noises. He loses himself in gels and foams and conditioners and textured scrubs, remembering at the very last possible second to stop himself from first singing, then masturbating. He considers moving into this house. They'd refuse if he asked, and of course he'd never ask, but what if he just brought his stuff over in a truck and took up residence? They wouldn't even notice him. He's been invisible to them all his life; when he was a child he was often convinced he really couldn't be seen, he was a ghost, a POV camera. A floating whisper adrift in a hurricane.

He feels the grime on his clothes when he puts them back on, his body clean and smelling like a fancy spa. The house is filling up: there are voices everywhere, echoing up from the ground floor through spotless corridors as Rudra shuffles through, staring like a tourist at the smartpaint sculptures growing in their cocoons. The smell of incense floats up, with strains of classical music. Some kind of chanting. He finds his brother's bedroom. The AC welcomes him, speakers start playing some waily Punjabi pop. Rohit doesn't appear to have changed at all since they last met, so if he remembers correctly . . . yes. From a shoebox on the bottom shelf of one of the cupboards, he extracts three neatly rolled-up joints. It looks like there are sensors on the box: Is Rohit getting an alert? Best to be prepared. Two joints go into his pocket, and he lights up the third, not even bothering to open a window. A long, burning, deeply satisfying drag: if Rohit handles his money like he handles his rolling it's no wonder business is booming. Pure vegetarian. He opens a long-unused productivity app on his phone and makes a note to eat some token-defiance beef.

He opens Rohit's cupboards and exhales on his clothes. Carbon nanotube sportswear and fertility-regulating briefs, what an unbelievable asshole. The mirror starts overlaying outfit options on his body; he tries to instruct it to make nudity the default setting but he doesn't have admin privileges. He stubs the joint out on the mirror before sinking onto the bed: it wouldn't do to burn the house down on his first visit.

He wakes up with a start to the sound of loud moans: it's Mehta Uncle, call centre owner turned click farm magnate, and . . . his new wife? Someone else's wife? They're making out by the door, hands wiggling everywhere. They have those absurd mood-sensitive smartatts, both glowing bright pink. He's lying right there, in broad daylight, and they haven't even seen him. It still works, this invisibility cloak. Mehta Uncle's friend seems nice, and it would be nice to see a live naked person for once, and her blouse is about to come off, but this seems bad form for a funeral, so Rudra coughs loudly and they yell in shock, covering up.

"I haven't seen anything," Rudra says, rising swiftly. "Got to go."

"Jesus, you look just like your father did at your age," Mehta whispers. "Almost gave me a heart attack. Where have you—"

"This has been a pleasure," Rudra says, bowing—and wishing mid-bow that he didn't behave this way when embarrassed—"but I have a pressing family engagement." He catches a glimpse of himself in Rohit's mirror—poor little rich boy. So edgy, living in a multicultural low-rent neighbourhood full of people whose histories he's scared to ask about, whose lives he couldn't have endured for an hour. Behind every door in that warren is a different alt-universe horror story. Like every Useless Culture Colony Younger Son—there are several downstairs, he knows, all fashionably bored and cool—he's not even a real person, he's handed his identity over to his family. If he looks himself up right now—he ignores the impulse as usual—he'll find he's doing very well in whatever career he supposedly has. Good Rudra has spent the last five years at Harvard studying bio-augmentation instead of dropping out and slumming it, being all self-reliant and independent but so inherently obedient that even his rebellion is budget-friendly. It's just a phase, he'll come around eventually. One day, he might even get to wear his own smartatt, though he'll never be as physically fit as the company employee who proxies for him. Rudra is the human equivalent of a shell company: If he dies today, how long will it be before his family notices?

Mehta Uncle and his friend stare at him—do they think he's

expecting an invitation to join in? He leaves, his high wholly vanished. He wanders around corridors, a lifelong pastime: in the house he grew up in, there weren't many doors, but there was one that led to a "backside" balcony full of decaying cartons. Rudra would keep opening and closing the door, hoping that if he got the timing right, it would open into another dimension: a mirror city, a fantasy paradise, a time-traveller's ship, another planet. This mansion has many doors, but he doesn't really want to look inside any of them anymore.

The family ghost enters the hall largely unobserved. The shraddho rituals are in full flow. A priest reads out shlokas while inaccurate translations in English and Hindi float up on everyone's phones. Rohit sweats in front of a fire, surrounded by a vast array of flowers, fruits, mounds of rice, and ceremonial paraphernalia. Rudra catches his first glimpse of his mother. She's Flowing in a corner, flanked by two of her most formidable Colony aunty friends. Large tears stream down her face, and her sari is on trend as always. Rudra has blocked most people he knows, and stays off the meatspace data stream as much as he possibly can. Sometimes he worries about being the last person to learn about a war or a tsunami because he's silenced everyone who might tell him. But his mother always finds innovative ways to force her daily ruminations on clothes, spirituality, current affairs, and high-end travel and living down his throat. She actually hires spammer agencies to make it difficult for people to block her.

His father had been the one who kept him informed about really big-news events. When they tore down the KRP Industries Taj Mahal and Changacom Khajuraho six years ago, his father had pulled him out of a national intercollege gaming tournament because Hindus Weren't Safe. When allegedly-Canadian hackers had broadcast the names and addresses of Indian foreign-aid-theft kingpins and vaccine scammers, and his father's name had appeared on these lists by mistake, Rajat had tried to kidnap Rudra and smuggle him out of the country. Even after Rudra left his family, he'd relied on paternal newsbreaks—his relationship-with-father highlight reel could have been called Previously on National Trauma. The last time he'd tried to debate his father? The 2024 purge, when upper-caste boys all over the country had used mysteriously accessible data to destroy Dalit houses because a Dalit taxi driver had given a Brahmin a low rating in Jaipur. The last time they'd discussed meeting? The 2026 horror, when police and mobs torched the few remaining lower-income Muslim ghettos in Delhi, targeting survivor families with pinpoint precision. He'd pointed out the obvious: that all of this had happened before; that he wasn't Muslim and didn't live in a part of the city that was being recultured; that he wasn't even going out to do relief work, wasn't saying anything on the internet or out loud, so no one was going to kill him and throw him into a drain. He'd even sent pictures of the now-familiar visual of Hindu homes standing untouched between the charred husks of Muslim ones, but his father had wanted him behind real walls in case there were retaliatory riots this time. He'd refused. The last time he'd seen his father was in one of his mother's Flows: he'd seemed happy. It was his birthday, and he kept saying how much he loved celebrating with his whole family.

She's not the only one Flowing at the ceremony: there are her acolytes, various other guests, there's an official Flow being recorded by a cousin, live coverage plus specially made videos that Rajat's many, many friends have brought from around the city. A fitting farewell for one of Delhi's earliest social media influencers. There are lots of other fame-aspirants here, but this is not Delhi's elite. Those people are mostly abroad or in hiding, in transformative cocoons, reshaping themselves daily, keeping close tabs on the world they must reemerge into. This is the next layer, New India's young wave now middle-aged, first-generation players replicating whatever they can remember of the lives of those they envied growing up, because now it is their day out of the sun. Rohit's friends are huddled together in a corner, their hands grasping air in the absence of guns or whiskey glasses: one clocks him, whispers, and the whole group gives him ultra-Delhi pre-violence glares. They've still not forgiven him for that time he'd sent messages from Rohit's phone to all their friend groups, telling them recent studies had revealed that all fascists had micropenises, should they all pretend to be communists? It hadn't ended well: his shoulder twitches in memory.

His mother spots him and gestures from across the room: hundreds of eyes are on him as he walks over.

They hug. Padmini turns towards the camera and says, "My long-lost son." She grapples him firmly again.

"You stink of drugs," she whispers. "Even today. Get out."

"No," he says, looking deep into her eyes and finding nothing.

"Any trouble and we'll have you unpersoned," she says.

"No, you won't." And he detaches himself and walks away. She resumes her Flow, wiping her large, expressive eyes, murmuring about gratitude and unity being the core of her culture.

Reunion accomplished, Rudra wanders about unsupervised, enjoying the sights. The walls are lined with screens and tributes to his father, a Museum of Rajat: his warmth, his generosity, his humour, his honesty, his open home, his expensive tastes. His father would have wanted physical photographs too, though, even one of those fake oil paintings.

"Photos fade, babu, paper can be torn, but digital disappears— companies shut down, drives get hacked, bank accounts get locked, governments erase you with one stroke. Nothing is permanent, but never trust anything without a body. Always remember this," he would always say, but this was also a man who kept no records of his own transactions, and whose collection of alternate legal identities could have filled a small funeral hall. Rudra tries to remember what he's really learned from his father, and he can't think of anything, except the importance of always carrying cash.

The digital-only displays are his mother's design. The largest screen is hers, currently running an old clip-compilation of a trip they'd taken to Paris. They're in the Louvre, his father complaining about both the insults meted out to Indian tourists and the atrocious, nation-shaming behaviour of those same tourists, his mother taking pictures of herself in front of each painting, his brother sneaking videos of girls who knew exactly what he was doing. She's used the videos he'd shot, but as he waves through the rest of the tribute, he notices he's been cut out of all the others. He's overcome by a strange urge to find himself, and he tries the Roy family tribute, next to theirs, scrolling quickly through his father's childhood photos, and there he is, he exists, he's stuffing his face with ice cream, but just for a second, and then it's Romola Aunty telling his father to stop photographing the food, Rajat laughing a little too loudly and turning his camera on her.

The biggest tribute screen is reserved for the one from their guru's ashram. At least that monster is not here today. One of their biggest fights, definitely a top-ten contender, was when Rudra, still in his teens, had refused to prostrate himself before the godman and kiss his feet. His father had hit him then, kept hitting him until the guru graciously forgave him (he took his time). Rudra remembers the guru's benevolent hug. His flesh had been cold and clammy, like a fish. It had turned out later that the guru might not have forgiven Rudra: when he'd been severely infected during the third pandemic wave, the godman had insisted that Rajat feed him some strange quack herb mixture instead of getting him actual treatment. Rajat, fortunately, had decided not to sacrifice his son.

The godman's booth is special in another way: there's an in-booth camera and a QR panel for donations. He considers making faces, but people are watching.

The godman's network has been good for his parents, though. A lot of the most high-net-worth people here today are fellow cult members. One of the kids lurking outside the hall, chasing car-toon Augmented Reality collectible creatures on her phone, is a familiar face from old cult-social times. He'd had to babysit her when she was five or so, while his father tried to persuade hers, a media baron of some sort, to cover his first holistic-healing clinic. She'd been perfectly well-behaved, but had told him, at some point when the grown-ups were having dinner, that her daddy thought his daddy was a fraud. Her name pops into his head out of nowhere: Kyara. Her whole generation has names that sound like apps or shampoos. Her father isn't here: she's been sent as an ambassador. The other devotees aren't including her in their conversations about aligning spheres and resonant cosmic energy and indigo children. She's probably not one of the godman's cho-sen soul-daughters that go and live with him from time to time: lucky for her. She sees him watching her, and quickly changes apps: a video of Zaria Salam, the controversial Muslim investi-gative journalist, appears on her screen and she closes it quickly. Clearly she's going through a rebellious phase: he decides his babysitting inspired it years ago.

His smartatt vibrates. At first he thinks it's the usual noti-fication that his proxy-lifer has walked his diligent ten thou-sand steps, but there's activity on his phone: a message from his mother: Don't leave, your brother will speak to you.

Is Padmini worried he'll start some kind of inheritance dis-pute? That would be hilarious. But wait he does, for hours, as the funeral slowly transforms into a party. Competitive Rabin-drasangeet singers from his mother's side of the family caterwaul in turn. Rudra passes through the crowd unseen. Sometimes people talk about him, he can feel their eyes on him, but no one knows what to say to him, for which he's profoundly grateful. He starts a conversation with his long-lost cousin Hindol, pretend-ing to be unaware that Hindol had taken a vow of silence ever since his cult-procured Mizo bride stabbed him in the penis and ran away, but gets bored after a while. He finds unlikely allies: a group of teenagers brought here against their wills, white kurtas and kameezes dragged over their regulation clothes—he can see their T-shirts changing colour underneath. They're lurking on the landing discussing ways to murder various prominent guests. He approves of many of their choices: Tandon, apparently in the news recently for holding children captive in his workshops, gets eaten by cost-cutting robots; Satpathy, the mythology-astrology investment tsar and mainstreamer outrage ninja, has a sex dream about Mao and dies of shame; Shankar, the Chinese-made 3D-printed religious icon franchisee making loud, off-colour jokes about prostitutes with QR tattoos, gets an STD and is then clobbered to death by his corporate-Hindu-moral-instructor wife.

"Chopra, the positive propaganda thinktanker, is force-fed happy pills until he chokes," he contributes, at one point, forgetting he's a decade older than these kids.

"That's my dad," says the girl. The two boys with her size him up, consider punching him, but decide he isn't worth it. Or have they heard the rumours he's deranged, that he's been in rehab all this time? Is that what actually happened, has he just imagined the rest? He considers telling them about his imaginary friend Bon-Rui the Pangolin, an AR pet he'd fallen in love with as a child. He'd taken months to even acknowledge that Bon-Rui existed only on smartglasses his father had brought him from Japan; he'd been convinced the pangolin was just hiding. He'd grown so attached to Bon-Rui that he'd refused to take the smartglasses off, worn them all day and night for weeks, and they'd had to tear them off him as he screamed and kicked. He'd told them he could still see the bouncing blue pangolin for months after that, even without the glasses. They'd laughed, but he'd been telling the truth: he still sees Bon-Rui sometimes, but he's learned not to talk about it. He suspects these teenagers might not enjoy that story. They shoot him classic teenage dirty looks and slouch off, a clear lifelong pack of feral Useless Younger Children. They'll probably run the country one day. Rudra approves.

A quick foray to his brother's (fortunately empty) bedroom later, Rudra is relaxed, confident, and positively social. The family ghost drifts down the stairs and floats around the edges of clusters of conversation, accepting condolences with grace, wincing only slightly when the screenshades descend around the hall, cutting out the slanting afternoon sunlight and scrolling black-and-white graphics about his father. He is an ambassador from another planet, come to gather anthropological information about this place and time, and return to his own world with fascinating facts: it's not that much different from getting lost in wikis.

Most of the conversations are immediately discardable ones about numbers: square-foot costs, mileages, exchange rates, multibagger potentials, cash components. He stumbles into a group of women discussing their designer vaginas, and beats a hasty retreat. He's thrilled to hear that a long chain of murals on the highway depicting the transformation of Hindu men into gods through bio-augmentation have been burnt and covered in blood by unknown vandals, and the culture-terrorist E-Klav is a prime suspect. A man pitches a location-based mob aggregator app at him, thinking he's his brother. He meets a neuromarketer, a flying warehouse distributor, a portable crematorium arranger, a non-fungibility shaman, a viral mutation futurist, a detention centre designer, and a friend-renting social maven. He pretends to understand complaints from smart city investors who all bought land in the hills and seem surprised that construction is at least five years delayed, though this has happened every year for the last ten. They all want to move out of Delhi to find cleaner air. They will not. Everyone keeps complaining about the Chinese buying everything while scanning the room to verify there are no actual Chinese people present.

Rudra has always been skilled in knitting together the effluvia of other people's loose talk. He finds soon that he'd chosen, with his typical unerring accuracy, a very poor target for imaginary assassination: Chopra, whose daughter he'd recently offended, was just a medium-visible propagandist five years ago when Rudra last saw him, but is now access-caste elite, and the most important man at the party. You never know with people who claim to be access-Brahmins—some of them are just frauds claiming real connections to power to get invited to enough parties to launder their lies—but a quick look at Chopra's Flow Highlights reveals casually stockpiled one-degree relationships with real power. He's likely to be the real deal.

A single hour shadowing Chopra as he circuits the room, smoothly discarding unworthy networkers, and Rudra learns things he's sure he couldn't have off mainstream news if he watched it, and one of those things even he will remember: the social-credit rankings are coming back soon. His gaming circles had all been very excited by the prospect of limitless coding/hacking funtimes when the Indian government had tried to set up human scores in the early '20s. But the project had failed spectacularly, and it had been discovered that Chinese-owned shell companies were building India's surveillance infrastructure at a time when hiding Chinese land grabs from the public was growing impossible. And then the Indian technocrats handling the ratings system had decided that since India was still nominally a democracy, everyone should be able to rate everyone else in public. The resulting avalanche of online hate-mob attacks, offline revenge killings, and general furore over mass-downratings of every single well-known person on every point on the political spectrum had led to the project's sudden and welcome disappearance. But that was then.

"This time, the new idea is the old idea, haan? We're just buying the Chinese systems again," Chopra says. "Yes, I know, security concerns, but why pretend, sirji, the Chinese will find out everything anyway. All our data will be sold anyway, better we have some stake, no? What everyone forgets is that the Chinese are our friends now. We rename one neighbourhood after another—prime locations—to remind people this, bhai. No need to fight them all over the web anymore, but people forget."

This time, Rudra learns, your average Jyoti will never know what his rating is, or get to rate anyone else: it'll be wholly secret, wholly automated, based on every transaction, every observed adherence to or violation of every unwritten rule, every movement, every word spoken or messaged, every act of consumption, participation, or expressed emotion, and then categorised and filtered, obviously, by Jyoti's family, his community, his friends, his biometrics, and his overall performance relative to the ideal life he should be living as a Good Citizen. Only the Chopras of the world will have access to who Jyoti really is, will have a seat at the ceremony where Anubis weighs Jyoti's heart. No wonder everyone in the room is treating Chopra like a minor deity. Rudra's just grateful that he'll never see any of these people ever again. He wonders if Chopra's daughter and her boys were making actual death lists on the stairs: if this was the sort of job Daddy assigned them while he was catching up with new old friends.

There's just one major decision left as afternoon sinks angrily into evening: Should he have the last joint right now, or wait until after the long trek home? A decision he still hasn't reached when his brother's hand descends on his shoulder like the hammer of Thor.

Rohit semi-drags Rudra out of the hall, out through the kitchen where a small army of secret Bangladeshis is cooking for the guests, out into the farmhouse grounds. No doubt he has a small speech prepared about land and blood and how far they've come, but he checks the time and grimaces: always running slightly late, our Rohit.

"I choose to forget what I saw you doing in my room," says

Rohit. "It's not important, I'm just glad you didn't ruin the Mehta plan. Bastard doesn't even know he works for me now. Listen, let's just put the past behind us and talk brother to brother, okay? Baba's dead. The last couple of years have been difficult, you didn't know, but now the family has to come back together. Better days are coming again. So let me just ask you one question. Can I depend on you?"

"Yes," says Rudra on autopilot. Always agreeing with Rohit was something his lizard brain had taken charge of long ago.

"Do you know, when you were a child, Baba thought you were a retard? They were going to send you away, but I didn't let them. Whatever my brother is, he's my brother, I said. He's family. You'll realise this later, no one has ever been as good to you as I have."

"Yes."

"But I can't handle the whole family on my own anymore, and god knows Ma isn't any bloody help. We need you back. Playtime's over. I got mine too, I spent it neck deep in red meat and white girls in Berlin, and why you spent yours in Kalkaji surrounded by Africans and Bangladeshis—"

"May I point out that Bangladesh's economy has been growing faster than India's for a whole generation?"

"Quiet. Why you live like a middle-class loser stuck on your stupid computer I'll never understand. But blood is blood. Rudra, I was planning to tell you all this peacefully tomorrow, and move you back in here, and have the big meeting next week, with you properly prepared. But then you went ahead and showed up, so I've got to throw you in."

"In what?"

"Into your new life, idiot. You're getting a job. Now I can't let you fuck up the family business, but there's a huge expansion coming, and I need you to take charge of it in two years. You'll work for Chopra until then. Learn how the world really works."

"It's best for the family if I'm not given this sort of responsibility."

"Believe me, I know, and so does Ma. But it's good you've understood this. Means there's hope. This is a huge step up. It was supposed to be me, but Baba had to go and die ahead of schedule. This is everything we've ever dreamed of, so do not fuck it up, do you understand?"

He squeezes Rudra's shoulder, hard.

"I love you, brother," he says.

"I love you," Rudra says. It seems polite.

They hug. There's no time for further questions: Chopra steps out of the kitchen. Is there a Sinister Silent Entry app? Rohit introduces them and vanishes.

Chopra tells Rudra he's been watching the excellent work he's been doing at Harvard, while his eyes tell Rudra he knows absolutely everything about his real life, probably had a tracker inserted into his spine a few days ago. Rudra wants to run, and keep running, but his legs stay rooted as Chopra explains the job. The joints are kicking in now, and Chopra's talking really fast. Normally Rudra's good at just taking in words, leaving them in a pile in his memory to process later. But someone in the kitchen has switched on a massive exhaust fan; it's droning like a helicopter and he can't really hear anything. Is it all on purpose, so Chopra can't be recorded? Is he supposed to know how to lip-read? His throat is suddenly blocked: he can't summon up the courage to interrupt the access-Brahmin, he's flashbacking to childhood beatings from his brother. So much energy, even then. Chopra's saying something about human resources, competing with the Chinese on their turf, migrants, human utility and purpose, Kalkaji, domestic workers, missing children, opportunity, Rudra knowing how it is . . . the African exodus? Climate change? The Libyan slave markets? European blockades? Digital solutions? Immigrant control? The caste pyramid? Communist terrorists? Pragmatism?

It dawns on Rudra that he's being told about a slavery app.

His family is sending him to work as a slave trader.

The fan in the kitchen turns off.

"Formalities will be sorted next week, but I need to know if you're on board right now," says Chopra. He extends a hand. A blue pangolin appears on his shoulder.

And Rudra finds himself unable to speak. Chopra's eyes grow even colder. How is that even possible?

"Look, I'm really sorry to interrupt, Chopraji, but Rudra's hiding something from you," says a voice from behind the access-Brahmin.

It's Joey. Rudra's noticed her a few times during the day, running away from people pitching her Flow ideas.

Chopra raises an eyebrow.

"Rudra accepted a job offer from me this morning," she says. "I guess he's too scared to tell you? His family doesn't know yet. So, sorry if this is a problem, but he is taken, sir."

"Is this true?" Chopra snaps at Rudra.

"Yeah," he says. "Sorry, I—"

Chopra flashes his perfect teeth at them in the approximation of a smile, and silences him with a gesture. "Sorry for your loss, my boy," he says. "God bless, haan? Good luck."

"What a dick," Joey says as they watch him stomp through the kitchen. "Sorry, was that your dream job I just ruined? You looked like you were going to say something stupid, I waited and waited. But you weren't doing it, so I did."

"Thank you," Rudra says.

"So . . . my folks are finally getting the hell out of here and I came to see if you wanted a lift," says Joey.

"I do," Rudra says. "I also want that job you just made up. If possible. If it's not too much of a problem? Please?"

Joey spends a few seconds looking at him, and then shrugs. "Can you edit Flows?"

"Yes. I can edit anything," Rudra says. "Can you pay me in

cash? And can I live in the office? I think my family might un-person me. Or kidnap me."

"That's nice," Joey says. "Do you have any more of that weed you've clearly been smoking all day?"

He hands her the last joint.

"You're hired," she says.

CHAPTER 4

Late one night a week into his job, Rudra finds himself seated at a sprawling screen array watching in disbelief as his new Flowstar boss/flatmate has enthusiastic sex with his chief stylist.

This wasn't part of his schedule. The video starts autoplaying at 2 A.M., popping up over Rudra's Blockhead Combat multiplayer session. Possibly cued up by a two-person movement sensor? Indi and . . . he's forgotten the stylist's name: he was introduced to all of Indi's wellness team at one go, and he's never been very good at several name-face associations at once. He's often wished he could remember the names and faces of meat people instead of his immediate recall of every game character's full backstory and stats: rediscovery of those would have been so much nicer, so much less fraught.

Indi makes it worse by constantly referring to famous people by their first names like they're his closest friends: it took Rudra a while to understand that Toomas, some friend who said clever things about living in people's minds, was actually Estonian brain-tech icon Toomas Nigola, but Ailya the artist is not Hollywood MR-tist Ailya Kabaka but one of the makeup people. Indi is a mystery to Rudra, an antikythera device—he changes his own personality settings quite visibly, boosting his sociability, lowering his authority, channel-switching his humour like he's adjusting a photo for upload. He's sure Indi's sex-game is impeccably curated off top pornstars as well, but his ability to erase the men in those videos has rendered him incapable of spotting references.

He's seen the woman, the stylist, several times over the last week, walking past his editing suite on her way to the set of rooms that make up Indi's onscreen penthouse: she always smiles warmly. She's smiling now as she arcs acrobatically over Indi, spectacularly lit by the amber glow of his bedside mood-reading lamp set.

Rudra's fellow gamers shout in his ears in a range of languages, the auto-translator repeating their choice invectives a second later, but he ignores them: he's hypnotised. Behind Indi and his stylist, his forgotten Blockhead avatar abandons its cover, walks out into the open, and crumples to the floor, headshot by some amused opponent. He's never seen people he knows in porn before, and this is porn. They're on display. Indi's making sure her body catches the light as it changes colour off his smartatt reads, always a spectacular angle, never missing a beat, turning and placing his partner in an impressive sequence of positions, switching every few minutes in response to some internal timer, performing as ever for whoever his audience is: Does he see his own life in third person? Their bodies are impeccable, their movements in perfect sync, he wants to give them full marks, share, subscribe. This isn't their first time, and he has many questions: Is this another Flow that they're secretly recording, or is this how the audience-obsessed behave even when they're alone?

The video isn't going out on Indi's Flow, fortunately: he has no idea how he'd have stopped it. The live Flowscreens are all normal: a recap of yesterday's events, a visit to a robot-fighting contest, plus Indi and Tara doing couples yoga and some light scripted flirting. Tara's asleep in her bedroom right now, her smartatt readings all stable. Her onscreen boyfriend has clearly benefitted from all that yoga: Rudra watches spellbound as the stylist has a magnificent orgasm, all performance forgotten as she collapses in a heap on his bed. Indi lies staring at the ceiling, big smug smile on his face, breathing evenly, patting her shoulder absent-mindedly as she recovers. It makes no sense: Why would Indi be recording porn when there was already plenty of AI-generated face-pasted material featuring him and other Flowstars available? Is it just a celebrity hobby? Can he not perform unless he's on camera? But he hasn't looked into the camera, not even once. Does he not know he's on camera? Or does he know, and this is some sort of side-project passion of his that his last in-house editor, his cousin who got fired, was helping him with? Or does he not know, and the cousin was secretly collecting or even selling sex videos of him? Did Indi find out, and fire his cousin? No, the video wouldn't still be playing in that case.

Rudra tries to remember if Indi ever gave him some sort of secret wink, some unspoken bro-code signal, to let him know this was about to happen, but he's never been in any sort of situation like this, and he's never needed to know secret male signals. He can't remember when he last saw the penis of someone he'd actually met, and now he can't take his eyes off Indi's impressive specimen. Does it have its own social media presence, its own legion of followers, its own emojis? How much of a pervert is he for already having memorised every inch of the stylist's body? Is it less creepy or more because it's on a screen? He tries to shut the video tab, but it won't close. He turns off the screen.

Suddenly he's sure he's being watched: this is a loyalty test, an initiation ritual. An invitation from an all-seeing exclusive

Boys' Club, offices in London and Singapore. He looks around wildly, scanning the room around him with his phone, but there aren't any cameras that he or it can see. But there hadn't been any in Indi's room either: it's scanned every evening. Whatever equipment they're using for this is more sophisticated. Actual spyware, government or military or corporate-espionage level. Unless Indi or the girl set it up? Whether Indi knows about it or not, this is something Joey and the funders at least know nothing about. Or can they? Is this whole operation secretly a porn ring? How well does he even know Joey?

He turns his screen on again. Indi's on top now, pinning her arms down and thrusting violently, she's squirming and moaning under him. Rudra is both disturbed and relieved to find he's not even slightly aroused by this. That's not how this story is supposed to go: he's seen it a million times, Big Brother Surveillance porn has been the most popular category worldwide for three years running. The plots are always the same: government agent, usually male, surveilling forbidden lovers, then punishing them, then fucking them. He briefly considers barging into Indi's room and demanding an explanation, but he has nowhere to go after that inevitable firing: he left his old flat just in time in any case, another day and he'd have had to face the thugs his brother sent to look for him. This is his life now. This is home.

The video disappears after exactly half an hour, as mysteriously as it arrived. He looks around the computer but finds no trace of it, no recorded file, nothing in the bin, no hidden folder full of similar videos. Rudra is not any kind of real geek, or tech expert: he has no idea how anything really works. He scrolls through the open-area camera feeds, hoping to find some sort of Meaningful Clue. Nothing. The bodyguards are asleep in their off-set section cots. The night guards are asleep at their posts on the landing. The stylist doesn't leave Indi's room. He looks her up: her name is Neha. He puts the computer to sleep, and wishes until dawn that he could do the same to himself, but the memory of

Indi and Neha writhing ritualistically before their unseen god is burned into his brain, and it doesn't help that he's now absolutely sure there are eyes in the walls.

He doesn't remember sleeping, but when Tara wakes him it's almost noon; he's missed his alarm again and his arm is asleep. Indi and his squad left for some assignment early in the morning. They left her behind too, and she's not happy about it. If the whole point of her existence is to help Indi sell some sort of fancy sex measurer, how is she supposed to do it sitting in his flat?

"None of them have even bothered to hear my pitches for my plotline," she says. "Do you think that's right?"

He thinks it's terrible, but hastily lets her know he has absolutely no say in Indi's programming. "I know, but who does?" she says, but grins, and allows him to escape towards the coffee he needs to restart his brain.

He feels bad for her; they've made her do her guest segments, clean-ups, all the potentially sponsored bits Indi has no interest in: explaining freeze-dried biopharms, hawking self-repairing Yak-Yakshi T-shirts, being amazed anew every time she sees their luminescent fish . . . all very well, but how is this to transform her career, let alone her life? Rudra has no answers: all he has is residual guilt about the previous night—none of his previous porn-watching had prepared him for a situation where it was all part of a sitcom where he was a character, and had to have a conversation with the cheated-on girlfriend—and a yearning for the morning sounds of his old flat, where the walls were thin and he could tell the time by which neighbours were having family crises.

It's only after downloading two cups of coffee that he realises she wasn't telling the truth: he distinctly remembers her pitching her futurist character to Joey and Indi on his first day, and Joey at least had heard her out. They'd been eating lunch, delivered from a new Russian place: cold borscht, salmon kulebyaka, and an angry-looking golubtsy that everyone had looked at nervously before putting in the fridge, where it died. He'd not been paying much attention to the conversation, he'd been focussing on not developing an irrational and inconvenient crush on Joey: it had seemed unfair to expect her to sleep with him and meet his emotional needs, however minimal, after she'd already given him a job and a home and possibly saved his life. Tara had been talking for a while, something about how people were essentially good but also so pessimistic, and she wanted to spread positivity and joy. He'd only paid attention when she'd said, "Fun Fearless Female Futurism," and Indi had stopped her with a raised hand. They'd all watched him chew in silence for a few seconds.

"The show already has enough positivity," he'd said finally. "And I had to fight my own team to achieve that. People come and watch me because I say things that are real and meaningful, sure, but within limits—nobody wants to hear the stars who're just crying and moaning all the time, you know? 'Oh, look how we're fucking up the earth, killing all the animals, and all the people too.' Like if this ray of sunshine"—he'd gestured towards Joey with a fork—"were a Flowstar, we'd all be in depression. But we're already at the limit of—what was that, Joey?"

"The positivity-credibility intersection."

"That's the one. They measured it, and I aced it. It's science. Any more upbeat, and they'd think we don't care, or we're idiots. Filling space in between promos. It becomes Bollywood, or some guru shit."

"I want to reassure the audience that we haven't failed as a species, that humanity is doing a wonderful job. Together we will make the world less horrible," Tara had insisted, and Joey and Rudra had looked up from their plates and made eye contact.

"Excuse me?" Indi had been looking at Joey, not Tara.

"It's just a relationship segment, Tara," Joey had said. "People probably aren't tuning in to see if we're failing as a species?"

"The links are there, personal to global. We are transforming the world into a single organism, a hivemind, with one culture, one thought, one goal," Tara had said, not reading her lunch companions at all.

"Are you quoting something? Is this religion?" Indi had been watching Tara with a look Rudra recognised: he'd seen the same look of cold interest in his father's eyes when he watched stock market animations in the evenings.

"Tara, in your auditions you'd said you didn't have any strong political or religious beliefs," Joey had said. "Good interview strategy, but you're in now, and if you're here on some kind of mission, you need to let us know. I don't like propaganda of any sort on my Flows. Brand placement is bad enough."

"Joey turns down political parties all the time," Indi mumbles through a mouthful of borscht. "She thinks it keeps us clean."

"I'm just trying to tell you my vision of the future, if you'll let me," Tara had said, tears springing to her eyes.

"Oh, okay. You're a futurist. Go on."

She'd cleared her throat, very rattled but determined to power through. "It boils down to this: we are evolving into a creature beyond anything we have imagined. A superorganism, linked by algorithms and AI. This is our purpose and our destiny as the most brilliant animal, the most beautiful, the most responsible."

"The most responsible?"

"Why yes. We are building our own replacements, no? We cannot live in peace, we cannot learn from our pasts, we cannot agree on our futures. So we are building gods who can. We are teaching the machines how to be better than us. One day our children shall rule the stars, and they will be better than us. We did our duty, we should be proud. This is the message I want to share."

She'd looked around the table, expecting applause or at least argument, but Indi and Joey had both nodded and returned to their food.

"What do you think?" Tara had said.

"It's fine, I like it."

"But?"

"But it's not time yet. No one's ready for an Indian woman futurist," Joey had said. "You can try, Rudra will help, but you'll have to handle your feelings when they take your ideas and give them to some circuit dude."

"India's not one of the future-type countries, Tara," Indi had said. "Nice idea, though. I like how your mind works."

Rudra had felt bad for her then, but feels bad for himself now, because Tara repeats her whole idea to him, almost word for word, and then sits across the table, arms crossed, eyes full of rage.

"I don't know what you want me to say. I agree with you, I think," he says.

"I don't really care," she says. "Thank you for listening, at least."

She leans towards him, a rueful smile on her lips, and he's suddenly struck by how beautiful her collarbones are, and yanks his eyes away before they wander further. They always know when you're looking.

A lot of his week has been spent in taking basic Flow training classes with Tara. It's been easier than he'd expected: he'd thought Tara at least would be put through some sort of ballerina-schoollevel hardship. He's seen former K-pop stars do tell-all documentaries about the rigours of their training: the chaperones, the indoctrinations, the insane diets and exercise regimens, the body morphing. But no one's offered to add to Tara's height, or cut her eyelids: it's still India, and things are still loose.

All through the week, despite his trainers finding what he already knew, that he was bad at interpersonal communication (his results: he's good at avoiding using problematic words, but his references are too geeky for anyone else to understand), he'd been quite sure that Tara was flirting with him: a first for Rudra; normally the only way he learns of anyone being attracted to him is when they tell him five years later they thought he was cute five years ago. But there's something about Tara that still makes him feel that she sees him, and that he, and he alone, has her complete attention, that there's a special corner they lurk in together unobserved. But he now suspects all that was because she thought that as the Reality Editor and power-lunch companion he was actually someone whose approval she needed. When she realised—and he's vaguely pleased it took a whole week—that Rudra was largely superfluous to the whole operation, that Joey, Jin-Young, and the two Flow livestream-editors in Indi's OB van were in charge of how much screen time she got, she didn't drop Rudra entirely, but there was a very clear shift in her behaviour.

"You people are all confusing," she'd told him after a group meeting. "You all talk the same. Same words, same style. Same schools, same families, same friends. You see the same things, know the same jokes. It's hard to tell you all apart."

"I don't map into this analysis, but that's not relevant, I see what you mean," he'd said. "But you fit in perfectly well! I haven't seen you miss a single reference, or joke. And you wear better clothes than anyone else, as far as I can tell. I don't understand these people either, frankly. I don't fit in here either."

"That's because you didn't want to fit in, you chose not to," she'd said. "I wasn't raised to be a part of this group: I had to learn."

Not being flirted with is a condition both familiar and comfortable, but the urge to champion and protect a new human is unfamiliar for Rudra. Most of his Kalkaji friends have been through horrifying ordeals both while crossing the Arabian Sea and while struggling to make a living in Delhi. He knows at least five people who've been chased out of their flats by mobs, accused of being cannibals and demons and drug traffickers. But they'd spent some time getting to know him, playing his games and sharing his food, before opening up and telling him their worst stories, and he'd known that the guilt and rage he'd felt, and the desire to help them in any way he could, came from somewhere real. He'd brought a stack of CVs from his flat, handed them to Joey on his first day.

"I can't do anything with these," she'd said. But she'd kept them.

Tara keeps hitting him with stories of bad workplaces and exploitative situations she's survived, and he wishes he had the courage to tell her it's all too much too soon: he wishes he had the courage to really listen, or to tell her to see a professional. But he's grateful to have someone to talk to, even though Tara does most of the actual talking. He already knows how much of an outsider she is, how she grew up in Jaipur the daughter of proud-Hindu middle-class parents and ran away from a forced marriage and a dreary future to be a movie star, how at every stage of her life she's been gaslit by every elite she's encountered, how she expects nothing from Joey and Indi, how she is and always will be alone. He's seen her on the phone with her parents, though: they fight a lot, but they always call back. He's glad she has some strings holding her to the world, even if she cannot see them. Sometimes he feels untethered, floaty, even though he knows there are so many bindings he can't escape. It's like he's in an unconstrained open-world game with no map, and a smog as bad as Delhi's real-world one surrounds him while the streets shift and rearrange themselves anywhere he's not looking directly. Sometimes he wishes he had a smartatt actually monitoring *him*, maybe even medication of some sort. A few days ago, he'd spent hours speculating over ways to calculate exactly how many people had died in India over the last decade—off the map and off the books. And he'd been aware throughout that this was not something he knew how to do at all, that the world's best health statisticians had tried and failed at this quest because every official statistic that came out of India was a lie. He'd only realised that he wasn't okay, that he had gone into a void for far too long, stressing over an assignment no one had asked him to undertake or would reward him for succeeding at, when Bon-Rui had appeared, blue and bright and curled up over his monitor, looking soulfully into his eyes.

He's amazed at how much Tara still wants to belong, to fit in, after everything she's been through. He's spent so much of the last week feeling disappointed because life, yet again, had found a way to not give him his Chosen One moment: this new waypoint in his journey had not proven to be a gateway to some vast, shattering twist. None of the assorted costumed weirdos in the building have revealed themselves as a wizard or a kung fu mentor or a superhero recruiter waiting for him to arrive. His Reality Editor monitor array would have been perfect for a secret message announcing that all of the reality he knew was a lie, all his memories were false, that he was actually a cyberpunk anarchist trapped in a pod outside a simulated world, or an astronaut watching brain-TV in his stasis chamber on the way to some other planet, or a robot. He'd have made a good robot.

Tara's plan for their unsupervised day of fun is to explore their building: there are six whole storeys they haven't visited, each occupied by Flowco hubs in literally ascending order of importance. Indi is the only one who has a whole floor to himself, letting the others know exactly how high they can dream of climbing. The ground floor is full of constantly auditioning no-hopers, mostly gimmick acts: a walk from lift to lobby always involves avoiding performance artists, self-mutilators, streakers, jugglers, conspiracy theorists, animal/alien/celebrity impersonators, stunt people: Indi's Flowfunders are their landlords, but what they all want is active management, a team led by producers like Joey. Tara wants to find out everything about every Flower in the building, but Rudra has to decline: Joey's made it quite clear that the floors in the middle are off-limits until the funders are sure Rudra and Tara are not spies for another Flowco.

"As few selfies as possible, no replies on tags, no cameos, no being nice to strangers," she'd said, very firmly.

"I want to be part of the community," Tara had said. "People remember arrogance."

"And you want to be remembered," Joey had said. "Rudra, same goes for you. Don't be seen too much with the downstairs people, okay? Make all the friends you want, but keep it off cam."

He wonders if she knows about Indi's on-cam friendships: he can't get last night's video out of his mind. Worse, he can think of so many ways he could have handled the whole thing better— not watching the video at all, for one. He's just grateful he's not run into either Indi or Neha yet, just spent his morning pacing his room delivering low-stakes Hamlet soliloquies. Should he tell Joey what he saw? How? He's already heard she and Indi were an item in college, that's how she got her job. He hasn't spent enough time with his family to really learn how nepotism works. It's possible the team thinks he's one of Joey's exes as well. The whole point of his job is to be the one fired if anything goes wrong. Should he light that match himself? As the lift doors open and the low-level Flowers gape in awe at them, Rudra's dearest wish is to be as invisible as he's always felt.

A few Flowers recognise Tara and come and take selfies, and she poses enthusiastically, making a new friend every second: Rudra poses for some as well, not knowing how to say no, wondering if any of the people whose cams he's gazing blearily into has any idea who he is. A few seconds later, he sees Tara staring at him from inside an excited huddle, and is surprised to find the crowd parting as he steps forward, and leads her out. Somewhere along the journey from the penthouse, he'd acquired tremendous authority. Did they watch the lift to know what floors it went to? Had they ever accidentally mobbed delivery boys? That last answer is easy: there's a service elevator down a corridor from the lobby.

Tara had asked Joey for a bodyguard, and been very hurt by Joey's evident amusement. "Rudra will protect you," Joey had said, and so he's her appointed bruiser and companion on a discovery tour of ICB Market. This fits in with Rudra's schedule, which consists of exactly nothing except a compulsory journey outside the flat at some point because Joey thinks this will prevent him from going full hikikomori.

An unexpected burst of morning rain has cleared the air, it's actually possible to wander out without a mask for a few hours, an opportunity not to be missed. Tara has her AR headset and a booster strapped to her arm: this way she won't get mobbed, she explains. She gesture-plots their walk plan through the market, around the shrinking lake, past the ruins now being converted into an open-air theatre. She holds Rudra's hand completely unselfconsciously as they walk, and exclaims with delight as they cross a couple of air-dance artists and she sees, through her headset, the patterns they're weaving in midair with their smart styluses. Rudra's more interested in the shapes he sees moving swiftly from building to building, leaping across terraces and walking on wires. Monkeys, with shock collars attached to their necks, network booster packs strapped to their backs. He flinches every time one lands on the street and scampers past, but Tara is completely unmoved—she grew up surrounded by monkeys on the streets, and is amazed he's such a fragile creature. Rudra has vivid memories of the time he'd tried to defend his school lunchbox from a marauding monkey family, of the large circle of school kids that formed around them, laughing and encouraging them as they tore at his clothes and skin. Delhi monkeys used to be a huge menace until the government found a way to make them useful citizens: now they can't enter taxpayer houses without getting zapped. In less posh areas, homeless people make food money by acting as signal boosters, but homeless people aren't allowed in India China Brotherhood Market.

They walk through the market's lanes, stepping over mud-spattered spamphlets, rogue-drone-scattered sheets explaining, in plane-safety-illustration style, how to take out facial recognition cameras with laser pointers, or pole cutters. They avoid, with equal care, enthusiastic tourists with their lava-lamp spiritual T-shirts, their AR guides and tourist-company crowd handlers. Most of the restaurants haven't opened yet: by night these lanes are straight out of some exotic Hollywood Asian-fetish-exotic-tech-future movie, giant glowing signs, sexy holograms, colourful street food, smoke, filth, rubble. But by day they're just charming, photo-friendly and vaguely romantic, especially since the ICB Market area guards got stricter about letting locals in. His father would have approved. His father had once invested in a digital tourism company, where you lay down in comfy sofas in greenscreen rooms and travelled via Mixed Reality helmets, guided tours extra, while attendants of suitable ethnicities fed you Delhi versions of the appropriate country's food. Rudra had visited one of the parlours a few years ago, and hadn't been surprised to discover it was essentially a multicultural handjob centre.

He doesn't mind that ICB Market is an overpriced tourist trap. He avoided it all through school and college, but living in it has showed him it's also a portal between worlds: the Russians call this market Temno Kalingrad. It's where white immigrants gather to fortify themselves with alcohol before venturing out into the Delhi night in their retro-cool Crocs-and-socks. Plenty of the restaurants and shops are no-Indians-allowed: they're reluctant to admit even celebrities like Indi, who wouldn't be seen dead in any racist place, of course. He's heard that the Peach Blossom Spring, a very posh pan-Asian lounge, is where the upper end of the continent's human trafficking network operates. ICB Market is being recolonised by several countries at once, not that Rudra finds this disturbing: colour-coded colonisation is easier to identify and deal with than the other kind.

His phone rings: it's his brother. He lets it ring out, as usual. His mother has been calling every day as well, even sending him videos demanding to know what his plans are, and reminding him that all his betrayals will have consequences. They even tried calling Joey once, but she told them to fuck off in that really nice way she has.

He puts the phone back in his pocket, his hand shaking a little. Tara takes off her headset and gives him an enquiring look: he's tempted to pour out his whole life story to her, but resists. She draws him into her favourite coffee place, the trendy City of Cats, full of college kids running AR workgames and eyeing one another at retro-pirate torrentbooths.

"I used to dream of places like this, as a kid," Tara says. "Our local coffee shop was mainly a place for us to go to change clothes in before going to clubs. Then, of course, there was a scandal, there were cameras in the bathrooms."

Rudra stares at his matcha cheesecake a good while before speaking. "There are probably cams here as well."

"It's different now," Tara says. "Now we know."

An early batch of ad drones buzzes outside, promising Ladies' Nights and Lao Xiang tribe-finding socials, anti-pollution drones spraying the neighbourhood from far above: sometimes the sounds this market makes remind Rudra of his old neighbourhood, though they look nothing alike. Quite apart from the obvious upscaling of the buildings, he hasn't seen any African immigrants in the last week. The only thing in common is the kids in masks lurking in groups, phones out in every direction, recording everything.

The expats at the tables nearest them are posh-Asian, and Rudra's only helpful contribution to Tara's life so far has been helping her distinguish them by probable nationality. They've both already messed up with Jin-Young: in a rare burst of social initiative, Rudra had asked him where in Korea he was from, only to be told in Hindi that he was from Lajpat Nagar.

Jin-Young had told them how a very wasted Indi had met him in India China Brotherhood Market quite close to their current office, and had hired him on the spot based on Jin-Young's (actually nonexistent) resemblance to Comet5's lead singer. Why Indi had thought a billionaire global teen icon would be loitering in Delhi waiting to be hired by a rising local Flower, Jin-Young didn't know. But Rudra knows that's just how Delhi works: at his father's funeral he'd skimmed past several stories about yet another generation of white immigrants who just came to India to do drugs but ended up with top jobs, genius wives, and prime land. But these stories were just gateways to the ones they were really worried about: the ones about Chinese businessmen marrying Indians as well; now, no doubt, inspired only by true love and not because it was easier to buy land in their spouse's name. Rudra cannot imagine what the Culture Colony uncles would have made of Jin-Young's parents' North–South love story: his mother, a North Korean sociology student and drum-group performer at Delhi University, met his father, a Hyundai engineer from central Seoul on a five-year punishment posting, at a dorama club festival in Chennai, the heart of the Korean-Indian community. The Culture Colony kids would all have loved Jin-Young, though: nearly all of them are K-drama addicts.

"It's things like that AR history course you showed me that really make me feel my school life was wasted. I don't know if I'll be here long enough to finish it," says Tara, drawing him back to earth: it's possible he's missed a lot of her thoughts.

"You can access it from anywhere now that you have an account. I don't think the company will even notice," he says. "Just be careful with what you read, because even on the premium net there are always people watching."

"I'm not a child."

"I'm sorry. Of course you know all this."

But he's not sure she knows all this: how dangerous it is to open maps made in other countries, how news from India is completely different depending on where you see it. Does she know who actually runs the East? He doesn't. Some people in his gaming streams say it's China, some say it's Delhi, or a reunited Bengal corporate cartel funded by gods know who. All of these could be true: all these governments could be in operation at the same time. She hasn't grown up hearing about parallel economies, then parallel countries, then parallel internets, all stacked on top of one another like photo filters. He has. Though he can't claim he understood most of it.

"I know I can trust you to tell me the things I really need to know," Tara says. "Can I trust you? To tell me if I'm in any danger, even if it's a secret?"

He nods and smiles, but it's mostly because he's finally come to a decision. He's going to tell Jin-Young about the video.

"Then here's my secret. I'm not leaving anytime soon," she says, sipping her tea. "I'll finish the course."

That afternoon, while Indi and Tara flirt for the cameras, Rudra draws Jin-Young aside and tells him what he saw. He's never seen Jin-Young flustered thus far, and is disappointed that he doesn't seem even mildly surprised to hear that someone, possibly Indi himself, is running a sex tape operation out of Indi's bedroom.

"I'm glad you came to me," Jin-Young says. "We should take this to the funders at once. Ask them what should be done."

Rudra often thinks of himself as a fool, but he can spot an obvious coup in progress when he sees it. And he'd thought Jin-Young was the one person in the team who'd definitely be loyal to Joey. It's a shame: Jin-Young had seemed so nice, they'd bonded over living in South-Del immigrant neighbourhoods, about knowing what the warning signals for a police crackdown were, knowing how to get along with and occasionally shelter climate change refugees and medical immigrants from Burkina Faso, Gabon, Zimbabwe, and Eswatini. Jin-Young had been very impressed with him for being able to tell people from different African countries apart.

"I thought Indians were as racist as Koreans," Jin-Young had said, and had then endeared himself to Rudra considerably by spending at least ten minutes trying to come up with a nonracist explanation of what he'd just said, despite Rudra assuring him repeatedly that he wasn't offended in the least. He'd thought they could become brothers in awkwardness, even if Jin-Young was light-years ahead of him in terms of faking style. That they could sit together for years, watching the bar for minimum acceptable human behaviour standards slide lower and lower, and occasionally make off-colour comments about it, preferably while drinking. Even the idea of this is the best friendship Rudra has ever had.

But there's no excuse for this nakedly Joey-undermining plan, and Rudra knows he has to go talk to Joey at once: he has committed himself to a life of endless intrigue. Perhaps Jin-Young senses him withdrawing, because he corrects himself.

"By funders I mean Joey, of course. Everything through the proper channels. I've heard of this happening many times—the talent putting the Flowco in danger." Jin-Young is disappointed to hear that Rudra hasn't got any actual evidence: Rudra can see him wondering if all this is a trap, and is mildly pleased that he isn't the only completely paranoid person in this building.

"I believe you, but no one else will. We need video proof," Jin-Young says. "You must record it all next time. On your own phone. And stream it to me."

"So I'm supposed to stay up every night with a camera pointed at my screen?"

"Every night Indi has a guest, yes. If you like, I could move in and wait with you."

"No need," Rudra says. "I'll come to you and Joey when I have something."

Jin-Young nods. "Don't discuss this with anyone else," he says. Rudra wishes he hadn't brought it up at all.

Over the course of the week he's been impressed by Tara's shapeshifting abilities, something he's noticed in other people who grew up with a better sense than he had of how feudal the world actually is, and how much they'd have to do to fit in. To Joey she's a wide-eyed student, to the entourage a polite but demanding superior. With Indi she'd been playing it mildly mysterious—flirtatious, attentive, but distant enough to let him know he needed to woo her a little. Joey had stopped using their attraction stats off the smartatt extension within a couple of days: "It's like the government's air-quality index numbers, the truth is bad for morale." They'd just been faking the whole relationship for days now, based on audience comments. If their physical readings are to be believed, Indi's attraction to Tara has fallen drastically, and Tara finds everyone in the building repulsive: the Flow's lead romantic couple isn't compatible at all.

But that was then. Now, it's like Tara's downloaded an update that's reprogrammed her to see Indi as an object of absolute fascination. His every utterance is hypnotic, his every movement breathtaking. Under her rapt gaze, Indi absolutely blossoms: he's revealing dreams and aspirations that have Joey shaking her head.

"I've always wanted to be an animated character," he tells her as they hang out in the penthouse drawing room. "I want to teach my people how to dance, how to fight, in VR worlds."

"You can dance too? I love dancing, I trained in—"

"In VR, I can do anything, and so can my fans. They'll play as me in adventure games, I'll pop up on their phones when they're drunk and tell them to take a cab instead of driving."

Joey has to cut away to a recap after a few minutes of this, to tell Indi not to give away their entire programming schedule before the sponsors are locked. He's visibly irritated by this, but when he's live again he switches to personal stories: how he'd moved to Bombay to become an actor and moved back because all the male stars he'd hung out with kept showing him naked photos of themselves and he didn't enjoy the company of narcissists. Tara has stories as well, about growing up in Jaipur and running away during the 2026 water riots. It turns out they'd been auditioning in Bombay at around the same time, and they run various scenarios about how they might have met in audition lines. The viewers eat all of this up: already people are reFlowing recent Bollywood hits with Indi and Tara as the leads.

Rudra watches Tara in wonder: she seems to have genuinely fallen in love with Indi over the course of one day. Is this Stockholm syndrome taking effect? In the story breakdown the writer team has given them, Tara hasn't moved in as yet: her room is not a part of the floor section that's used as Indi's penthouse. But if their chemistry keeps working at this level, it's only a matter of time until Indi reaches the move-in plot point. Unless he's being cynical and Tara's just responding to Indi's charm? Rudra has felt a bit of it himself: it's not like he and Indi have actually hung out this week, but even their few minutes together have involved Indi providing useful mentorship, excellent male-bonding punchlines, and occasional inspiring quote-drops. In his presence, Rudra finds himself very fond of Indi, laughing or groaning with the rest of the crew as he goes about his Flow. It's only when he's alone in his suite, watching Indi on his screens, that he wishes he could edit the Flowstar clean out of his life instead of helping to build his image, pixel by pixel, moment by strategic-charisma moment.

"What brought me back here was not just the rejection, or the struggle," says Indi, staring into the middle distance as the sun begins to set over the ICB Market rooftops. "It was the need to be near the people I understand and trust, my spiritual community. I'd done so much free work for people I admired, for 'exposure,' before I saw those people were going to drain me of anything that might be unique about me, and I almost lost myself to them, you know? It was the emotional labour, not just the physical. I swore I'd never do that to the people in my life if I ever became someone important."

"I also believe that collaboration is the key to humanity's future," Tara volunteers, but Indi's in Flow. He raises the stakes at once, and turns to the cam.

"I'd find my people and stick with them, and together we'd

build something new and amazing. So I know I'm not supposed to say this on my Flow, but I think my fans will understand and forgive me. You people, yes all you behind the camera, who give up so much for me and the people who see this? You're my family. I thank you. And I love you."

Rudra looks around the room, and everyone's staring at Indi with real love in their eyes. Jin-Young applauds silently. Joey shakes her head, hiding a reluctant smile. Tara's almost in tears.

That night, when the video tab pops back up on Rudra's screen, of course Tara's in Indi's room, and Rudra feels no surprise.

For a single second that lasts forever, he watches Indi pull her T-shirt over her head. Then he's up, out of his room, forgetting to breathe as he sprints across the hall. He bangs on Indi's door like the house is on fire.

"Go away!" Indi calls.

"I'm sorry, something's wrong. You need to stop."

Indi pulls his bedroom door open a minute later. Tara's on his bed, wholly clad. She doesn't meet Rudra's eyes.

"What the fuck do you think you're doing?" Indi's voice is ice.

"A video appeared on my screen," Rudra says. "Showing images from this room."

Indi considers this for a second. "Is it going live?"

"No."

Indi walks over to the edit suite, Rudra a step behind. He stares at the tab, which shows Tara hugging her knees on his bed, rocking back and forth.

"How long has this been happening?" asks Indi.

Rudra considers his options. "Once before," he says. "I didn't know what to do."

"When, yesterday?"

"Yeah."

He watches Indi wondering whether or not to hit him: he clearly wants to hit someone.

"Get the fuck out of my house," Indi says finally.

When Jin-Young finds Rudra an hour later, he's just wandering the ICB Market lanes, watching drunk people stagger out of clubs, watching tearful farewells and breakups, watching policemen and criminals wait in shadowy corners for their chosen prey, watching a pair of holo-ad dancers loop relentlessly in invitation over rolling giant dice at a casino entrance. Rudra's been mistaken for many things in this time: a drug dealer, a driver, a pimp. He stares hollowly at Jin-Young as he approaches, blue hair reflecting bright neon signs around him.

"Where were you?" Jin-Young shouts. "I've been calling you for ages."

"I don't know," Rudra says. "Just . . . I didn't have anywhere to go."

"Well, stop this drama and come back to the house," Jin-Young says. "Everyone has questions."

The meeting is in Indi's bedroom. He's asked Tara to wait outside. They've found the hidden camera: it's tiny, and was embedded in the room's smart sensors, which is why the scans missed it. Joey tosses it from one hand to the other. She looks half asleep: Rudra notices her Yak-Yakshi shorts with something that will turn into amusement one day.

"Joey says she trusts you, but I still think you fucked up," Indi says. "Looks like it hasn't leaked, so you're not fired. Yet."

"Do you know who it is?" Rudra asks.

"I think it's my bloody cousin, but obviously he's not answering." Indi glares around his bedroom as if to yank out more hidden surveillance equipment with the power of rage alone.

"So here's something to ask yourself, Rudra," Joey says. "Do you think that friend of yours, Chopra, could be behind this? He's been trying to invest in the Flowco since we met, and also to hire me for some government thing. I looked him up, and he's really not someone we can fight."

"I don't know," he says. "I don't think I'm important enough to matter to someone like that guy. I'm nobody."

"Some political thinktanks have approached our funders as well. They're actually very pleased about it," Joey says. "Maybe we made more of an impression on him than we realised."

"I don't think this is about Rudra or you," Indi says. "Obviously one of the big companies got to my cousin."

"Obviously," Joey says. "Listen, I never asked you why you fired him, but if there's anything that puts the whole team in danger, you need to tell us. Now would be best."

"We had a fight about something," says Indi. "Actually, that's probably why he set up the camera in the first place. I don't think we should worry about it. Even if he leaks some sex video of mine, it only helps our ratings. And we can always say it was faked. Right? I've heard of people putting this stuff out there on purpose."

"Would you prefer talking to Legal?" Joey asks. "I understand if you're not comfortable telling us, but I need to stay ahead of whatever story's coming. I'll have them come in and brief you."

"No, absolutely not, I hate those guys. Just . . . forget about it, okay? We need to have better security, though. Rudra, I'm putting you in charge of that."

"Really," Joey says, her face so impassive everyone in the room flinches.

"And Joey, I don't appreciate that tone. I've had a few people over, but there's no story you need to worry about. You have no idea how much stress it is, being me."

Rudra looks at Joey, and winces in anticipation of whatever she's going to say; across the room, Jin-Young does the same. But Joey says nothing. Indi glowers at her for a few seconds.

"Are you pissed off, or is it one of those times where you shut down and restart and then talk in jargon that no one else understands because you've gone into expert robot mode?" he asks.

Joey stays silent.

"Don't look at me like that," Indi snaps.

He rolls his eyes as she storms out.

Later that night, Rudra sits alone at his screens, playing Block-head with another international cabal. There's a soft tap on his shoulder. It's Tara. He pulls off his headphones.

She puts a finger under his chin, tilts his face up, and kisses him, very quickly, very gently.

"I'm glad you're here," she whispers, and walks away.

Rudra wants to run after her, but doesn't know what to do when he catches her, or what to say, and every wall has eyes.

CHAPTER 5

Virtual Reality meetings are the kind Joey usually hates least. She loves the idea of spending more time alone in her flat, of not having to worry about body language signals or enemy-turf micro-emotion facial scanners. She would have taken all meetings in her bedroom, dressed in carefully defiant pyjamas, naked on formal occasions. But of course Indi doesn't like to do meetings alone. He used to be mystified, in college, when she insisted they spend some time apart. The first time they'd slept together, it was only because he'd timed it perfectly right, and told her he was scared of sleeping alone, and all the traffic lines on her phone were red.

It hadn't been a good morning. She'd run out into the lobby to find two building guards pushing a maid around. Someone had robbed the Israeli couple's flat, and they needed someone to blame, and were interrogating the maid. She'd yelled at the couple, who were standing to one side, watching, shaking their heads like they were very sad about all this, but what else could be done? She'd yelled at the guards, who'd asked her to file a complaint with the Association, and promised not to beat the maid too much.

The maid's face, first when Joey intervened, and then when she looked at the time and ran, stayed with her all through the quick drive to ICB Market. That, and for some reason, the girl who'd left the audition after Uma, whose name Joey's already forgotten, if she ever knew it.

"You're all monsters," she'd said.

It's just her and Indi in the meeting today, and they're sprawled on beanbags in the penthouse living room, helmets on heads, haptic gloves covering most of their arms. She'd taken a certain pleasure in leaving Jin-Young out. She's chosen to believe he was trying to protect her from Indi's home-porn venture, not using it to upstage her. But she's learnt very quickly to send clear signals to her teams when they've overstepped, which they do quite often. When she'd started out, she'd been all about building that second line, training her replacements for the good of the organisation and all the other things her mother had taught her. But she learned very quickly that the best way to acquire a reputation as the best in the business was to make sure she never taught anyone everything she knew, and to make everyone think she had many secrets and buried skeletons, even when she didn't. Assuming they thought about her at all—she hadn't found a single way to determine if other people found her mysterious and enigmatic. One couldn't just ask.

Another thing Jin-Young doesn't know—and they'll all get fired if the funders find out—is that Rudra's added Cyber Bazaar pirate plug-ins to their Mixed Reality sets, so they can record the meeting, and even share it live.

Rudra's hooked into the meeting as well, from his edit suite. He'd pulled the extremely illegal pirate-tech out of a decaying rucksack quite casually, and told her he'd used it to share streamed shows and games with his always-broke neighbours, mainly so they would get off his sofa and go back home. Joey had hesitated a long while before asking him to participate, but she needs him for a very specific reason. The Flowco's mysterious new investor is leading today's meeting, and she needs Rudra to see if he's an access-Brahmin friend of his family.

When their Narads are done setting up and testing everyone's connections, Joey and Indi warp in, to discover their virtual selves sitting on mats on a tropical beach. Before the others arrive, Joey does the customary once-over of her sim's yoga-influencer body, and resists the urge to jump up and launch into lewd dance routines.

The sea is calm, and there's a perfect digital sunset behind them. There are dolphins in the distance, taking turns leaping out of the water, squeaking in identical audio loops each time. Joey's never seen a single meeting environment without at least one overdone element. The others appear one by one: Funder Radha, Founder Karan, and three strangers. Joey and Indi are evidently the least-rich people in the conversation: they're using scenario-determined avatar bodies (beachwear-clad, in this instance) with their faces awkwardly pasted on the heads, but all the others have hologram avatars of their real-world suit-clad bodies. A tragic waste of Indi's many abs, really. The funders introduce them to three representatives of their new investors: Li Yun, a celebrity-incubator mentor from Hong Kong; Stephen, an election consultant from London; and their leader, Nikhil "Nick-to-Friends," from a private jet but originally from Delhi. They all look as if they're in their early thirties. Joey's seen far worse. She's impressed by the extensive work Nick-to-Friends has had done on personalised rotoscoping, so his avatar always seems slightly better defined than the others, his features just that little bit more chiselled. He must be very important.

—They put us on mats and got stools for themselves, Indi growls on private chat.

—Let it go, Joey messages.

—Our backs are to the sunset. Petty shit. Always petty shit.

—Doesn't matter.

She knows it's pointless trying to hold Indi back when he feels like he's not being treated well: he's told her several times she doesn't understand this aspect of the business, and should just leave the primate-dominance manoeuvring to him. They've argued about this before, it's always ended with her ragequitting after Indi's use of the word "nuance." He tells the funders he doesn't like this beach, and asks for a more interesting background. Joey's glad Li Yun's present as well: once, before face ID in meetings, Indi's location-shift demands had led to a producer switching on a strip club backdrop because he hadn't realised Joey was a woman.

—I don't know any of these people, Rudra messages on superprivate chat. Can I go?

—No. Be useful. Stalk them, get background.

The funders change the setting: it's now some sort of Greek ruin, surrounded by hills, and they're all seated on pillar stumps. High-res birds fly in perfect circles around purple clouds above them. She and Indi are now in toga-clad avatars, faces now starkly brown over white bodies, their hosts in somewhat more ornate togas draped over their holo-suits. Fortunately Indi doesn't notice the imbalance, and now the actual work can begin.

"Everything in this conversation's covered by blanket nondisclosure, standard procedure, the forms should be arriving on your screen now. Sign them," says Nikhil. After they've wiggled their fingers dutifully, a slideshow starts playing between two massive Corinthian pillars behind him as Nick-to-Friends explains who he is.

If he's to be believed, Nikhil's the man behind most of the innovations that have kept mainstream Bollywood theatres alive over the last few years. He claims he's responsible for the segregation of screenings into "Proud Patriotic" and "Luxury International," forcing every filmmaker to shoot at least two versions of their stories. Joey's less convinced by his claim to have invented the new half-hour Emotion Moments screenings, that just show fights, songs, and assorted Loving Family, Comedy, Sad, Inspiring Lessons, and Indian Feelings Moments. And she's absolutely sure he's lying when he says he's behind India's first AR-integrated film franchise, a small-town remake of a noughties religious children's animation show. She knows the two women who actually made that.

She's always impressed by the casual confidence with which the Nick-to-Friendses of the world simply take credit for other people's work and ideas. It's not new, but it really never will go away—and she suspects Nick, like other operators she's seen, genuinely thinks he invented everything he stole, especially from invisible women. She's learned, over time, that actually executing any of her plans usually involves three people above her in the food chain claiming to have come up with her carefully documented and publicly delivered idea. One of them is usually Indi.

"Here's something no one knows about me," Nikhil says with the air of a man who's told this story in a thousand meetings, "I was also the lead investor in the Pure India open-world game. My partners thought I was crazy—do you know why?"

"Yes," Joey says.

"Nick, no matter how much money you make, don't do it, they said. Like, we all want to run around shooting the anti-national types of the day, sure, but a game where you do it and post your videos? The woke elites will fuck you up, they said. I told them they'd just do our marketing for free. They came on board then, because they know me. I bought a mansion in Berlin when I sold my stake. Investors don't understand this country, man. You can do anything here, as long as you don't make powerful people look bad. That's the only crime."

"Was this before or after people started the actual killing videos with the game's music?" Indi asks.

"Well before. Listen, the game had nothing to do with that, people have been posting kill-vids for like ten, fifteen years in India. Point is: I change the playing field, whatever the game is, and if you stick with me, your life changes. You're not an Icon yet, Indi Mathew. Why is that?"

Joey can't remember when she's immediately hated anyone more. Rudra returns with information: there isn't any real data available on Nikhil, or Li Yun, or Stephen, nothing on the web except corporate press release jargon-pits. All personal socials locked, no Flows, no pictures—though Li Yun face-matches closely with one of the Chinese pop singers who went missing recently after a social ratings fraud scandal. They're a corporate assassin squad, they leave no traces. She asks Rudra to tell his AI to look harder, and is surprised to find he doesn't use an AI assistant, so this is all he can get her. So either they're access-Brahmins with the ability to control their public data trail, or they're just made-up avatars, shell people, and anyone could be behind them. Neither of these are good options.

—Can I go now, Rudra texts.

—No.

"I've been watching your Flow, man, from the very beginning. I'm a massive Indi stan, but I'm going to put my fandom in a box. I have to talk straight, pure business, man to man. We've got to relaunch you. Your brand is dying."

Joey can almost hear a prerecorded beat in the background as Nikhil takes them through a quick presentation about Indi's career so far. She agrees with all of his insights. And that's because, predictably, they're hers, repackaged from her reports and proposals to the funders. A lot of the slides are direct swipes. They haven't bothered to change the text, but they have changed the animations, and the colours on the graphs. The funders are lapping it up, and Indi seems enthralled as well. They're probably seeing them for the first time.

—This is all stuff I've told you, she messages.

—Relax, I know, he texts. Put your hand gestures on Auto. You're looking hostile.

Thanks to his excellent advice, no one can see Joey giving them all the finger in the real world a second later. She can't see her hands, but she can feel them sweating.

Unmoved by her withering gaze, Nikhil delivers his essential pitch, a standard new-boss move: that Indi has everything it takes to be a global Flow Icon, and the only thing holding him back is his present strategy team. Joey would have panicked if she were less used to this. It's quite evident Nikhil is far too big a deal to really care about who manages Indi. All of this is just a stone tossed in the waters.

"You've been brainwashed by Hollywood," Nikhil says. "It's such a trap for global Indians like us, they make us think they're better and we copy them."

"Maybe your generation," Indi says, and Joey fist-pumps next to him like a child, "but we grew up seeing bad news out of the West. Corruption, racism, Nazis, disaster capitalism, the military-industrial complex, all the stuff we have here. They've been letting the world know who they are since I was in my teens. Old people didn't know, but we never thought America was better than us. We're brainwash proof. I'm a minority here as well, but I never tried to move."

This is news to Joey, because Indi had most definitely tried to move, and she had done all the paperwork, but she sees how bringing that up might not be a great idea.

"Nice try, bro, but I see right through it," Nikhil says. "Of course you don't want to change, you've worked hard, it's worked out, you're a star. But you're smart as well, that's why you've been chosen. All you need to do? Understand the real India."

"Oh man, not again. People keep telling me I don't understand India," Indi says.

—Indi no. Not Meaning of India, messages Joey.

About India debates can go on for days once Indi gets into them.

"Well, tell me then. What is India about?" Nikhil asks.

"I feel like you're going to tell me."

"India is about staying the same but acting like you're going to change soon. That's all it is. You're an insider, Indi. Minority, English-type, whatever. You stay in, because you follow the rules. You see what you need to be in line with, and when the rules change, you change faster. You serve the king until you're king one day, and then you make the rules."

—How much will you pay me if he brings up the Ramayan within, say, five minutes? Joey asks.

—Two minutes, how much you want?

—Just lunch.

"Look at the biggest stars, all the Icons in any field, all through our history," says Nikhil. "They can come from anywhere, but in the end, for them to rise to the throne, the people must see them as Ram."

—That's worth two lunches at least. Should I order? Joey hasn't smiled this much at a meeting in years.

—Shut up.

—What do you feel like?

"Sushi," says Indi, and realises too late he's said it out loud. Nikhil stops his presentation: his digital face looks irritated.

"This is like sushi," Indi improvises. "It's neatly packaged, solid ingredients, but frankly we've seen this before—a little obedience, a little disruption, whatever. I have now understood India. What next? How do I become a global star?"

"You don't," Nikhil says.

"I'm sorry?" Indi sounds really confused. Very few people ever tell him he can't have something he's said he wants, that's Joey's job.

"Indi, Indi, Indi, please tell me you're not an Indian who thinks the rest of the world might find you interesting," Nikhil says.

"I totally am, Nikhil."

"Bro, you have to stop! The Americans don't care about you. Except the desi ones, who will hate you most. Look. If you want to be West-facing, there are specific roles you can fill. And you need to customise your content to fit those roles, and you're not doing that."

"Specific roles?"

"I assume you know? You have to be a Spice Boy. There are five. Hot Exotic, Mystical Guru, Suffering Savage, Culture Professor, and Tech Savant. The slots are taken, there can be only one of each. And obviously you have to move your ass across the world."

"There are exceptions."

"First-generation ones? Where? You could take a crack at it, maybe, but you'd start at the bottom. It's a long climb. I suppose you could get there, but the return on investment is very low. We won't take that journey with you. You think immigration categories and border controls are just for your body?"

"What do you mean?"

"Do you really want the rest of your career to be a visa form? In India, you're a demigod. In the West, you'd be another useless immigrant. They'll want to measure you, test you, give you cavity searches, put you in a box, send you back. Even if they let you in, they'll tolerate you at best. Just for the third-world eyeballs you'd bring. Your children might be stars, but you'd be B-list for life. That's not what you want."

"People have broken through before, Nikhil."

"Sure. They're geniuses right out of the gate. You know I love you, but you're not a genius."

She can hear Indi growling. She wonders if he knows he does it out loud.

—Can we not fight with the new boss? Joey asks.

—Who the fuck does he think he is?

—Just say yes to everything, let him move on, we go back to normal.

Nikhil is far from done. "The fact is, bro, you don't have it made in India either. The people here who like you now, your biggest fans? They're high-end, trend-conscious, always need to discover some fresh trophy. But one day—and this is about three months away, for you, we see the numbers—they'll find the next trend, and they'll drop you."

"I guess I should check and see if any other Flowco wants me," Indi says.

"Please, don't even go there," Nikhil says. "Like, just skip those moves. This Flow trend? It won't last. It'll get buried by fucking billions of three-second videos from nobodies. And then the Chinese will figure out some way to automate even that. New shit is always on the way, and the hoops you have to jump through keep getting smaller. You'll have to spend the rest of your career leaping from bubble to bubble, hoping the audience comes with you, while younger and hotter kids snap at your heels."

"Nice to know I'm valued."

"This is the best day of your career, Indi. Day Zero."

"Because you're here now to save me?"

"Yeah. And we're going to absolutely crush the competition. You and me, we're the same. We're monsters, baby."

And Joey finds she can't breathe.

Her smartatt goes berserk. She takes off her helmet, slowly, and the cool air-conditioned air hitting her face is the most pleasure she's felt in a long time. She places it on the floor, ashamed of her trembling hands. A few deep breaths, and she feels a little better, though the room's spinning slightly. She's sweating all over. She reaches for her phone, and another spell of dizziness hits her, this one worse: she rises, and totters towards the bathroom. Indi pulls off a glove and gestures: what? She reaches for his hand, squeezes it, and stumbles away.

She turns on her phone in the bathroom. Narad has much to say, about panic attacks and heart attack risks: she's already sent Joey's doctor her readings. Joey swipes Narad silent, and grips the comfortingly cool washbasin, reminding herself how to breathe. Her ears are pounding and bright red.

She calls her building, and asks the manager what happened with the maid in the morning. "It's all right," the manager says. "They left their window open, and some birds flew in and made a mess, and they think we are all thieves, na madam?"

"The guards can't push the staff around like that," Joey says.

"Oho, madam, don't worry, they are all friends."

"I'm serious."

A long pause: she knows he's biting back insults. "Do you wish to file a complaint with the building society, madam?"

"No."

"Thank you. Are you all right, madam? You sound unwell. Have you eaten?"

They're still at it when she puts her helmet back on. It's possible no one even noticed she was gone, except Indi, whose angry chat messages and increasingly indecipherable notes on the meeting are all she can see on her view.

—Where the fuck were you? Indi asks.

—What did I miss?

—I wrote notes.

He wants a gold star. She can see the sulk in his messages, they're practically vibrating. There's nothing Indi hates more than having to write things down, and she wishes she weren't so used to this that she has no problem understanding what he means through his labyrinth of typos and misplaced autocorrections. Nikhil thinks even Indi's most loyal fans will switch to Japanese laifu-VR or Chinese neo-wuxia. Joey actually agrees with this, and what Nikhil says about Indi not being the type who'd ever attract "real" Indian superfans, who build temples to their idols, attack people who say bad things about them, tattoo their faces on their hearts. Indi's never done anything terrible enough for her to wish that life on him.

—But what does he want? Joey asks.

—Fuck knows, Indi says. I was waiting for you to get back.

"You have to understand we live in overlapping realities right now," Nikhil says, pulling her back into the conversation. He's swaggering around the virtual Parthenon, no doubt imagining he's some kind of ancient philosopher. "You can change the reality you live in like switching channels. And all the realities want to eat each other."

—Is he pitching a movie or just drugs? Joey asks.

—I'm going in.

"I'm going to stop you here," Indi says. "Look—bro—I can see you're a brilliant guy. But there's one problem."

"What is that?" It's difficult to tell from avatars, and for all Joey knows Nikhil's got emotion-masking tech in play, but he's certainly signalling interest.

"If I told you that you were getting everything wrong, and you asked me how I could fix it, and I basically negged you and then started talking about the multiverse, what would you say?"

Nikhil laughs out loud. "I like you, Indi Mathew," he says. "You and I, we're going to make magic together."

"Can't wait," Indi says. "So we're good here?"

"No. I wasn't joking when I said you're heading towards a massive downslide."

"Right, and you're the only one who can save me."

"You're riding high right now, and you don't see the cliff you're heading towards. On your way down, you'll meet four generations of next big things, faces of the New Global India. All your teen crushes. Still alive, still around, hosting sports and travel mainstreamer shows. Lurking outside gyms, waiting for paparazzi. Reality show cameos. Yoga, candles, inspo. Fighting over dressing rooms with the kids competing in the music contests they're judging. Pretending they're still famous and relevant on their Flows."

"I'm better than those guys."

"How many examples do you need? All those genius new-wave

filmmakers, slum rappers, woke comedians, videosplainers, where are they now?"

—He's looping, switch topics, Joey messages.

Indi doesn't respond. He's twitching so hard his onscreen avatar is glitching.

"I know what I'm doing, and it's working," he says.

"You don't, and it isn't," Nikhil says.

It's clear they're going to dance-fight for a while, so Joey takes her helmet off. She puts on earphones, and lies back on the beanbag, staring into her phone. There are several missed calls from her mother, followed by priority messages telling her to ignore the calls, everything's fine. She'll have to call Romola soon, it's been a while. The news, otherwise, is no more terrible than usual. Today's crisis is a drone that has flown—from Russia, it's rumoured—all the way to Gurugram, and into the house of a retired singer. It has shot him, his family, his staff, and even his dog, and powered down. No one knows what to do with it, and so it's now in jail.

In her ears, Indi and Nikhil are doing a round about how people are fundamentally stupid (Nikhil) or good but programmable (Indi).

The messages in her Abuse-filtered inbox are the usual: a parade of strange penises, a torrent of invective, death and rape threats. She swipes them away lazily, pleased at how much space she's clearing up despite knowing she has unlimited space. There's shouting in her ears: she forces herself to listen.

"The things you're telling me now? I've heard them at every audition in Mumbai," Indi says, his voice shaking more than it would if he were acting. "I still hear them in most meetings. You live in a bubble, Indi, you're not real. Right from the first day I started Flowing, people who weren't storytellers tried to teach me how to tell stories. All the success I've found has been because I'm smart enough not to listen to them."

The messages in Joey's Low Priority inbox are a different story.

Thousands and thousands of audition videos, idea pitches, port-folios, photoshoots, CVs. Complaints, pleas, outbursts, hate mail cleverly worded enough to escape her content filters. What puz-zles her most are the people who send her pictures of flowers, landscapes, movie stars, babies, hundreds upon hundreds, all of which bear only the words "Good Morning." What do they hope will happen? How long will they keep at it?

"All the people I really admire from this part of the world have gotten where they are by ignoring the suits. They've had no choice—they've had to invent their own paths," Indi says. "So no. No scripted mainstreamer soap. No slapstick-melodrama garbage. No laugh tracks. No politician guest appearances. No Bollywood promo special episodes. No South Indian comedy character. No token Christian liberal beef-eating sex-mad friend. I'm not doing any of it."

"Well, I think we can all agree this is a fascinating discussion." It's Founder Karan's voice, and Joey tosses her phone aside and scrambles for the headset, stepping back into the virtual world just in time to see Indi's toga-clad avatar vanish as he logs out of the meeting. "I'll, um, be back," she says, and logs herself out.

They go to the kitchen and drink the freezing water their Narads have waiting for them in amicable silence: by the time he's drained his, Indi's all cheerful again. They let two calls on Joey's phone ring out, then one on Indi's.

"So—did we achieve anything there?" Indi asks.

"Work."

"Then why did it take so long?"

Joey shrugs. "Meetings."

"What were you doing, anyway?" Indi asks. "Did you need to take a shit or something?"

"Do we have a plan?" Joey asks as they put their helmets on.

"They need us," Indi says. "Never forget that."

She never knows whether it's inspiring or worrying that he knows how to deal with these people. It's convenient, they often win, but it always reminds her of the time Indi had taken her to an insiders-only no-phones private event called Desi Power Chakra or something even worse. She'd been worried it was a shady-politician networking event, or a gateway cult thing, but it had turned out to be something far worse: a presentation. Some Indian-American hair-gel-reservoir type had mashed together pickup-artist techniques and wikis about Indian political strategists, Chanakya onwards, to put together a very predictable set of self-help tips for neoliberal sociopaths, no doubt using the already-everywhere blockchain.

She'd half slept through it, and dragged Indi away from the post-presentation drinks schmooze, but on the drive back he'd completely shocked her by revealing he'd actually enjoyed it, that if he'd known how to use the enemy's tactics against them, how to make the enemy think he was a friend, and how to always think three moves ahead, his life would have been much better. And that he was going to use these techniques, use the tools of evil but for good, and thus transform himself into a global superstar. He'd laughed at her completely horrified face and said he was joking, but she'd been worried, and still is. Not about Indi turning into some kind of multi-step schemer, he doesn't have the attention span to be strategic or forward-thinking, but for herself: that somewhere inside her is a Desi Power Chakra Joey, just waiting to break free.

The next phase of the Nikhil meeting is set in an underwater paradise: everyone's hovering in incredibly blue water, surrounded by schools of cute digital fish. Presumably this is supposed to be calming, but all Joey can think of is drowning, of unimaginable amounts of pressure crushing her into the ocean floor. She calms herself by thinking of Toons, who'd been to Thailand recently, to shop for vast quantities of seamless innerwear and perform in some pan-Asia traditional dance thing. She wishes Toons were here right now instead of these idiots, swimming about in front of the replica of the Great Barrier Reef that lies in the far background, a burst of splendid twentieth-century colour. The tiger shark that floats above Nikhil's head is a bit much: it cannot possibly be a coincidence, but it's not like anything else about him has proved particularly subtle thus far.

"Joey had some ideas she wanted to pitch to you," Indi says before Nikhil can get in a word. She's used to Indi suddenly throwing the ball in her court in troubled situations, and so she launches right into it. The new investors stay eerily quiet as she outlines Indi's wants: the animated avatar, the video games, the AR expansion, the interactive tutorials, the smartatt apps.

"I don't see the vision," is Nikhil's response. "Anyone can be popular. Multimedia expansions are boring now. They'll get done, but they're for mid-level people."

"You need to stop gaslighting Joey," Indi says. "Or anyone else in my team. We're like a family."

—No worries, Joey texts.

—I mean it.

—He should have told us his vision by now. It's weird he hasn't.

"I'm going to let you into a little secret," Nikhil says. "We all know what the keys to success are, right. And you've got most of them down. Your team's the best in the business. If I thought they weren't, I'd fire them. I don't have time to send them hugs. They work hard, and they have good ideas, but they're missing one thing. My personal key to the big wins is pretty simple—a killer combo."

"Like in fighting games?"

"Yeah. A quick set of wins, perfectly timed, as flashy as they need to be, and you break through to the next level. Everything else is maintenance. Necessary, sure, but nothing I need to supervise."

Joey can think of a few killer combos she'd like to perform on Nikhil—and everyone else tossing out banal insights for big paydays—but she knows he's not wrong.

"That's what I bring," Nikhil says. "I deliver the winstreak. I break it down into a few steps—never more than five. We line them up, we execute them in a chain combo. We win."

It sounds to Joey like it's only a matter of time until Winstreak Deliverer becomes a trending online bio phrase. There's a nice bank heist/prison break plan vibe to it, and she's not pleased with the parallels she can immediately make between these and her job.

"Let me tell you what my vision for you is, Indi," Nikhil says. "The line between fiction and reality is gone. Entertainment, news, it's all the same. While you people were kids, my generation saved the country. Not just on the streets, but in people's heads. The idea of India had been murdered, and what rose in its place had to be destroyed, so we did it, now we're building a new and better country. It was like a second independence movement. World-changing. And that's the level I need you to be at. Someone so central to the culture he can make governments do what he wants. Sometimes you'll be the opposition, sometimes you'll be the one explaining why bad shit needs to happen. A face this country can present to the world, to explain what's going on in a way everyone understands."

"You just said the world wasn't interested."

"I'm not talking about the entertainment game anymore. There are powers who want to build their empires here, and are looking for partners. Some of these people are Indian, some are not. It doesn't really matter where they are. People with real influence, whose faces you'll never see. People who can make governments back down, people who can stop riots with a phone call, lift economies, make judges change their decisions mid-sentence. We're going to make you someone who can shape the future of this country."

—Um, a politician? Joey texts.

"I don't want to be a politician," Indi says. "I've had offers before, from all the usual parties. Too much blood for me."

"If I wanted a politician, I'd buy one right now," Nikhil says.

"If I wanted a movie star to use as a megaphone to draw in the masses, that's where I'd have gone. Listen to what I'm trying to tell you. It's never been about the numbers. Indian culture flows from the top. Elections are irrelevant: I already know how the next one will go, seat by seat. I know where the voting machines will disappear, and which hotels they'll keep kidnapped seat-winners in, and how much they'll buy them for. We'd have stopped having elections long ago, but rituals are important. What the Years Not to Be Discussed should have taught India is that you don't leave the actual running of a country to politicians, or corporations, or, fuck, citizens. If you keep remaking a country every few years, it cracks. The whole culture gets broken. Well, a few of us learnt. Out of these ruins we're going to build something new, and you're going to play a huge role in that."

"I don't see the vision here," Indi says.

"You'll get it in time, that's what I'm here for."

—Don't like, Joey messages.

—I know, Indi replies. What now?

—Well, no one's ever told me I had a deeply masculine aura before. So obviously I'm a bit stunned, Rudra texts.

Nikhil does a bit about shifting cultural landscapes and true insiders. Joey misses it completely as she stares at Rudra's chat bubble.

—Sorry, Rudra says, after at least five half-typed and deleted messages.

—Wrong conversation?

—Yeah.

—Keep it together, Rudra.

—Sorry.

—Who thinks you're deeply masculine?

—Typo.

—Are you sharing this meeting with someone else?

—No. Sorry. Leaving now.

—Rudra!

—What now? They're all looking, Indi texts.

—Wing it.

"I'm excited to see where this goes," Indi says. "But I want you to promise me I will have creative control, and I get to pick my team."

Joey's pretty sure that the tooth-display on Nikhil's avatar's face is supposed to be a warm smile.

"We'll let the lawyer dudes earn their pay with all this shit. Listen, I hate meetings, this is the longest one we'll ever have. But the stage management of public opinion in your segment—of media, civil society activists, lawyers, students—is a tricky-AF dance. Much trickier than—what are you doing now? A sex tattoo? If you learn the game, the rewards are endless. I can teach you. What we're starting here is something special, if you're up to the job."

"I am," Indi says.

"Fantastic. You'll look back on this moment as the one that changed your life."

"Amazing," says Founder Karan. "I'm just so happy for all of us. Now will you tell him the best part, or should I?"

"Dude, this one is all mine," Nikhil says.

—Now, the catch, Joey messages.

—I know.

"So, we were looking at your Flow together, Indi, and we figured out the perfect way to make it bulletproof. We're going to get you a partner. Someone whose relevance scores are off the charts, and will give you the credibility boost you need, while you get the casual audience to fall in love with her. Brace yourself—we're getting you Zaria Salam."

—Who? Indi texts.

—Act happy, not so bad, Joey says.

She's not surprised Indi's not heard of Zaria Salam. The truth is she hasn't seen much of Zaria's work either, but her name is one she's seen with increasing frequency. Her friends' gossip groups have been full of Zaria for several months—twenty-two, former college troublemaker, controversial politician's estranged daughter, risk-junkie journalist or stone-cold power climber or boyfriend stealer or stuck-up bitch, depending on which group Joey's watching. The rumour is that watching Zaria's videos on foreign sites gets you under special surveillance. What she must have given up, or what blackmail material she has, to be allowed to work at a leading Indian Flowco, Joey cannot imagine.

"We think the idea of truth is due for a comeback, and we want to be its personal manager. And the combo of Zaria and you handling the Return of Truth? Chills, bro. Can't wait," Nikhil says. "I presume you're already a fan?"

"Normally I'd pretend I know all about this person," Indi says, "but you said today's a special day, so let me stop you right here. I'm not giving away my audience to any partner. She can appear on my Flow, we can see how we get along, and we can take it from there. You want to build a new Flowstar, let her earn her own fans, not hijack mine."

"We need both of you for this to work. We need India to take you seriously, and not think you're just another seasonal woke-bro. You need a strong, edgy woman by your side. But there's no question who the star of your Flow is."

—What do you think? Indi asks.

—Ask for time. They're rushing you.

"I need to think about this," Indi says. "Maybe when we're done with the Tavata project. I need to see what the plan is, go over it with Joey."

"Yeah, details, all good," Nikhil says. "Do you know what a pika is?"

"No."

"It was the latest animal to go extinct. Last week. Looked like a hamster, cute ears. There are memes. It didn't get killed by predators, or humans. It got killed by climate change. We live on the top of a mountain, Indi. As the world gets warmer, the animals that live on the lower slopes move up, or die out. And the world is getting warmer."

—This is from a douchebag-motivation book called Cultural Warming, Joey adds. Straight lift.

"I will think about your animal facts too, if you want," Indi says.

"Don't take too long," says Nikhil, "and okay, one more thing, it's mostly technicalities and boring shit for the lawyers as well, but I wanted to tell you so you won't be surprised when it comes up."

—Okay, no, this is another catch, Joey says. Weird.

—Can you handle it? I'm tired.

—Hang in there, I just hope it's the finale.

"Let's not lose sight of the good news. While we prep your up-grade, you don't have to give up anything you said you wanted, your whole list, it's all going to happen. It's nothing. We're going to amp up your avatars and start burning on our scheds, you should warn your bank they'll need a bigger vault, and figure out what you're going to do with all your free time. Not just games and apps like you said—we're talking shows that you won't have to bother shooting, big-screen movie franchises that never end, because you'll never age, where you can be customised to look like whatever gets each of your fans going. We're talking action figures, merchandise, international, you name it. As the tech im-proves, we'll be able to control micro-expressions to a point where you can win Oscars without stepping out of the house."

"So I become an entertainment Icon digitally, and a society one in real life?"

"Exactly. It's all lining up. We've already started making mov-ies without Bollywood actors in them—they were having so much CGI bodymorph work done anyway that we started just cutting all the flesh out, which meant the films got made much faster, lazy bastards. And the audience doesn't care, acting quali-ty's the same. Hollywood will take a few more software updates."

—This is a trap, right? Indi asks.

—Oh yeah.

"Who controls my digital bodies? Are you going to hire them separately?" Indi asks.

"Own, not hire. But that's all manager stuff," Nikhil says.

"Joey's right here. Tell us!"

"It's an industry standard now, really—no one signs actors up for franchises anymore without acquiring their digital identities. You'd be doing that wherever you worked, it's boilerplate. Zaria, who's already on board with it, actually had much more to worry about."

"Super, so take full ownership of my digital image, and of what I say as well, I guess? So basically you buy me."

"That's not how it is. You always have a say, especially with the nonfiction. We can't have you doing anything off-brand."

"And, what, all media and all future media across the universe?"

"That's just standard contract language."

"Boilerplate, right? Sure, sure. But what if I didn't want to be the Future Hot Buddha or whatever you're trying to build?"

"We're all friends here. We see you as a core part of the family. But there are still investors."

"Of course. But still, what happens if I don't want to say the things you want me to say?"

"I guess we'd part ways as friends, like with any other IP deal? You'd be free to do whatever you like as a person, subject to behaviour clauses, but we'd still own your digital selves, of course. Your new employers could acquire your rights from us, like any other asset."

"Or you could sell me to whoever you like. I see."

"Try and see this as the incredible opportunity this is, because the next generation, the one you'd have to worry about otherwise? They might not even get it. In a few years we'll just be creating public figures from scratch, without needing to sign up an actual human. So you're among the last wave of human stars, which is amazing, I think, because if things go well you might be a star forever. One of the first. Definitely the first from this part of the world."

"I do feel lucky," Indi says.

—Is it time? he asks.

—Yes, says Joey.

—You with me?

—Yes.

"Thank you for this talk," Indi says. "I'm afraid I'm going to have to say no."

"Don't say things you'll—"

"Also fuck you."

Indi signs out, and so does Joey. They take off their helmets and wipe their sweaty heads.

"Admit it," Indi says. "You want me right now."

"Did we just quit?"

"No. We won. Sure, Nikhil hates me, oh no, what to do. He can't be me, though. And he hates that."

Joey checks her phone, to find her Narad has good news: the sushi Joey won in her bet was not only ordered, but has also arrived.

Their phones start ringing simultaneously: they silence them.

"Hungry," Indi says.

"Me too. God, that was a lot of talking. Why is there so much talking?"

Indi stares at her and decides not to say anything.

"What?" Joey asks.

"You barely talk, Joey. I don't know if you even realise how quiet you are."

"You do it better in these situations."

"I don't know." Indi shrugs. "Talking is all we can do, right? And even that is measured and recorded all the time. But not as much as anything we do with our bodies. I feel like meat, mostly. I'm just saying you should talk more. All you do is react."

"Your feedback is noted. Should I smile more, too?"

"Forget it, let's eat. Will you invite your nerd and my wife, or will I?" Indi asks.

"I have to call my mother," Joey says, and grimaces when Indi attempts a feeble haven't-seen-her-in-so-long.

Romola picks up on the second ring. "Just missed you, that's all," she says. "How have you been?"

"What's wrong? You've been crying."

Romola laughs. "It's always strange when you actually remind me you've grown up," she says. "It's nothing. I just had a bad moment, but it's gone now. I'll see you this weekend."

"What happened?"

Romola is reluctant, but Joey pushes harder.

"I went to the market because the crab guy called," she says finally. "And they were burning some tyres."

She doesn't need to tell Joey more: it's not the first time this had happened. Romola had gone to northeast Delhi to do relief work with some friends after one of the bloodbaths, when Joey was still in school, and had never really recovered from what she'd seen and heard that day, the stories of children who'd been chased by bloodthirsty mobs and survived by leaping from roof to roof, of families who'd lost everything and had just been standing in the street next to the charred husks that were their houses, asking journalists and aid workers what would happen next. One family had led Romola inside, into the ruins, up a staircase into absolute darkness, and shown her what used to be their daughter's bedroom, where everything had been slowly, systematically ripped apart and then burnt. The daughter had never been found.

The memories have faded over the years, except one: the smell of burnt rubber, from the tyres they'd lit to set fire to the girl's room, has not left Romola still, she cannot stand it even now.

"Are you going to be all right?" Joey asks. "Do you want me to come over now?"

"No, it's fine, really. I'll see you this weekend. Joey?"

"Yes?"

"Stay out of trouble, please."

"Always. But we're safe, you know."

"I know."

Joey knocks on Rudra's door, then enters the room when he doesn't answer. Rudra and Tara sit on his bed, helmets on, side by side. No doubt they're walking in some romantic VR world, space, Paris, who knows. By the alignment of their haptic gloves, Joey can tell they're holding hands in VR. She wants to go and knock on their helmets and yell at Rudra for letting Tara see a meeting she had no business seeing, but something about them makes her pause: they've had to go to an imaginary digital world to have their moment, whatever it is. They've found a private corner under Indi's shadow. And there's a certain innocence to that which Joey hasn't seen in a while. It's just what she needed after that meeting.

And then Tara pulls her glove off, and sticks her hand into Rudra's shorts. Joey suppresses a squeal, and is out of the room before their helmets come off.

CHAPTER 6

It's a high-forties day outside the Grand Ganesha Cosmos Mall in South Delhi, and Joey's grateful to be indoors, under the aegis of what a large banner declares, under the pictures of a dozen politicians, is the World-Record-Winning Biggest Air Conditioner. There's a World's Biggest Aquarium somewhere on the premises as well: there always is. What the owners of the mall hadn't built, and haven't yet figured out how to remove yet, is a massive E-Klav holo-sculpture that floats in the sky above it: Ashoka's four-lion pillar, but E-Klav's changed the lions. One wears a judge's wig, another army fatigues, another a suit, another a politician outfit; their lower halves are animated, wearing shorts and boots and marching in unison.

Joey and her team are here to Flow a standard mid-morning collaboration with a large supermarket, Indi and Tara pushing advice-enabled trolleys down the aisles discussing modern romance, full outdoor crew in pursuit, two new drones, Indi's reward for recent badassery, flying above the shelves taking interior panoramas.

Most luxury locations hate letting Flowstars perform on their premises because of the wreckage they leave behind, not to mention the chaos the more famous ones create with their flash-mob fan gatherings. Indi has a good reputation on both fronts, because Joey always brings a cleanup crew and more security men than strictly necessary. The cleaners aren't working fast enough today: there's an asteroid belt of loose wires and scattered merchandise forming in a spiral trailing Indi's orbit, because of course her experienced team can't walk through a supermarket aisle without demolishing every single shelf. Much of the damage is from the extra bodyguards she's hired for this mission: they've been warned about wrestleFlowers who wanted to make a name for themselves by attacking Indi. They seem completely unaware of how much physical space they occupy.

Joey's impressed by how everyone's conveniently forgotten the virtual-meeting argument of two days ago. It had taken just a few salmon-and-avocado rolls to wipe Indi's brain of all record of conflict: he'd started Flowing as if nothing unusual had occurred. She'd called Funder Radha that evening to ask her what to do next, and learned that Nikhil had been absolutely thrilled to finally meet Indi and his team, and very excited for whatever was next. "Am I the only one who remembers a massive argument?" she'd asked, and Funder Radha had laughed and told her that was the most docile she'd seen Nick be in years, all part of the game, just a friendly initiation ritual, and Indi had been amazing as always. Nick liked to test his biggest stars from time to time. He was a hilarious prankster, wasn't he?

"Do you think everything I do is frivolous and irrelevant?" Indi had asked her last evening. He'd been quieter than usual all through the segment, watching Tara and his friends hit their banter beats, completely skipping most of the punchlines his writers typed in his glasses.

"No. But I actively produce more of your life than you do, so I'm biased," she'd said. "If it helps, you have the most sought-after audience in the country. That's why your life is so dramatic."

"I think I'm going to take Nikhil's offer," he'd said. "Better us than other people."

"There's this Russian power model where the state funds and controls the resistance," she'd said. "So there's really no left or right, everything's a distraction, everyone's observed and under control. We've had versions of this in India before, this just sounds like an upgrade. Do you really want to be a piece in that game? Because I don't."

"No, I have to be in charge. So we stay where we are?"

"We need to evolve, but in our own way, at our own pace. We can focus on social relevance if you like. More welfare projects. More education, human rights, all of that. I'd like to."

"I don't want to become some intellectual leftie type. Preachy and boring is great for in-groups, but we managed to hit that balance, Joey—"

"Think about it. Think about what you want to do now."

She can see him almost make a joke about not needing to do that while she's around, but he stops himself, as always, on the brink of too much honesty.

She keeps an eye on the Tara-Indi patter: there's trouble brewing there. Rudra swore he hadn't let her see the meeting, they'd just been wandering around VR worlds together and chatting, but she's not sure she believes him. Tara's decided to take up more airtime on Indi's Flow, but her dialogue needs work and professional writers: Joey has always refused to allow accent coaches for any of her charges, but it really shows when Tara does rehearsed bits; she overperforms, and then overcompensates by improvising, and keeps interrupting group conversations to tell the audience things about herself and her struggle. How she learned English via correspondence course, how she got assaulted by police at a Jaipur student protest and is scared to go to Delhi ones, because she's terrified of getting caught in another mass student killing, how previous boyfriends and bosses and family members have exploited her because she's trusted them too much.

Joey can't bring herself to stop Tara. Why should she not talk about what she's been through? And what better opportunity could she have to pitch herself to her next employer? But if she's doing it to win over the audience, it's not working, and Joey can't find a polite way to tell Tara this. She's had to talk Jin-Young out of warning Tara about her dipping numbers and increasingly irritated live feedback: it just seems wrong to silence someone talking about their trauma. But the crowd is muttering today, even harsher than usual, because Tara couldn't have chosen a worse place to talk about student protests.

The Ganesha Cosmos stands over the ruins of what was once Delhi's most prestigious post-grad university, demolished after three years of demonstrations, terror strikes, and bloodshed the city pretends hard to forget. The campus was vast and green, full of peacocks, tea stalls, handmade posters, redbrick buildings, and odd characters. The mall and the religious amusement park being built over it are an attempt at dazzling the city into distraction. They're uglier than the new government building complex, still under construction as part of the traditional new-era new-palaces power demonstration. The nicest thing that could be said about the Ganesha Cosmos is that there was a decent gap between the razing and the new building, which allowed the city to mourn.

Next to Joey, Rudra shuffles awkwardly as he tries to stay out of Indi's eyeline: Indi's already stopped the shoot once to yell at him. Joey hasn't asked Rudra how the love triangle in Indi's penthouse is working out: it's none of her business, and she's overcome the temptation to look at the living room footage to see which bedroom Tara's slept in the last two nights. She suspects it's Rudra's, and that's why he's here, staring at Tara with a stupid smile stuck on his face. He'd made a big deal out of asking for permission, as if they weren't all perfectly aware how he spent his days.

Jin-Young reminds her that Indi and Tara haven't yet done the required promo about the supermarket's cashier-free frictionless checkout and how it works. They should have walked out of the doors by now, while explaining how the store was automatically scanning their groceries and billing their accounts, but instead they're arguing about monogamy in front of a wall of cereal boxes all displaying a grinning criminal billionaire's face. Since Joey appears unmoved by the delay, Jin-Young takes charge and waves towards the supermarket's sliding glass doors in a frenzy. Indi glances towards him, then towards the doors, and achieves genuine enthusiasm for the first time since morning.

Breezing in, surrounded by her all-female security crew (the Six-Pack: six gorgeous fitness models from different parts of India, possibly the subjects of the most AI-generated porn in the whole Flowstar scene) is one of Indi's closest rivals in the Delhi Flowstar charts, MC Sharmila, known for her out-there style palette and with-it wokeFlows. She's also one of Indi's oldest friends, they went to school together, though their respective round-the-clock schedules haven't allowed them to stay in touch over the last few years. Joey's known her since her time with Indi: Sharmila had a habit of popping up and making not-very-subtle references to unspecified school events that made Indi sweat.

"Did the venue double-book?" Joey asks Jin-Young, who runs off to check. Indi waves at Sharmila mid-Flow, and she winks at him. Sharmila's Flow crew springs into action. Three cameras, different angles. Sharmila snaps at one of the Six-Pack, who's in the way of a shot, and Joey winces: the girl, for all her muscles and supremely sexy-confident outfit, looks terrified. But when Sharmila turns back to her, her smile radiates charm. She leans in and gives Joey a warm, lingering hug.

"I'm sorry," she whispers.

"What for?" Joey asks.

A drone flies up. Sharmila's live.

An assistant hands Sharmila a bucket full of black paint. She flings the paint at Indi, a perfect cast, a shimmering black wave that hovers in the air before enveloping Indi, captured from multiple angles into ultra-hi-def to be replayed forever in super-slo-mo. Future generations will comment how it almost looks like a lady in a flowing dress embracing an old friend; in real time it's just a resounding sploosh, and Indi's covered from head to toe. Tara screams as the splatter hits her, zebra-striping her in an instant.

"Rapist!" Sharmila shouts. Her assistant hands her a bucket full of pink paint, which she hurls at Joey, who's still watching, frozen, too stupid, too slow to escape. Open-mouthed, which makes it worse.

"Gender traitor!" Sharmila shouts. She turns to her cam.

"To find out why I did that, stay on this Flow," she says.

Joey spits out some of the paint in her mouth and halts Indi's advancing bodyguards with a gesture. The Six-Pack, all in battle-ready stances, look vaguely disappointed.

Sharmila blows them a kiss and leaves with her crew.

Everybody taps their wrists to shut up their smartatts.

Indi realises he's still live. He wipes his face, achieving very little, and gives his cam a big smile and a splutter.

"I have no idea what that was about, but Sharmila is an old friend—as you all know—and this is probably some kind of joke, or performance art," he says. "She got me! Pranked! But there's no doubt about one thing. Obviously there's no truth to—She's joking, okay? I'll be back when I've cleaned up. Until then, I hope you enjoy this recap."

For the first time since Joey joined, Indi's Flow goes blank. In his OB van, his editors scramble to find the right package.

"Don't say anything," Joey says, pointing at the store's cameras, feeling paint run into her clothes and down her back. "Jin-Young, settle up with store management. Get Legal. We're out of here."

She's glad she hired more muscle than usual, because main-streamer crews are lined up in the car parks along with the usual paps. Every mall shopper nearby has gathered to watch this circus, and there are more cameras up and pointed at them than she's ever seen before: it's like a pop concert. Whatever this is, it was well planned. She'd been a fool for thinking she had any goodwill in the industry—a hundred people could have warned her about this impending crowd-shaming, and had chosen not to. The mainstreamers don't know what Sharmila's Flowing any more than Joey does, but someone tipped them off—they don't know what they're looking for, but that's never a real problem. They taunt Indi and shove mikes in his face to get reactions to unasked questions, but his bodyguards fight them off. Everyone's just recording, stacking their footage: the edits will come later.

Rudra and Tara ride off with Jin-Young in a decoy SUV. Joey scans her driver thoroughly before entering another SUV with Indi, and is relieved to find he's not a possible spy, he's one of Lax-mi's boys. They take the secret VIP exit, huddled together in the back, smearing paint all over the new seats. On Indi's other side is his stylist, Neha, extracting one product after another from her capacious tote bag and breaking new ground in chemistry in her efforts to get the paint off his face. Nothing works.

Joey can feel the bubblegum-pink layer drying on her own skin: she's sure, for a moment, that it's a balloon that she's trapped in, the bubble that she'd heard so many people tell her she lived in, shrinking and tightening, wrapping her like in cellophane, tighter and tighter, choking her. She can feel her smartatt warm and confused on her wrist, feel her clothes stiffening as well, flakes forming when she moves, like a monster in a wall, but she knows it'll be a while before anyone can tend to her. There are many things she wants to say, but she can't get them to line up in order, even though that's her job, she has to remind herself, the timeline is her operating theatre, she's a fucking producer. The driver turns up the radio, another pandemic wave scare, fortunately a hoax. She switches it off with a gesture.

Indi seems shell-shocked as well: she's seen him at a loss for words before, but never like this. Since their hasty exit from the supermarket he's just been staring into space. His phone is still off, and occasionally his eyes dart towards its blank screen, but he doesn't switch it on, or say anything. Perhaps it's for the best: there'd been no time to bug-sweep the car, and they can't stop anywhere either: there's probably a bounty on pics of a paint-shamed Indi anywhere in the city right now. She'll have to have the car cams wiped as well. She lets her parents and friends know in emoji that she's fine and has no time to talk. She's going to have to conserve words. She's distracted by a series of heart emojis from an unknown number that have somehow made it past her filters. There's also a message.

—Don't let the bastards get you down. And don't call this number. U.

U? For some reason the first name that pops into Joey's head is Uma, but that makes no sense: Desibryde has been in her thoughts a fair bit, but there's absolutely no reason she'd message Joey. But there isn't time to dwell on this, because a priority message comes in, and Joey's heart leaps as she sees it's from Toons, Toons was watching over her all along, Toons would make it all better.

—Saw the news. Very disappointed in you.

Toons follows this up with links to a documentary about harassment in India. Joey's already seen it.

—You need to do better.

Joey deletes the message.

Narad's attempts at instant therapy aren't of any discernible use, but Joey appreciates the effort. Narad's abilities as a work assistant are invaluable, though: she's shut off all nonessential messages for the moment, and her if-you-messaged-X-consider-messaging-Y suggestions are all on point. They achieve smooth, balletic, silent communion, her fingers flowing across the screen, putting out fires, aligning schedules, deflecting curiosity, coordinating traffic routes with the rest of the crew.

Neha's the only person present with the wherewithal to open Sharmila's Flow on her phone. She hands it, and a bunch of paper napkins, to Indi, and they watch it together.

There's a video of Indi playing on loop, Indi on a bed with a girl who looks familiar. Joey's forgotten her name, but it doesn't matter because it's right there on the screen: Simran. Another stylist. Neha's team. They're in Indi's bedroom, at night, lit up by Indi's amber mood lamp.

It's been a long time since she last saw Indi naked, and she finds herself watching him from a great distance, like he's just another college friend who's resurfaced with a Flow. He used to be so skinny, back then. He looks better now, less awkward. And then it hits her that he's right there, right next to her, they're in a car covered in shame-paint watching a video where he's supposed to be raping someone, and it's so deeply strange that it's gone full circle into normal, like a nature documentary, as if this is just a new segment pitch and they're sitting with the rushes. Except that her heart is thumping so hard it feels as if it's only the paint that's keeping it in place. The girl, Simran, is on her elbows and knees on the bed, back arched, ass up high, Indi behind her thrusting violently, eyes shut, grimacing. Joey's seen that face. There's no audio, but Simran looks like she's screaming. Indi smacks her, grabs her hair, yanks her head back, speeds up. She looks like she's sobbing.

"Stop the car," says Neha.

"No, we can't—"

"Stop the car!" Neha yells, and the driver swerves towards a service lane. Neha opens her door before the car comes to a halt, and as the smart alarm starts yowling Joey reaches across to grab her wrist.

"Let's just go back, calm down, and figure out what to do next," she says. The car's already full of smog, they're all coughing. Joey shuts her eyes, refusing to cry.

"Don't get your shit on me," Neha says. She grabs her phone from Indi and jumps out. The tar on the street is melting, and she's wearing heels, but they don't get to see what happens next, because she slams the door shut and bangs on the side of the car until the driver starts it up again.

Joey considers leaping out of the car as well, and just running after her, a bright pink blob slowly sinking into the tar, melting into candy swirls.

"I didn't do it, you know," Indi says, and she flinches. "I didn't rape her, Joey. She was—she wanted it. Consensual, all of it."

"We don't have to talk about it now." Joey feels sane enough to turn off Narad's safety protocols; within seconds her phone is blowing up with notifications and messages. She can't access Sharmila's Flow, and her hands are shaking. Narad is all over her screen, making emergency suggestions, all useless.

The driver switches on the seat smartscreens. She finds Sharmila's Flow. Simran is speaking to the camera now, with the sex video playing in a corner. Simran's pretty matter-of-fact about it: Indi promised her a Flowstar career, gaslit and manipulated and exploited her in every possible way. Worst among these: he raped her repeatedly, and she'd kept quiet about it for a long time but couldn't stay quiet anymore, couldn't stand him being all over Tavata's advertising, the dream mate, the face of true love, the perfect Indian partner. She has more videos.

"She's lying. Totally trapped me. Everyone's watching anyway, I assume," Indi says.

Everyone is. Sharmila's Flow is trending all over India, and is one of the top ten personal Flows worldwide.

"Always had consent. That's why there's no bloody audio—she's saying yes in this clip. Right there," he says again. "Joey. Joey, you have to believe me. I didn't."

"Don't tell me this. Legal is coming to the office. So is your lawyer. And your business people. Tell them."

"No, I mean, she was Raj's friend. Raj set up the spyware. They set me up. My own cousin, and that sly little . . . they were blackmailing me with these videos."

"Just give me some time, okay?"

"That's why I sacked them. I wanted to tell you, but—"

"Indi. Shut the fuck up."

"Joey, you believe me, right? I don't care about what anyone else thinks. I need to know you believe me."

Joey stares out of the window, through the haze, at dust and dead trees and more cars and flyovers, always more flyovers.

"How do I make you believe me? They can make up any evidence. Everyone's already used every possible response. Everyone's already made up their minds. What is the point of all this tech if it can't tell us what's true?"

He grabs his phone, as if to throw it out of the window. But he doesn't.

She reaches inside herself, to pull words of comfort out for him, but they don't come. She pulls at them, and they hurt, like the paint stuck in her hair. But she has nothing for him, and nothing for herself.

—Don't come to ICB Market. Drones and media everywhere, says Rudra.

It's the first sensible idea she's seen in a while: she's even had a text from an unknown number offering to release a herd of cows into traffic to help them escape, for a really ambitious sum of money. Everyone except Joey decides the place to meet is Joey's house, and so the convoy reunites at her Harmony Place flat. Everyone remarks how clean and well-maintained her home is, so much nicer than theirs.

When Joey emerges from her bathroom, there's still traces of pink in her hair but she's managed to rub her skin clean, thanks to a stockpile of Flowco gift baskets. Indi's in her bedroom with a phalanx of lawyers and publicists and stylists, and Rudra and Tara whisper in a corner on her carefully handpicked but never used mood-curve smartchairs. Most of Indi's crew have been sent to the office to keep attention focussed there, though some body-guards have been dispatched to create diversions and rumours of Indi's presence all around the city. The celeb-locator apps are running wild.

Joey manages, in a while, to find the right remote from her vast collection and switch her TV on, and is relieved to find that while he's all over the Flowverse and the entertainment channels, the news mainstreamers aren't talking about Indi, and it's not just because they can't play the video: another mass grave found in a riverbank, thousands more victims of the Years Not to Be Discussed, another set of conspiracies and accusations. She knows this is supposed to be horrifying, but her primary emotion is relief: her filters do their job, the burnt corpses are blurred, and Indi's not today's national crisis.

"I need to ask you something," Rudra says. He holds out a placatory iced tea from her kitchen. "Tara wants to put out a statement, and I'm going to help her Flow it. We'll check with you before broadcasting."

"No," says Joey.

"I won't be censored," Tara says, failing early at pretending to not be in this conversation.

"Your contract gives me control of your Flow for another two weeks," Joey says. "And your nondisclosure agreement gives the Flowco control over any reference to your time here for the rest of your life."

"To hell with your rules," Tara says. "You people all do whatever you like, and I get lists and regulations and auditions. By the way, I'm trying to help. I'm going to defend him."

"You're going to sit tight and wait until we all figure out what the plan is."

"You know, whatever your job title says, maybe you're aware you don't actually control reality? It's already far too late. I remember the first purge, I spoke up against a teacher, it's a lot harder to do in Jaipur than it is here, by the way, and he wasn't even a powerful man, but he got away. You people will be fine. Your type always has somewhere else to go. You know whose career will end? Mine. Second purge, I stayed quiet, lost my job anyway because I didn't show loyalty. Some token heads roll, the real powers escape, then the men strike back. I won't get shut out this time. I need to say something. I need to take charge of this."

"By circling the wagons and defending Indi? They'll say you're as bad as him."

"Who? That girl, Sharmila? She doesn't even see me. You'll all make some deal, and two weeks from now I'm finished. This was supposed to be my big break, Joey. I can't just sit here and watch it die, do you understand?"

"Yes. But wait until we assign you a writer."

"Please. I don't need help, it's all very simple. If I attack Indi, my career is over. If I say nothing, I vanish. He'll get rehabbed at worst, but I'll get attacked by both sides. I have only one option. Are you going to help me?"

"As soon as I'm able to," Joey says.

"But if I went and did something without your permission?"

"Can't react to things I don't know."

She watches them scurry away with mild concern.

After Indi's entourage departs, she finds him in her bedroom, examining himself in her smudgy mirror. The stylists have done their job well, turning the clock back to his Morning Look.

"It's all good," he says. "Nikhil's going to sort it out."

"Did you talk to the funders?"

"No, they're not involved, Nikhil's taking care of it. Mainstreamers, Flowstars, meat-world A-listers will be speaking in support. They'll make alibi videos, showing me doing a bunch of other stuff at the times Raj claims I was doing whatever. The white dude's taken charge of my team directly, so you don't have to. I know this has been difficult for you."

"The whole system's worked out now, huh."

"Thankfully for us. Really, after all we've given this art form—"

"You've got to see it's a little weird that your cousin and his friend should release this video so soon after you told Nikhil to fuck off. And that he had room on his schedule to fix everything at once."

"What, you think Nikhil's behind all this? That's really paranoid, even for you. He's saving my ass, Joey. Him, not you."

Joey shrugs.

"But it turns out you're not that far off the mark," Indi says. "So Raj had approached Karan and Radha with this garbage before, right when I sacked him, and they'd turned him away. They should have told us about it, obviously. But Raj isn't going to be a problem anymore."

"How so?"

"Nikhil said he'll talk to one of his influential friends who gets things done, and he'll find Raj and this girl and make the problem go away."

He waits for Joey to ask him how, but she just stares at him.

"As in, he'll get them to confess in public that they made all this shit up. And it should take a couple of days max, because even if they're hiding, they can be found. Sharmila will give them up, plus whoever else they gave the videos to. We don't need to know."

"Nikhil's friend is going to send gangsters after Sharmila as well?"

"No, he's just buying her whole Flowco. Buying? He's already bought it. She works for us now. And guess who her new Reality Controller is? Nikhil says hi, and welcome to the family."

"And have you already agreed to his plans for the rest of your career?"

"Please, it's not like that, Joey. He didn't even bring that up."

"But you're going to do it, right?"

"I'll think about it and make a call. The lesson from today is that at this level, I'm not safe. I mean, this audience I have now, they were just waiting to find something wrong with me, right? I looked. There's a bunch of angry feminists who don't know anything about this world trash-talking me right now. And at this level they kind of matter—the fanFlows as well—but if I scale up they won't."

"Some people attacking you for a few days shouldn't be able to scare you into major career decisions. You've been through far worse in the early days. So have I."

"They can troll me and hate me for the rest of their lives, just like the fascists. It's not about me, it's about them and whatever brand they're trying to build. And I'm tired of having to care about their shit. I've proved I'm a feminist many times, it's never good enough. I won't change myself to please anyone."

She wants to tell him that he's been jumping through rings of fire to change himself to please his audience, any audience, since the day they met. She doesn't.

"I've been a strong feminist since my fucking mid-teens," Indi says. "I didn't have to unlearn anything. We used to joke about old people, you know, how they were having to learn things we already knew. That's why you never had to teach me feminism, when we met. I'd be the first person to say always believe the woman, never blame the victim, fuck the patriarchy, cancel abusers. So, of course, this happens to me. Nikhil said this is a common thing now, standard blackmail package. Countries, companies, everyone's running honeytraps. Every rising star's at risk, because no one will believe them, no one will support them. I just never thought someone could get me like this."

"I never thought I'd hear all of this out of your mouth," Joey says.

"Look, why don't we talk about it once this is behind us?" Indi says. "We still have to get through the day. Until Nikhil's friend wraps up Raj and Sim, and the support Flows start trending, we're still in a crisis."

"Did Nikhil tell you who his friend is?"

"I think so, but I forgot. I can ask one of the guys if they recorded the meeting, but it's unlikely, you know? Some Delhi name—Khanna or Mehra."

Joey's smartatt buzzes. She swats it into silence.

"Chopra?" she asks.

"Could be," Indi says. "I'll ask him again later, or ask him yourself? Why?"

"Just curious."

Joey imagines alternate universes. One where she hadn't taken a sudden dislike to an access-Brahmin's face and stolen Rudra from him on a whim. One where Rudra had gone on to be a slave-market trader before moving on to running his family's shady clinics. One where Rudra hadn't gone to his father's funeral, where no one had wanted him in the first place. One where she'd never taken this job. One where she had Delivered a Winstreak, instead of what seemed like the exact opposite. In all of these universes, she can still find ways to make everything that's happened her fault, ways to forget that none of this would have happened if Indi hadn't felt compelled to sleep with every woman in the National Capital Region.

"What happens to the girl?" she asks.

"Which girl?"

It's a good question. But before she can answer it, her doorbell rings, and Jin-Young's face pops up on her phone, staring into the void.

He comes in with a woman who looks extremely familiar: Joey's seen her online, and has her filed mentally under Vaguely Important and Unfairly Beautiful. Narad flashes her data in response, and Joey almost punches herself in frustration: of course she knows who this is. Zaria Salam, global lecture-tour over-achiever, gossip group staple, intrepid journalist, troll magnet, death-threat meme maker, upper-class rebel icon, and constant presence on India's Top People Under Arbitrary Age lists. Zaria shakes Joey's hand with vigour, showing off an elaborate custom-ised Urdu-calligraphy-around-zenana-miniature smartatt, and presents Indi a dazzling but wary smile.

"First day at work and I meet a K-drama hero and a drone tries to fly in through a window," she says. "What's next?"

"I couldn't leave her at the penthouse," Jin-Young says. "We were supposed to present options for her Flow launch this evening."

"But of course I understand if you can't, today of all days," Zaria says. "I have a lifelong habit of showing up in the middle of a crisis."

"There's no crisis here," Indi says. "Just an angry ex-employee trying to make a name for himself, and a woman he's tricked into telling lies. She's the one whose life will be damaged most by all this. She's the only one I feel bad for."

"You look ready for camera," Zaria says.

"Why don't we skip the presentation and just start your Flow-star career with a no-holds-barred exclusive interview?" Indi's gone into instant-charm mode. Joey's always taken a second to roll her eyes any time she's seen him do this since their college days, but she's too tired today. She watches her new Flowstar con-sider Indi's proposal as she looks him up and down.

"Nah, I'm good," she says.

Jin-Young's mouth falls open in a pleasingly cartoonish way, and Joey finds her mouth is slightly agape as well. She shuts it with a snap. Indi's face is a study, and she can see him struggling not to burst out in an impassioned speech: Does Zaria not un-derstand what a magnanimous gesture he's just made? How much every journalist in the country wants to interview him right now? How incredible a beginning to her Flowstar career this exclusive would be? How stupid it is for a young journalist to turn down a rising star? He's learned something in all this time, though. He doesn't make it worse, just gives her a half smile and turns away.

"I wouldn't mind interviewing you two, though," Zaria says. "What do you say, Reality Controller?"

"No thanks," Joey says.

"You, K-Pop?"

Jin-Young just shakes his head, unsure where to look.

"I'm going to stick around and observe the rest of your day," Zaria says. "Just a fly on the wall. I want to see how you steer your way out of this mess."

"You're going to do nothing of the sort," Indi says. "Also, don't call Jin-Young K-Pop. That's racist."

"Is it? Have I hurt your feelings, Jin-Young?"

"I don't know," Jin-Young says.

"Well, tell me when you figure it out. Joey, do you need any help? No? Okay. I'll be waiting for your presentation then. I understand you're the one in charge of making me likable?"

"No," Joey says.

"Well, who is then? I can't wait to be popular."

"Not me. Did you sign away your digital identities to Nikhil?"

"Fuck no. Why would I do that? If you're sure you don't want me around, I'll be in your office. K-Pop, you're with me."

"Jin-Young stays here," Indi says. Zaria shrugs, and makes a graceful exit, pausing at the door to make sure everyone's watching her leave. They are. There are two hulking bodyguards outside Joey's flat, dressed in black kurtas, who glower at them as the door slams shut.

"Another self-made icon who happens to be the daughter of a rich politician," Indi says.

He clears his throat and stretches.

"Okay, time to get to work. Jin-Young, I need you on your A game right now."

Joey watches with reluctant appreciation as Indi instructs

Jin-Young to go and track responses to apologies, flat-out denials, counteraccusations, distractions, and other responses in all celebrity sex-assault accusation cases. He is to find out what worked, sort results by region, profession, and age, and then show Indi projections for whether, if he does respond, he should tell his fans this is a blackmail attempt with a few details, or run a distraction ploy—corporate conspiracy, attack on minorities—or whether he should just keep quiet and wait for people to forget. She couldn't have organised a defence any better herself: it's nice to know he was actually listening at all those crisis-response strategy meetings. And that he isn't immediately thinking of getting into bed with Men's Rights Activists, or anti-woman politicians.

"I need to also check, let's see, whether I should apologise to the fans for the pain they've had to feel because of these false allegations," Indi says. "Give me charts and numbers. On paper, I need paper right now. Joey, I assume you have a working printer?"

"No."

"Of course. Projector, then. Jin-Young, go."

Jin-Young has no idea where to go, and looks at Joey in panic until she gestures to her bedroom. He rushes off.

"Joey, I need you to set the writers to work on all these scenarios. Pick the ones who'd relate most to each, yeah? When you're done with the assignments, we'll go through the key points of your statement."

"My statement?"

"Yeah. Nikhil's lining up some top feminists, but then I was like, we also have real talent in-house. And that Zaria wanted to interview you for a reason. Don't stress about it, just get it done. Remember how we used to perform together back in the day? The camera wants to see you again."

"Thanks," Joey says. "You know I'm not going to do any of this, right?"

His shoulders sink. He takes a breath, reloads, and assumes what he must think is a tired and appealing stance.

"Joey, I don't have time for this. I've always taken care of you. I've been there whenever you needed me. I need you now."

"Taking this job was a mistake." Her phone's ringing, somewhere in the room, she wants to drop everything until she's found it.

"Don't say that."

"No, it was. You know, when you asked me to work with you, I went and interviewed at a few other Flowcos. Because I didn't want to work with you, I knew it would be complicated."

"I'm so glad you changed your mind."

"You know why I didn't join them? It was all guys. Just a bunch of bearded horny dudes with headphones, staring into their screens, checking me out openly, not saying hello when they were introduced. Just room after room full of sweat and deo and splainboi music and just . . . vibes. I thought your space would be better. Safe."

"And it was always safe."

"I don't know. I was fine, I was protected, you were my friend. But a lot of women came to work here because of me. And I've let them down. Every time I looked the other way, every time I didn't want to see what you were doing, I let them down."

"They didn't need to be protected! They were adults, with agency, and doing what they wanted!"

His body language is right on point, and she feels a certain pride in how much he's improved with all those classes. Or perhaps it's all genuine. She can't tell anymore.

"You were giving me some privacy," Indi says. "I've had none. None at all. I need some, right? Everyone needs some. You taught me this, years ago. I was very grateful to you for giving me that space."

"It was a mistake."

"Joey, you know me better than anyone. You know I didn't do anything wrong."

"I am not going to put out a statement defending you."

She finds her phone, and can see, for a horrifying second, what his face would look like with her phone smashed into it.

"Why? Why won't you stand with me?"

"Why should I? Haven't I been through enough? Do you realise what happened today, Sharmila's great gender-traitor reveal—that's the first thing people will find when they look for me online? That's who I am now. That clip, that paint-shaming. For the rest of my life. Whatever I do, wherever I go. I chose this life. I chose this public humiliation. It is all a result of my decisions. There aren't any excuses."

"This is not about you, Joey."

"Not about . . . you know, I can't even talk to you. And also? Hey, Indi. Indi, look at me. I don't know if I believe you."

"How can you stand there and say that to me? You think I'd touch someone without consent?"

"You've touched me without consent."

"What? What are you talking about?"

"More than once! When we were together. No, don't pull that face, I've seen them all. There were nights, I was tired, I was sleeping, I told you, I told you I didn't want to, but you just had to fuck something, didn't you? You always have to fuck something because how will you know you're a winner if you don't?"

"That's so unfair. First of all, it was years ago. I told you I was sorry. So stop flinging that in my face. And look, there's absolutely no comparison between this and that!"

"I am not putting out a statement defending you."

"Fine, please don't! I'm sorry I asked. I can't believe you."

"I don't know why you even need this so much. You know you're getting away with it."

"Getting away? I didn't do anything!"

"Didn't do anything. You were her boss. You had power over her, and abused it. I looked away. I was part of it. I deserved what I got. Now leave me alone, Indi, please. You're fine. There are whole systems lined up to help you out, and they've had so many years of practice. There's no punishment. There's no process. You're fine. People will forget about it by tomorrow if they haven't already. So just go home and enjoy your victory, yeah?"

A loud, deliberate cough from her bedroom: Jin-Young is in their midst. He's been listening for a while.

"I have the charts," he says.

"That's good. Now help Joey with her statement. We're wasting time," Indi says.

"It's not going to happen, Indi. Let it go."

"Joey. You work for me and I'm ordering you to do it."

"Thank you for that," she says. "I quit."

"Just calm down. Take some days off, you're really stressed," he says.

"No, seriously. I quit."

"Joey!"

"No."

He reaches out to her. She shrinks away.

"Just tell me you believe me," he says.

"No. Stop pushing."

Indi shrugs. "Jin-Young, you'll take charge of the whole thing then."

"No, I won't," Jin-Young says.

Both Indi and Joey stare at him, aghast.

"I would also like to resign," Jin-Young says. "I have decided to . . . no. Actually, I just hate it here."

Indi's phone rings. He stares at it, then at her. "It's Nikhil," he says. "I have to take this, but—You know what, fuck it. Leave. I don't need you. Get out."

"You're in my house," Joey says.

She watches him walk away, phone to his ear, each stride more confident, more enthusiastic than the last. Her smartatt doesn't indicate high levels of stress, so Joey knows she must be fine.

CHAPTER 7

Rudra's still not used to waking up next to another person, but over the last week he's discovered it's his favourite thing in the world. He now has a morning routine that extends beyond pulling himself out of bed and shambling towards coffee: he now opens his eyes before the alarm goes off, reaches out his left hand, and switches off the alarm while reminding himself to remove it altogether once he's properly up and about. He then celebrates quietly because his right arm is asleep, and waking it up would involve waking Tara, and Tara's next to him, she's still there, huddled up and snoring and mumbling, and it's so unbelievably good to wake up next to someone. To wake up after deep sleep, body achy but incredibly alive after nights of intense sex. Tara's taken him on a journey of a lifetime over the last few nights, taught him things he will probably never get to do again. He can't remember when he was last this aware that he had an actual body, that it felt and experienced its own moods, that it was more than some sort of organic locomotion device to carry his worries around in. He can only imagine what this week will bring, and wish that he'd done a few years of yoga to prepare.

She's told him very strictly not to fall in love with her, because this is just a two-week fling, and they're already halfway through it. She doesn't know where they'll be once her contract with the Flowco runs out. And, of course, he hasn't fallen in love with her, the very idea is ridiculous, and clever, funny, ambitious, charming, beautiful, athletic, naked celebrities aren't his type anyway. She's probably just sleeping with him because she's bored, and lonely, and he's there. Because he doesn't talk a lot, and avoids doing absolutely stupid things for the most part, and local male standards are very low. Rudra's aware this has been key to most of his past relationships—in school and college, everyone in his social circle had dated everyone else, you had to collect the full set, and in Kalkaji, he'd tried to be kind to his neighbours—and all he has to do, for the next week, is to focus really hard on not fucking it up. He knows he can manage a week, though he wishes he could move that week to sometime in the future, just to somehow transform himself into a better, upgraded version. She makes him want to cut his hair and clean the house, to learn new skills and possibly memorise the Kama Sutra, to figure out ways to somehow improve the parts of his body she's very clearly told him she likes—eyes, lips, hands, arms, shoulders, ass. She's also given his penis glowing reviews, though maybe she was just being polite.

A week is a good length of time. Not long enough for Tara to find his unmeasured adoration annoying, or his constant attention tiresome. But long enough for her to train him to give her pleasure, and remember him when it ends. Long enough for her to start to feel the affection he's addicted to, maybe even feel it when they're not together, not long enough for her to find his habits disgusting, or for either of their best-self facades to crumble enough to repel the other. He's been storing mental images of her every day, building an imaginary album to remember when she's gone: Tara lost in contemplation of her own body, patting her stomach in front of the mirror to make sure it's as flat as it looks. Tara moving her lips in silence whenever she reads. He's terrified he'll miss her terribly when she's gone, but all through the week his smartatt readings have been consistent with new high scores for happiness.

She wakes up, and he forgets all about smartatt readings as she pulls him on top of her. It's less confusing each time: they have a routine now, they're a team. And when they're done, and she pushes him off and lies absolutely still, grinning at the ceiling, he's absolutely sure he's going to get his heart broken.

He doesn't want it to end. He wants to run away with her. He's got it all planned out: the well-executed heist on his own bank account, the fake identities sourced through his old neighbours, the flight to . . . where? Where are they to go? What are they to do there? He wants to just head to someplace with a beach that's low on the tsunami-risk list and high on the fresh-squid list, but there isn't any such place in the subcontinent that isn't already crammed with slow-boiling retired Russians.

His gamer friends in other countries have been encouraging him to join an augrel, an AR-based religion where you gain points by performing daily acts of virtue customised and assigned via app and supervised by an AI priest, and these points win you, first, passes to exclusive cult utopias scattered around the world—there's one near Mussoorie—and then, presumably, to the gates of personalised paradise. There are millions of people worldwide, and several thousand in India, already in these augrels, but he'd be at an advantage because his accumulated fortune in game credits is transferable. He's resisted so far, pointing out his family's already in a cult and he finds that lifestyle unsuitable. His gamer group asks him to at least try it for the affiliated discounts, accuses him of living in a bubble, and logs out.

But even if he finds a place to go, why the hell should she want to go with him? If she wanted to escape, there's a wide variety of sexpats available in the local market, all looking for amazing, pliant Indian brides. They approach her whenever she's out getting a drink, offering her country homes, breathable air, and eventual boredom in a range of countries. But she's right where she wants to be, laying the foundations of her own empire.

When they're not eating or sleeping or going at it, she talks about her plans constantly—what should her solo Flow be about? What demographics should she target? What are her top strengths and weaknesses? How should she be the bridge between mainstreamers and that mythical global audience? Could Rudra do some research, and figure out a list of alternative paths for her? Could Rudra actually manage her, or should she get Jin-Young?

Getting Jin-Young is no longer an option, though: he's disappeared. When Joey and Jin-Young quit, the management had simply refused to accept Joey's resignation. She's still reluctant to tell Rudra the details, especially on the phone. He acknowledges this makes sense, she's his boss, she knows he'll tell Tara everything, were they even really friends? And isn't the growing distance between them completely his fault? Has he been anything but trouble to her since they met?

But he's put the story together from the fragments that Joey's shared. They'd pushed her with clauses and threats and praise and a barrage of messages about how essential she was, how they couldn't even think of letting her go to a competitor. She'd tried to tell them she had no intention of switching teams, she just didn't want to do this anymore, but they'd refused to believe her: everyone wanted what she had. Nikhil himself descended from on high to tell her about the special connection between them, give her raises and empty promises about employee protection committees and better workplace cultures. She hasn't accepted any of these yet.

"Don't worry about Joey," Tara had said when he'd tried to talk to her about it the first day. "The whole good-girl thing is an act, she's just negotiating. She'll fail upwards. Don't get involved."

He hadn't stopped calling, but he'd stopped telling Tara about it. The rest of the team tells Rudra with absolute confidence that Joey will come around eventually, she always does. Their confidence hadn't faltered when she stopped coming to work, they'd told him she'd feel guilty about doing nothing and suddenly one day she'd be running around pretending she'd never left, would he like to bet? He hadn't: he'd have lost his money three days ago if he had. And it was only after she came back—and he still can't believe she came back—and she asked where the hell Jin-Young was that anyone noticed he was gone. They'd all assumed he was lurking quietly either in her shadow or Indi's.

Jin-Young's just gone: his phone's dead, his flat's empty. The Flowco's decided to wait for a few days before notifying the authorities, because if they look for him by face tracking he'll end up on some Suspicious Foreigners list. Joey even went to Little Korea to investigate, but no one in his neighbourhood had anything useful to tell her.

Rudra and Tara have the house to themselves. Indi's team has taken all his things away—he's been moved to some secret location to prepare for his big stardom push, and his Flow has been playing mostly recaps, interspersed with games, travel, and exercise for all demographics. He appears sometimes, face to cam, telling his fans he's excited about the big announcement. He never said good-bye to Tara, and Rudra knows she's still upset about that.

She stretches, and rolls out of bed, and as always he's amazed by how beautiful she is, and how astonishing it is that she's there with him, and tries not to stare. This is the plan: she's going to the bathroom, and he's going to make them some breakfast, then they're going to figure out whether round two happens in the bedroom, or in the shower. Afterwards, he's going to laze around and try not to stare at her, and she's going to be on the phone with her agent, yelling at him for not fixing up secret appointments with rival Flowcos now that her week is free—the Finnish chastity-belt smartatt sponsors have pulled out of the Indi-Tara relationship, fortunately; Indi must have been getting several infidelity notifications of late.

A loud thumping on the glass-window wall distracts them: Rudra quickly connects to the public streetcam view of their building, but there's nothing there. He calls out asking what it is, but there's no answer, just urgent hammering on the glass. They draw up the digiscreen with its two-colour display of the Manhattan skyline, blinking as the harshness of the morning outside floods the room.

There's a monkey trapped on the narrow ledge outside the glass, banging in a frenzy at the invisible wall separating him from them. There's something wrong with his collar, it's zapping him even though he's outside, probably a network glitch. Sparks cascade from the collar to the glass. Tara wants to open the glass pane and let him in, she really has no fear, but he stops her. The monkey's in great pain, eyes bulging, rolling wildly, mouth foamflecked, limbs askew.

Rudra searches on his phone for a number to call, but by the time he's found it the monkey's passed out, eyes locked with Rudra's in baffled rage as he slides down the glass onto the ledge. Tara's sobbing, but then two drones fly up, and she squeals and makes a run for it. Rudra wonders why, and then remembers they're both still naked. The glass is supposed to be photo-proof, but it's best for Tara not to take chances. He doesn't have a leering audience of thousands, though, so he just stands there, staring back at the drones, until their operators lose interest and fly away. Outside the glass, the monkey's collar pings: he leaps up, and takes off, apparently recovered.

Rudra's left alone, staring out at the grid of ICB Market roof-tops, each one a perfect square covered with smartiles. He'd heard a lot about the ICB night games, when the market roof-top transforms into a gigantic board, on which celebrities play board games. The plan was for it to be visible from space, but they hadn't factored in the Delhi haze when they built it, so they just do it all with CGI instead. Rudra and Tara spent their first night together with the screen up, listening to the strange mix of music drifting up into the sky out of the clubs below, watching the glow of the market's signs filtered through the dust, and the rooftops lighting up one by one.

"Honeymoon's over," Tara says behind him.

"What do you mean?" She's looking at her phone, scratch-ing her stomach, and he realises he'd completely forgotten about breakfast.

"Phone was silent," she says. "The new girl's moving in today."

"Zaria? When?"

The doorbell rings.

Rudra's obviously disappointed to have his morning plans de-stroyed, but he's also very excited to meet Zaria, and he suspects Tara is too. They've watched the hell out of her videos on the pre-mium net, and haven't managed to see them all because Zaria's been breaking big stories since her mid-teens: she once exposed a government oxygen-cylinder scam from a hospital bed. Rudra's seen some of her global-viral reports through his gaming friends who follow her from around the world: he had no idea who Indi was until quite recently, but Zaria he's known of for years. Tara, on the other hand, has been tracking Indi's career since his first Flow, but has had no access to Zaria's videos, which face mass downratings, complaints, and lawsuits within seconds of release in India, often get blocked by the big telecom companies and dis-appear entirely off the Indian internet, or lose traction because of troll-blasts about special surveillance of Zaria's followers. She's been chased out of cities by murderous mobs, shot at by riot police, gone entirely underground for months, been doxxed multiple times and assaulted quite a few. She's faced death threats from a sea of internet trolls, members of Parliament, religious leaders, and major CEOs. She's survived actual assassination attempts. She shot to national fame after Hindu extremists put a price on her head, after a series of stories about cow corpses blocking highways because nobody dared to touch them. She had to leave India after a video series where she travelled along the border of actual Indian control, measuring its distance from the official border, taking selfies with Chinese soldiers deep inside officially Indian turf. No one even knows what she did in Kashmir to get her whole family thrown into jail. She got deported from Mozambique after infiltrating a child-trafficking ring in Mumbai and following it to an international slave auction. She's completely blocked on the Chinese internet after a story on the brain-modification joy-camps of Xinjing. Rudra is a fan.

"Why would she want to work with you?" he'd asked Joey as soon as he heard Zaria Salam was actually going to move in.

"First of all, thanks," Joey'd said. "What do you mean, why? You were there for the meeting."

"I didn't mean to be disrespectful. And no, I wasn't listening to the meeting after the first few minutes."

"Not important enough, huh?"

"Sorry again. I just meant, wouldn't someone like her see what we do as a step . . . as a very different line of work?"

"How would I know? Maybe she's tired of putting her life on the line? Maybe her family, or the government, or any of her many enemies has found a way to stop her doing what she's done all these years, and this is her only option now?"

"I've heard that all the news organisations have been given instructions to not work with her," Rudra says.

"Well, there you have it. Maybe she needs a new point on her CV before she moves to another country. Maybe she wants to be a politician like her dad. If she tells me during a pillow fight or when we're getting mani-pedis, I'll text you."

"Joey, please stop being angry with me, I wasn't suggesting any of this was easy," he'd said, widening his eyes and putting a finger on his lips and pointing at the walls theatrically. She'd laughed.

"If anyone's listening, do you think they haven't thought of all this? It's all over the Flowverse, every kind of theory about why Badass Zaria fucking Salam should descend to the level of us shallow trend-chasers. What could have gone wrong? All I know is I'm tired, Rudra. I'm trying to quit and they won't let me. Everyone's cleverer than me anyway, everyone's always two steps ahead."

"Why did you come back, if I may ask? I was so happy you'd gotten out. I mean, sorry, not happy—"

She'd silenced him with a gesture.

"Did they threaten you?" Rudra had asked.

She'd turned towards the walls, and addressed them directly.

"Whoever's secretly watching or listening to or, I don't know, smelling this, I'd love to work for you," she'd said. "You know I'm the best, you've seen it all. Just get me out of here."

He'd just stood there, not knowing what to say to her, and she'd given him a sympathetic grin after a few seconds.

"Okay, okay," she'd said. "If you really want to know what I think, she wants to infiltrate the Flowco, hack into all our systems, find out something about Nikhil, or Chopra, or whoever our real boss is. And they probably know this, but have signed her up for whatever fucking above-our-pay-grade reason anyway. So as soon as any of these people get whatever it is they want, she'll leave, or disappear. Whoever wins, it won't be us. And she'll probably be an asshole to us. Most Flowstars are. So don't get too attached to her."

And then he'd made her a kiwi-dragon smoothie and she'd

wandered off, and he'd watched the new Desibryde video, which featured her sitting in a cage reading the preamble to the Constitution out loud, while all around the cage, men in god masks had angry sex with one another.

Rudra opens the door and lets Zaria in, hating himself with a passion for not being able to summon up one second's worth of suavity. In Tara's enthusiastic greetings he can sense a simmering hostility, but that makes complete sense: Zaria's strolling not just into their love nest, but into a slot that Tara had hoped, unrealistically, to occupy, and Tara's been working really hard to climb up to it. Joey's there as well, with Zaria's two hulking black-kurta-clad bodyguards, Faiz and Husain.

"Did you put on clothes just for me?" Zaria asks Rudra by way of greeting, and he realises his T-shirt's inside out. He mumbles something about not being fashionable, but Zaria's already moved past him. She saunters around the house, Husain and Faiz always a step behind, scanning devices out and surveying every possible direction. The kitchen appears to win her approval, Indi's room elicits a raised eyebrow and a smirk, Tara's room a few deep, significant sniffs, a slow stare at the unmade bed, and then a quick look at Tara and Rudra. Rudra's room, unused for a week, is where she spends the most time, tapping the wooden surfaces, touching the start control panel and somewhat theatrically drawing a finger over the dust on the computer screen.

"I'm taking this room," she says.

"The star gets the big bedroom," Joey says.

"I always sleep where the monitors are, not the cameras," says Zaria. "How long will it take to clear this space out?"

"Not long," says Rudra. "But I need this equipment for my work."

"And we can't fit the double bed in here," Joey says.

"Don't need a double," says Zaria. "Where's K-Pop, by the way?"

They break the news to her that Jin-Young is gone, and she

expresses deep sadness. "I wanted him to teach me everything about Flowing."

"Rudra's here for that," Joey says. "He'll be your editor."

"Nikhil should have told you, I'm bringing people I trust," Zaria says. "People are actually trying to kill me, so if this is my HQ I'm going to need to run it. I've checked you out, Joey, so that's all good, I said I wanted the best and here you are. But I need to look you two lovebirds up before I let you be on my team."

"I'm not on your team," Tara says. "I'm another Flowstar? And he's not available, he's with me."

"Great. So you're moving out?"

Everyone stares balefully at Joey, who keeps her face impressively still.

"You'll figure that out, I'm sure," Zaria says. "Now I need you to log in to all the computers in that surveillance centre, and give my boys a couple of hours to bug-sweep the house. Stay away as long as you can, actually. I have a presentation to work on."

"We had the house checked," Joey says.

"Yeah, I saw how well that worked with Indi. We can measure our dicks if you like about this, Joey, but it saves us all time if you go and get some coffee—try City of Cats, it's great."

Rudra watches open-mouthed as Joey considers this, and accepts. She'd told him Zaria would try to get into their systems, but like him, she probably hadn't anticipated it would be within her first few minutes in her new base. And it's definitely her base now. He can see in Tara's eyes the same uncertainty he feels: Do they even live here anymore?

"I woke up thinking today was going to be a good day," says Tara later, glowering into her phone. Her agent isn't taking her calls. Joey and Rudra aren't at their best either. Two mugs each of diabolically strong Costa Rican coffee, drained far too quickly, and their heads and smartatts are throbbing. Tara's smiles for stranger selfies have all been bordering on grimaces.

"You really don't need to worry," Joey says. "I know that sounds stupid, but I've met a lot of actresses and Flowstars, so believe me when I tell you that you're going to make it. It just takes more time than any of us want to accept, that's all."

"Easy for you to say," Tara says. "You have a salary. I have another round of bloody auditions to set up, and all they'll want to talk about is Indi."

"I won't have a salary once they finally accept my resignation."

"You're not going anywhere," Tara says. "You're here because you choose to be, and you love your job. You're the best in the whole industry, didn't you hear? Bitch pretended she didn't know who I was, like she hasn't been watching my Flow since it started. She'll want you, though, and you'll stay. Might as well face facts."

Joey shrugs. "I might surprise you one day."

"Oh, fuck, no," says Rudra.

They turn to him, and find him staring aghast at a man sitting across the café, several empty mugs with fruit-juice smears on the table in front of him, face covered by a tablet. A powerful-looking man, bulging out of a business shirt. He sets the tablet down, rises, and approaches their table.

"If you ladies can give us a minute," Rohit says, "I need to speak with my brother."

The Peach Blossom Spring pan-Asian lounge is just a few doors down and a few flights up from their coffee shop. All Rudra knows about it is that it's rumoured to be a child trafficking hub, but he doesn't know what signs to look for, and it's not even lunchtime. The guards at the door seem to know his brother. A sharply dressed manager walks them through an extremely trendy and empty Sinofuturist-design restaurant, through a sliding door in a metal facade, and up a dark and narrow flight of stairs with dragons dancing on the walls beside them. Rudra's heart thumps harder as they ascend into darkness: Where the hell are they going? Why is there a walk-in Hong Kong 1960s gangster movie experience available ten minutes away from his bed?

Another door, a giant bouncer, and they're in a bizarre reconstruction of somebody's imaginary old-school Chinese restaurant,
dim, smoky, noisy, large red lanterns, stained carpets, embroidered
wooden partitions, stunning red-robed waitresses, an explosion of
delicious food-smells, elderly red-faced men around a gambling
table, every Orientalist cliché he's ever seen. He looks around
for opium addicts and rival kung fu schools, but maybe they're
late-lunchers. They sit in a booth, red velvet sofas, large menus in
Mandarin. His brother doesn't need them: he chats with a suit-
clad waiter for a while, and lights a cigarette.

"I didn't know you spoke Mandarin," Rudra says.

Rohit shrugs. "Baba had to learn Hindi. His dad had to learn
English. We do what we have to."

The waiter appears, replaces their wooden kuàizi with titanium
ones, and sets cold appetisers down.

"You've put on some weight," Rohit says. "Living with girls and
all, it happens. You look good, overall. Are you finally getting
some sex?"

"How did you know I was going to be at Cats?" Rudra asks.

"I always know where you are," Rohit says. "I've always known,
ever since you left. We're family. I assumed you would come to
me when you were ready. But you've never claimed your blood
was thicker than it is. The fault is mine."

"You're being even weirder than usual," Rudra says. "What do
you want?"

"Calm down and watch your tone. We are the city's elite in a
place of power, where we may speak freely, but remember there
are always eyes on us."

"A place of . . . do you know how shady this Peach Blossom
is? It's a child trafficking den."

"Jealous outsiders gossiping. Learn to see the city's great
durbars for what they are. The details are irrelevant—if these were
colonial times, this place would look like the Gymkhana Club.
It used to be an American diner until five years ago, jukebox

and milkshakes and all that nonsense. And now . . . well. Look around, breathe. Don't stare, just observe our surroundings. Sense the power of this place."

"You're clearly high. Why are we here?"

"You know, I really thought Baba's death would bring you back, show you where you belong. Then that idiot Bijoyini had to stick her neck out, and, of course, you had to jump—when have you ever said no to a chance to make a fool of yourself?"

"Rohit. Why are we here?"

"To talk, you fool. I could have had you pulled into a van and brought home, but you're too old for that now, and there is no time to fight and then make amends. We have to move forward like adults."

"You sent that van to my old place, I hear."

"No. I went myself, to bring you home, but you'd run away already. I've always tried to let you have your freedom."

"What did you mean, you always know where I am? Do you have a tracker on me?"

"No."

"I don't believe you."

"I was waiting for you in that café because I thought you might visit it. And I wanted to sit down across a table from you. That's how things still get done, you know. All your virtual meetings and remote work . . . nothing moves until two men meet face-to-face and sort things out."

"What do you want to sort out?"

"You. Ma's a wreck. I can't handle it all on my own anymore. You have duties, you know. It's time to step up and be a man."

Rudra gives Rohit his most withering glare, but the effect is wholly ruined by the arrival of a waitress with a tray on which a magnificent crispy duck, pancakes, and hoisin sauce lie in state. The brothers stare at each other through a cloud of gentle smoke.

"I thought you were vegetarian," Rudra says.

"I am," Rohit says, digging in.

In between skilfully rolled pancakes and a predictable hogging of the sauce, Rohit explains what he wants. Things had gone downhill since Rudra turned down Chopra's incredibly generous offer. You didn't insult Chopra the way Rudra had and not suffer consequences—Chopra had not only taken over Rudra's Flowco, but handed it to Nikhil, a direct rival of Rohit's. But even this punishment could be an opportunity—now they had, for the first time, a chance to find out more about Nikhil's plans.

"You need to keep Chopra and Nikhil thinking that there is a rift between us."

"Not a problem."

"Nick's going to make his move soon, and promote you to a spot where he can try and turn you against me, and find out more about our clinics. You're going to say yes. And together we're going to trap that private-jet bastard, and drive him completely out of Chopra's circle. Stop looking at the wall every time I say their names—we're safe here. If the Peach Blossom's secrets come out, all of Delhi burns."

Rudra waits until the next pancake goes into Rohit's mouth. "I don't care at all about any of this melodrama."

"You remind me so much of myself," Rohit says. "If you think about it, you'll realise you don't even really hate Ma and me the way you think you do. Your problem was with Baba. But we don't have time for tantrums now."

"Can you not just hire someone else to be your corporate spy?"

"I already own three people in his teams. As he does in mine, no doubt, but this is not about him. I need my brother. I need you to wake up and start using that brain of yours. To see what the world we live in is really like. Nikhil is just another rival—we'll meet his type at every stage. And the truth is we're friends. Allies. Magicians, because advanced politics is magic. And the country is being rebuilt by our magic."

"So you're both turning all our lives upside down over some—friendly rivalry?"

"Yes. Because only one of us can pass through a gate at a time. The country's changing faster and faster, and we have to make sure our family is inside the wall when each new storm comes. I can't do that unless you grow up."

"Sorry, I'm lost now. What wall?"

"Delhi has always been a city of seven walls, and the men who live inside each. No, they're not demolishing CP again, focus, use that famous imagination of yours. The walls are invisible. You could only guess you'd crashed into your wall before, when you couldn't go further, but now the walls can be mapped and measured, the tools exist. Just look at a 3D map of the data that counts—real estate prices. Water supply. Family influence ratings. Anything marking class—therapist location density. It's like those old geography maps—isotherms. The walls are isothermal. You can see who's inside and who's not. A lot of the first-city people can't even be tracked in this way—only other first-city people know who they are. They're on some global power map, or on an island somewhere the satellites aren't allowed to show."

"And I thought I was the family nerd. What wall are we in?"

"We're in Delhi's third city. Chopra's in the second. Delhi's third city is, let's say, Asia's fifth city. It took our father his whole life to get into the third city from the fifth. You have no idea how difficult it is to jump two levels."

Rudra chews his food solemnly, but can't stop a slow grin from spreading over his face.

"Have we tried not jumping a level?" he asks.

"Very funny. It'll be less hilarious when a big crisis hits, and the second city decides to abandon everything outside it. When systems fail so badly that even people like us become ordinary. Have you already forgotten the last time? Sometimes the inner cities have to attack outer ones, for the good of the whole. That's when the walls become visible, even to idiots like you."

"You should come make geekFlows for your friend Nikhil. This will go down well with the superfan gatekeeper crowd. Seventh circle, fourth wall, fifth building. City inside city inside city. Conspiracies, secret societies. Amazing."

"I always knew you were slow, but I'm honestly shocked you don't even see the city you live in, even after living near poor people. You lived fifteen minutes away from the dark places, the torture chambers, the camps, the respectable-looking colonies where they put up the IDs of tenants on the gates for public examination, like restaurant menus."

"Right, but I lacked context. I wasn't aware my whole purpose in life is to help you go through an invisible wall."

"Not me, idiot. Our bloodline. So one day, our children can rule the city, and the country, and invade the rest of the world. New Gupta kings. I know this sounds funny to you, but you'll find, one day, that you're settling down into the life that you're meant to have. You'll marry someone, you'll have a kid, you'll see everything differently. I'm going to get married next year."

"Congratulations."

"Thank you, brother. She's a second-circle industrialist's daughter, she was there at the shraddho. She doesn't know yet. We're going to fall in love, make the whole city jealous, have the best wedding our family's ever seen. I'm not going to lecture you about fate, or destiny, we were both brought up to be modern, progressive people. But you'll find out one day that ultimately we are the tools of something larger than us."

"If this is leading towards accepting your guru . . ."

"No. Forget him. Baba needed him, we don't. We're both strong-willed men, who believe in shaping our own lives. Baba didn't really believe in tradition either. He thought he was some American-type entrepreneur. But you cannot escape your destiny—both of us ended up exactly where we would have if we'd just been the kind of traditional people who do everything by caste."

"I don't know what our caste even is."

"That's called privilege. We might not believe in caste, but caste believes in us. Your friend Bijoyini, do you know even she does a caste-appropriate job? 'Roy' means a family of small rulers, zamindars, land administrators managing turf for the local king. A Reality Manager in an age where data and attention are real estate? The exact same thing. She thinks she has that job because of what, her talent? She's allowed to have it because of her name. How many Dalits and Muslims do you think have jobs like hers? She thinks she's where she is because of her own choices, chance friendships, hard work. But she's ended up where destiny sent her. As we all will. Unless we escape to some foreign country and break the chain. But they have castes there too, it's just invisible. It's going to take generations to get inside their walls, to put down roots strong enough to withstand their storms. As a younger son, that option was open to you. But Chopra was your last chance. You didn't take it."

A flash of blue in the corner of his eye distracts Rudra: he turns, and sees either a bright tail disappearing under a velvet sofa, or nothing. Sometimes Bon-Rui plays hard to get. He shakes his head, and turns back to his brother.

"Good talk. Listen, Rohit—"

"Quiet, I'm talking. When they hear Gupta, cowbelt types think we're baniyas, business people. Bengalis think we're baidyos, royal physicians. And we're both royal physicians and businessmen, bhai, that's how destiny works, you can fight it, you can strike out on your own path, exercise all the choices you want, but in the end you will come home. We're royal physicians, building the next generation of rulers for our country, even the world, if things go well. Do you even know what we do in our clinics, why we're so powerful? We're building perfect children for the richest of the rich."

"That sounds . . . wrong. And dangerous."

"It's the exact opposite. Baba was a clever man; he found the safest thing to do in this world. No matter who's in power, no matter who needs land or blood, no matter which country's secretly running ours, there's one thing all sides agree on—the children of the rich must be protected. The scientists making them perfect must be safe. We're on the way to hacking mortality itself, regeneration, replacement, human–machine integration. Maybe we'll get there within our own lifetimes."

"You want to be immortal."

"Of course I do! Why try to be a billionaire otherwise? But this isn't just an idle dream. We can get there, and we already own some of the tools. No one's regulating us, the whole world's just investing, and trying to grab a piece. The Chinese were ahead of us, but their best labs were in Africa, and they lost so much when the shit hit the fan there. We might be the top line of clinics in the whole world. I want to show you, I will, soon as you're ready. You and me, brother—you have no idea how much of the future we own. Maybe we'll never even have to die! Can you even imagine how much power that gives us?"

Rudra finds he has no words. A waitress arrives with beef, rice, and steamed fish. She asks him how the food is, in Mandarin. He nods, and smiles, opening his mouth too wide, and she backs away.

"I know this is a lot, but you needed to know," Rohit says. "I was shocked too, when Baba told me everything he'd accomplished. I took all that on, and, Rudra, you won't believe what the last five years have been like for me, or for Ma. And you just weren't there. I protected you as much as I could—people have tried to abduct you seven times. Seven. And you wouldn't take our fucking calls."

"I'm sorry," Rudra says. "I just . . . I don't know what to say."

"Then just listen. Storms are coming. We don't know what they are. We live in a country that's so conformist even the fucking terrorists work for the government, but despite this everything manages to be completely impossible to predict. The walls are going to crack, because a tide of people will try to break them, just billions of people who are useless, lost in the world, people who are angry and desperate to survive: they're going to try to take everything down with them, burn it all. Climate change will break walls. The robots will break walls. New diseases, tech disasters, all these things. They're all coming, all at the same time, until one day there's only one wall, and the people inside it are gods, and the people outside it are monsters, or dead. It's going to get fucking mythological. I'm going to be inside the wall. And I want my brother with me. Do you understand now? Have I woken you up?"

"Yes," Rudra says.

"Are you going to do what I tell you?"

"Yes?"

"I don't believe you, but it's a start. Now eat your fish."

"What the hell is wrong with you?" Tara asks him that night.

"Nothing," he says, turning towards her, and noticing, far too late, new nightwear that he should have enthusiastically ripped off her a long time ago.

"You've barely said a word all day. Is it me? Are you upset with me? Are you obsessed with Zaria? Do we have to move out tonight? What's happening?"

He hasn't discussed his family yet with Tara. Or with anyone else. He doesn't know how.

"Something my brother said. Family issues. I'd prefer to not go over it again."

"Tell me."

"Not this week," he says. "We still have this place, and our jobs, and some time. I don't want to ruin it."

"Why would I ask you about your family if I was planning to leave you after this week?"

"You're not?"

"No, you dumbfuck. Oh my god, you don't know. We're a couple now."

Ablaze with joy and relief, he kisses her, but when he goes further she pushes him back.

"Talk," she says.

"I don't know where to start."

"Why did you leave?"

It wasn't something he'd ever thought he'd tell anyone, but he tells her. About how he used to sing and dance as a kid, and his family would encourage him, just make him perform in front of stupid clapping audiences. How there was one time when the whole extended family had gathered, and everyone had insisted that he dance to the new Bollywood hit, and he hadn't wanted to because he'd needed to pee, but they'd made him do it anyway, and just keep at it, and they hadn't let him stop until he'd pissed himself, and started crying, just dancing wildly around the living room peeing and crying, and his father had recorded it.

His memories of the incident are a muddle, just the sound of clapping and music and laughter turning into shrieks, and a feeling of immense confusion and excitement, and how when it happened, it had felt warm, even pleasant, and not even wet, until later. He'd forgotten about it somehow, no one had brought it up, until years later, when his father had been obsessed with being a first-wave social media star, had put that old video up, and it had gone viral. Everyone he knew had seen it. He'd been in his mid-teens then, a tangle of limbs and awkwardness and hormonal explosions anyway, but he's sure he'll go through his whole life without ever again feeling so much shame, so much betrayal, so much pure rage.

"I'm sorry, but that's it?" Tara asks. "This is your big trauma?"

"Yes, it does sound quite stupid now. I was very upset."

"I mean it's sad and everything, but I thought it would be far worse."

"I guess so. It's why I left. I don't know if it's why I stayed away."

She reaches out to him, and kisses him again.

"This is the past, baby. He didn't mean any harm. It's nothing," she says. "I'm going to fix you."

"Yes."

"Take my clothes off now."

"Yes."

CHAPTER 8

He hears Tara laughing as he wakes, and lies there listening, not wanting to open his eyes because that would mean starting the clock on the day, and it's the last day of her contractual relationship with Indi, her last day as a resident of the penthouse. Possibly his as well—the Flowco's going to go with whatever Zaria wants, but she hasn't deigned to tell him whether he has her approval. No one's asked Tara to leave the house yet, but she doesn't have his gift of invisibility—they're going to notice she's still around.

She's not in bed, though, she seems to be walking around the room, probably on the phone. He opens an eye and peers at her: she's wearing one of his T-shirts and has a mug of coffee in her hands. How long has she been up? She's in Actress mode, delivering a rundown of her career thus far to some hopefully spellbound producer.

The Flowco hasn't offered her any kind of new project, and she's angry with Joey because she'd been expecting solutions from her, not general life advice: she wanted a door, and all she's found is another wall with a motivational poster on it. Joey's told her to think of something that best expresses who she is and what she wants instead of chasing the market, which Tara says is classic gaslighting—whenever she's done that, starting from Day One with her futurist plan, Joey's told her the market doesn't want it, no one's ready for her. The market doesn't care about Tara and her ambitions, and has made this clear.

Rudra thought Joey's offer to help Tara structure a solo Flow pitch was generous, especially given Joey's general sentiments about the Flowco at present. But all this is useless, Tara's explained: she needs to know what people want her to be, and then she can be the hell out of that target. Joey's just doing what every smug insider has done when they have nothing to offer her, pretending that Flows are commissioned on the basis of some sort of unique personality, not just matched with a shopping list of what's sellable at the moment. Joey knows what that list is, Tara's sure of it, but is withholding that information because she has a problem with Tara.

Rudra has learned the hard way that defending Joey to Tara is a stupid idea, and he needs to work on his listening anyway, so he just listens as Tara explains to her mystery producer that she represents a new generation of exciting, authentic urban Indian voices. He finds Tara's performances on these calls amazing: her chameleon abilities both fascinate and vaguely frighten him. Every Flowstar has to calibrate their personality settings for public, business, and private, he's seen Indi flip those switches many times, but Tara can go further: her movements, her voice, her vocabulary are micro-customisable, she's like a Design Your Avatar pregame section. He's even discussed this with her: she's explained it's because she's so high-empathy she can't help partly becoming each person she talks to, and mirroring them. It's what made her want to be an actress in the first place, before she learned those doors were closed or involved abuse she refused to take.

"Empathy is like a superpower I can't control," she'd told him. "I think that's why I like you so much? With you, I'm myself."

It sounded like a compliment, but did she mean that he had no personality?

Whoever she's talking to now is getting the full force of her charm. Rudra wonders for a while whether he should be worried. The possessive boyfriend is not a role he feels up to playing, but is it something she expects? Are there alpha male patterns that she wants even if she keeps telling him she adores him for not being like all the others?

It sounds like an exciting job, but she needs to figure it out, and she can't wait to meet. She's noticed he's up now, and blows him a kiss. She makes a series of animated gestures, but he can't figure it out, he's always been bad at guessing games, so he just smiles and reaches for his phone. It isn't in its usual spot; he looks around and finds it on his bed.

He's slept through his alarm again.

"I still find it hard to believe, I had no idea," Tara says. "And you're mean! He's not like that at all. You'll see."

Suddenly he's wholly awake. He waves at her, and she winks at him. He checks his phone and his worst fears are confirmed: there's a received call from his brother.

"You have a pool? That's crazy! I'm there, what are the house swimwear rules? Oh, like that. Your mother would kick me out! And yeah, of course Rudra's coming too. Don't worry."

"Are you talking to my brother?" Rudra asks.

"He's up! You want to talk to him?"

She holds out the phone to him, and he just stares and shakes his head.

"Yeah, he's grumpy when he wakes up. Chill. I told you, I got this."

He's already out of bed, and heading for the living room,

conscious only of a burning need for coffee. She's still on the phone when he returns, now talking in a murmur. She says her good-byes when she sees him, hangs up, and beams at him.

Dozens of questions jostle in his throat. "What did you do?" emerges first.

"Okay, okay. Don't be mad, but I was up, and he called, you wouldn't wake up, so I just said hi on impulse. God knows how long you'd have waited to introduce me. Baby! Don't be pissed? Tell me you're not pissed."

"I'm . . . no, I guess. It was just a bit of a shock."

"He was really sweet. Took my number, called, and . . . okay, we'll discuss this properly later, but he's really fond of you, okay, and the moment he heard we were together he wanted to know all about me, and he knows Jaipur really well, all my local politicians, but even the best chaat places, and, you know something, it's so weird, your brother is like halfway between you and all the guys I knew growing up? Anyway, that wasn't even the exciting part, it turns out he needs someone to start a Flow about your family clinics, like be their official spokesperson, and actually be creative head for all kinds of shows about post-human upgrades and the hunt for immortality. I couldn't believe it!"

"I don't believe it either."

"He just told me."

"Didn't say a word about this yesterday."

"Well, you're not a Flowstar, are you? He said he's seen my work, he's actually a fan, even before knowing about us, and if this Flowco doesn't have me there's always a place for me in your family businesses! You didn't tell me your family was starting a Flowco!"

"It isn't."

"I guess you didn't know about it. Must have been planning to surprise you. It was amazing, Rudra! It was . . . no one's ever been that welcoming to me, and I have you to thank for it. I was really sad when I woke up today, but now . . ."

She gives him a kiss that would normally have reduced him to jelly, but he pulls back. Her eyes actually glitter in excitement—he's never seen anything like it outside anime.

"I think this might be it. He's sending a car over," Tara says. "Get dressed. Take me home. Show me everything."

"I don't think this is a good idea," he says.

It's like he turned off the central power, and he's immediately engulfed with remorse.

"My brother is not to be trusted," he says. "He's involved in some kind of . . . okay, I shouldn't talk about this here. But this is a trap."

"He said you'd say that. Let's talk about it on the way. This means a lot to me, Rudra. The wellness space is insanely huge, it's secure, it's something I would be great for, and, my god, I've always wanted creative control, I have so many ideas, and for the first time someone's listening? Like I even told him the futurist ones, and he thought they were amazing. He just got it. You guys, you're just well brought up, it's something else. It's those strong feminist mothers."

"I don't—"

"And best of all I wouldn't have to worry all the time, I'd be working directly with the owners. What owners? With you. With my boyfriend. My Reality Editor. You have no idea how great this is. It's the dream. It's like everything's falling into place."

"Tara, I want you to succeed, I really do. But you know enough about my family to know this is very clearly my brother trying to push us into an argument, and to provoke me."

She almost throws her phone at him.

"I do not fucking believe you just made this about you," she says. "Do you know how worried I've been? What my situation is? I can't just sit around and do nothing like you. I don't have wealth to fall back on."

"I don't—"

"A god-given opportunity comes to me and you're trying to kill it because you don't want me to meet your family? Because this is inconvenient for you?" Her voice is raw, cracked: she looks like she wants to hit him.

She pauses, and each second that passes then is heavier than the last. He sees everything he wants to say scroll up and delete itself in front of his eyes, he can see her recalibrating, like a phone restarting.

"I'm sorry. I'm sorry. I didn't mean that," she says, her eyes filling with tears. "Rudra, I promised I'd fix you. And I'm here for you. So trust me, and come with me? Sometimes the best way to bring a family back together is an outsider."

"I thought this was about your career, not my family."

"It is, baby. But it's something that can help both of us. And I want to help you, not just myself. I know you think I'm greedy, and don't know my place—"

"I don't think either of those things at all."

"Then can't you just trust me? Why won't you let me in? Did our time together mean nothing to you?"

"It meant a lot. Means a lot. And okay, maybe I've already ruined this, but I wanted us to do something together. If my brother is serious, he'll still want you for this project tomorrow."

"If you care about me, so will you."

"It's your last day today, and I actually have a whole day out planned. All your favourite places, all the places you said you wanted to go to but couldn't. I have the whole list. You said I never take you out. I wanted to change that. I know I'm boring and I want to be better. I want us to have a day."

"That's sweet, and I totally appreciate it."

"But not today."

"Ideally not? I'm not going to risk annoying Rohit. He's a powerful man. He can change everything for me. And for you. And you can tell who the powerful people are quite easily—they don't wait. They know there's no time to sit, and think, and analyse things. They act. Other people wait for them."

Rudra nods and rolls out of bed. It feels ridiculous, pulling his clothes on under Tara's cold gaze.

"Thank you," she says. "Have a shower as well? You kind of smell of us."

"Oh, I'm not going," he says. "Just putting some clothes on."

"I want you to do this with me," Tara says. "I want you to step up, and be happy for me. I promise you, I'm going to make you so happy in return it'll make your head spin."

"My head's spinning just fine already."

"Your brother said you wouldn't come," she says. "He said you refuse any attempt at therapy, healing, you don't want to belong to your family, to your family's community, to your guru, to society at all. He said you might be past hope. I told him I believed in you, he said maybe I could help you. Don't prove me wrong."

"I can already see our day together, the three of us with my mother doing crazy cameos. He wants you to be impressed by the house, and show me how you don't fit in. He wants me to get angry, and he wants you to watch him humiliate me."

"You know, there's obviously a lot that's happened between you that you don't talk about," she says. "You need to talk about this stuff with a professional, but that's for another day. I'm not going to get angry. I'm not going to ask you why you think I wouldn't fit in your house, because I'm going to. You think your family is a challenge, after the places I've been?"

"That's not what I was saying."

She blinks back tears, and he hates himself for wondering if she can cry at will.

"I'll fit in a lot better than you ever did," she says.

"I'm sure you will," Rudra says. "And I wish you both joy."

She laughs at this, and reaches for him, and kisses him with much tenderness. "I keep forgetting I haven't known you forever," she says. "I haven't seen you sulk like this before. You know what, it's fine. Forget it. You're probably right, and he's probably just using me to irritate you. And I'm sure I can get another job. I mean, look at me."

They hold each other, perfectly still: as stalemates go it's the most comfortable one Rudra's been in. A little too comfortable, in fact: it's morning, his body is clearly not aware they are fighting, and he knows he'll agree to absolutely anything in a few seconds.

"You should go if you want," he says. "I don't want to get in the way of your career."

He loses count of how much time he spends lost in VR games after she leaves, dimly aware after a few hours that he's very hungry, but he's hovering too close to full immersion to step out. His American friends are delighted to see him: it's been a while since he last attended one of their all-night sessions. They're mer-clans fighting in the ruins of submerged New York today/tonight, and Rudra finds in his gameplay a certain recklessness that's been missing the last couple of years. He leads his clan through a particularly dangerous raid, berserking his way through a subway-tunnel trap-maze full of newbie shark-men, engages their leader in solitary combat, hammering his head with a fire-hydrant-based mace, and is on the verge of a glorious kill when the screen goes dark.

He curses freely, punching his haptic-gloved fist into the endless darkness, and is rewarded by the sudden appearance of a group chat window. A stream of emojis pops up, several active speakers. Assuming it's a glitch or a hack, he shuts off his helmet. Too many people he knows have lingered in unfamiliar virtual environments and accidentally helped in organising droneswarm attacks in the Balkans.

He wipes his face, waits a minute and restarts the helmet, but the start-up screen doesn't show: it's still a chat conversation, emojis and animated GIFs and segments of texts, friendly picture-appreciation-comment banalities: "Hot!," "THIS," "Stunning," "Crying rn." A memory pops up: the link to Joey's VR helmet must still be active. He hasn't played since her meeting with Nikhil. Is he now creeping on some chat with her girlfriends? But Joey isn't even here.

He's about to take the helmet off again when he hears Zaria's voice.

"Rokheya present and secure," she says. "Requesting entry to New Tion."

He knows this is his cue to leave, so he tells himself to leave. Spying on his first Flowstar got him kicked out of the house, even though that was by accident. This time it's absolutely not an accident, and Zaria's a lot more dangerous than Indi. He takes off the helmet. He puts it back on.

A sim environment opens up, a Blockhead open-world setup, one of the new ones they've made for women gamers. Rudra remembers a recent online controversy because women weren't at all happy with the Blockhead-for-girls design, with its shiny pastel colours and overwhelming cuteness: they'd wanted safety regulations in mainstream Blockhead sim worlds, not a separate enclosure. This build is a generic city, clearly a work in progress: flat-colour skyscrapers line textureless grey streets, a building-block playground under a sun with an actual smile drawn in it, staring fixedly down from a sky-blue sky. Zaria walks into a Sadface café, where another woman waits for her, a default starter avatar, completely uncustomised.

"Olamina," Zaria says, and hugs her.

"The others are on their way. Are you safe? Are you alone?"

"As alone as I need to be. And yes, safe. The new crew's completely harmless, I've never seen anything like it."

"You all ready for our session?"

"I'm hopelessly underprepared."

"Please, you'll be fantastic, you always are. Anyway, after the last session the bar is now set to: don't mute yourself by accident, or fight with your cat."

"I'm sure I'll do something even worse."

"I know you won't."

"Stop me if I go on too long, okay?"

"You know I won't."

Zaria looks at the Sadface café menu, and Rudra does too, through her eyes. He's seen this sort of thing before—the items on the menu pop up one by one, morose and quirky, Polyamorous Matcha, Himbo Cheesecake, Microaggressive Mocha, Anxie-Tea. Truly his generation's idea of fun. The café itself is incomplete: one of the walls is an untextured flat surface, another seems unfinished; she can see the city outside through glitches in the walls.

Other women appear and are greeted, all names Rudra feels like he's heard before, or seen used in games: Khutulu, Jingwei, Safronova, Marmokreb, Aineko, Patasola, Mekatilili, Huli Jing. They're all using standard avatars: if there are spying eyes on the café, eyes other than his own, they see ten identical smiling animated girls sitting around a Sadface table, and occasionally exchanging places.

When Rudra was really young, his father had often tried to entertain him with a game where he shuffled three overturned paper cups around, and Rudra had to spot which one had a marble trapped under it. He always failed, and cried, which amused his father greatly, and this when his brain was young and sharp. Watching these women roam around a café is far worse. He wonders how Zaria tells them apart, if she even can.

Perhaps there are clues in the chat stream, which has not stopped for a second through all of this. If anything, it's sped up: multiple conversations through a vast range of animated images have spiralled into patterns of dizzying complexity. Using his nonexistent hacker skills and far too extensive experience of cyber-thriller films, he deduces they're probably using complex live encryption that translates their inputs into girl-chat code that most surveillance men would ignore, or dismiss. A Brazilian anarchist group had recently been caught trying to smuggle their messages in porn video backgrounds: this is probably just a less-attention-drawing, more-history-book-friendly alternative.

He convinces himself that not trying to break their code makes his presence in Zaria's shadow easier to justify—he's not actually spying, he's just watching with idle interest, like when other people's gameplay videos stack up, one after another, and hours pass by because he's too lazy to turn it off. This is really unconvincing, even to him: he has to try harder. He didn't ask to be here? True, but he could just switch it off. It's not like they're doing anything particularly private? Please, this is the most secret secret society he's ever encountered. Zaria's bodyguards should have found the helmet link and fixed it, why aren't they better at their jobs? That's just victim-blaming, he knows perfectly well what he's doing is wrong. What he doesn't know is why he's so excited to be here.

"I'm delighted to introduce our newest ambassador, Omu-Ako of Ife," Olamina says. Her voice is lovely, her accent American. "Like us, she's here to listen to Rokheya's stories today."

"It is an honour to be here," Omu-Ako says. "I am still learning your language, so I may be silent today." She's using a live-translation plug-in, a freeware robot-voice, which seems really unsafe, but Rudra acknowledges that if this group's security were watertight he wouldn't be here.

"Please speak, whenever you want," Zaria says. "If there's any place you should feel free, it is this."

The avatar Rudra thought was Omu-Ako sits still. Another one, two chairs down, stands and bows in response, and Rudra would have smacked himself on the forehead if he weren't wearing a helmet.

"Welcome, ambassadors of New Tion, to this special session," Olamina says. "We thank, as always, our grandmothers in Hunan, who taught us to use our new shoes."

A couple of the avatars giggle, and Rudra suspects this will be the first of many in-jokes.

"Tonight, or today, we shall hear the stories of Rokheya, who represents us in the land of Swarga," Olamina says. "She is set to embark on a grand new adventure, so we thought it wise for all of us to hear her tales before she leaves." He can hear what she isn't saying as well: whatever it is that Zaria is about to do, she might never come back.

"Thank you, sister. My first story is about knowledge," Zaria/Rokheya says. "It begins, as do all my stories, in Swarga, a land of peace and plenty, ruled by a great and powerful king."

He notices she's not using her regular voice, or her journalist-video voice: this is a deep, solemn, slow voice that reminds him of times his high school classmates dragged him to poetry open mics or art openings because they wanted to hit on college women and he had a car and a driver. No doubt it's meant to convey deep meaning and gravitas, but it's a voice that makes Rudra's brain want to spin a cocoon around itself, emerge years later with wings, and escape to the Himalayas. He shakes himself into the story, but it's a struggle.

Zaria's story is about a happy nation where the king ensures his subjects' bliss by learning absolutely everything about them through magic. Two children are born into a village in this country, and live a charmed life until they meet an evil witch who persuades them that the king was not to be trusted, and the nation would actually be happier if people kept secrets. The witch, who's also old and ugly, tricks the children into quest-walking to the country's capital to find ways to stop the king's magicians.

Rudra zones out in the middle of the story, trying to follow Zaria's surveillance metaphors instead of the plot: she's sending encrypted documents to the whole group as she speaks. He's played games with enough dark-webbers to recognise AI-created documents-as-images when he sees them: around the world, the ambassadors of New Tion will be running these chains of Good Morning messages, memes, animal pics, fan fiction trope lists, and Flow-etry screenshots through translators that reproduce them as . . . what? What is this secret society capable of actually doing? Who do they work for? How do they punish men caught perving on their resistance movement?

In the story, the children have escaped mobs of enchanted citizens whose love for the king has inspired them to remorseless bloodshed, and reached Swarga's capital, and discovered that city people are strange, and keep secrets from the king, but don't seem happy at all. The children are captured by the king, and find he's amazing, and the witch was lying. And then the kids team up with the king, become magicians themselves, and build even stronger magic, magic that they gift to all the nation's people, city and village alike, for their own good.

The story grows fangs: enemies of Swarga are found and executed, spies, traitors, infiltrators from other nations are put to the sword for the greater good. Later, Rudra cannot identify exactly when the story drew him in—was Zaria actually a skilled teller, or were there subliminal messages in the images that floated past him in the chatboxes? Were the New Tion society using a new form of communication?

Whatever it is, he finds, to his amazement, that he suddenly cares, that he's able to hear what Zaria's actually saying, sinking past the laboured alt-world fable plotline into an immersive reality. Beyond her words, he understands her message when she shares that the upcoming physical brain implants that will soon be forced on the poor will do more than identify and monitor citizens—they'll measure them, fortify the national Lakshman-Rekha internet, power the national blockchain, vote on their behalf in sham elections, store and share data, and eventually become their bearers' only source of education, income, and culture. They'll make the process of selling people's bodies wholesale to anyone who has use for them much more efficient.

"Ten years ago Swarga mapped their skins," Zaria says. "Now Swarga is under their skins. But it needs more. Swarga must be inside their heads, to guide all their actions for their own good, to give them real purpose again. They will get there, one day, it is just a matter of building the tools."

Already Rudra has forgotten what happened to the heroes of the story. They may have become the new kings, or perhaps they were killed by the witch? He's not sure how he missed the story's end, because he was definitely listening.

"What's happening in Swarga now already happened to us three years ago," Omu-Ako says. "You have long known, like we did, the pleasure of being the cradle for global experiments. Where the role of your country is for the world's rulers to field-test their strategies, and dump their waste, while our so-called global saviours look the other way, generation after generation. Where everything in rich nations' news has happened in your country before, but somehow their new tech takes a generation to reach you."

"Let us hear the next story—" Olamina's voice is wary, but Omu-Ako isn't done.

"How long will we sit by and watch East and West buy our leaders and carve up our lands? Watch our own chieftains sell out our people? The air and the water are poisoned, the bar for normal is deep underground . . ."

A burst of emojis, and Omu-Ako stops talking. Rudra glares at the icons as if the sheer force of his curiosity might cause them to transform into text. Did they just shut her up? Was the new girl saying something wrong?

"My next story is about death, and the lives we take to escape it," Rokheya says.

This story is about a hero from Swarga who befriends a lost orphan in its streets, and is shocked to find she is a witch in training. He rescues her from this life, and even plans to marry her, but his parents wisely intervene. A family friend, a magician, finds through a spell that the girl is not even from Swarga: she is from the dreaded land of Narak, opposite to Swarga in every way.

Discovered, the girl disappears, but the hero cannot forget her. He becomes convinced she has been abducted by a demon from Narak, and sets off against his family's wishes to bring her back. Going to Narak involves many difficult magic-enabled steps—portals, tunnels, oceans crossed on magic dolphins. Rudra knows the story's just a distraction, a bassline at best, but he can't help following it, since he can't read the real one scrolling on the screen.

Rudra remembers the time Chuki had come to his flat with a fresh set of scars, not the deep grooves on her shoulders that she'd acquired as a child during her crossing, but new ones, that ran from her torn ears down her neck, disappearing under her winking Mariam Marvel T-shirt. She'd laughed when he'd offered to go with her to the police, or to a hospital, or talk to former classmates now in the media.

"Give me beer. Give me games. And give me space," she'd said. He had. Later, after she'd gone, he'd realised she'd kept her hand on his thigh, and her head on his shoulder, for a long time while they'd been shooting aliens in space together. She hadn't come back for weeks after that, and when she had it was with a new boy. She'd refused to take her smog mask back from him after his father's shraddho. He needed to have a reason to come find her, she'd said.

Rokheya's fable's hero gets to Narak, and Narak is truly the opposite of Swarga. Slave markets, highways lined with brothels full of children, a brutal tyrant in charge, burning forests, poisoned rivers, no laws, hordes of barbarians roaming the land abducting women and children, or disguising themselves as noblemen and tricking women into slavery with promises of marriage. Our hero, in disguise, joins such a group of slave-herders, and journeys towards Narak's capital while setting many slaves free. He finds that the slavetrader captain is troubled: earlier, there was rich trade in sending slaves to other lands, but now no country will trade with Narak: they don't want slaves anymore; they have marvellous machines built by Swarga's magicians, and are building walls to keep the people of Narak out. Where are we taking these slaves, then? the hero asks. The trader merely laughs.

"Where's the girl?" an avatar asks.

"Patience," another says.

Rudra's either imagining things—but there's no blue pangolin in sight, and usually Bon-Rui shows up in times like this—or they've really invented a new way of doing things, because he can tell them apart now. Without name tags, without voice association, he can see them.

He realises the story has moved forward without him, and hurries to catch up: Rokheya has now moved to a great fortress and its deep dungeons, where the slavetraders take their catch. The hero wanders through pits of despair where Narak's people are tortured and reeducated into mindlessness, whipped into armies that the tyrant of Narak uses to attack his own people, and one day other lands. But deeper still, the hero finds worse: demons and sorcerers who perform vile magic, so far removed from that of the noble magicians of Swarga that the hero doesn't even recognise it as magic at first. Magic that is used to transform women and children into demons, demons who are then sacrificed to create creatures the like of which the hero has never seen before: perfect, beautiful, angelic beings that remind him terribly of the noble children of Swarga.

A cluster of link-balloons floats up in front of Rudra, and his impulse is to tap one and see what it all means, but he's terrified: What if Zaria sees? But how is he to find out more, find out how it all works, what they're really saying, what they plan to do about it, unless he dives into one of the links and sees for himself? What is the scale of this organisation? Who are its owners? Are all of the Sadface café ladies Zarias in their own countries, notorious, privileged, absolutely reckless? Is this all just some upper-class people in a digital club networking and politicking and letting off some steam while building career-expanding alliances, or a resistance that will one day change the world? How is this the only safe space they have to meet?

He doesn't need to see her links to know what's in them. He knows they're about trafficking, mass abductions from refugee camps and villages, concentration camps, and other things he's spent his whole life avoiding conversation about. He knows they're about perfect-child breeding projects using bodies from around the world, the birth-outsourcing industries booming in post-law nations, organ-growth sweatshops, body farms, womb-renting factories, sex slave training centres, cell-harvest centres, gene-testing prison camps. He knows humans will never go really obsolete, because there'll always be uses for their bodies, right down to the last cell, there'll always be people willing to use them.

He wonders how many times his family's name comes up in the reports behind the links.

The hero finds the girl and she tells him that Narak was Swarga all along, he just hadn't been looking, but the hero decides she's a lying witch, kills her, burns down the fortress, and returns to Swarga. Rudra had seen this one coming, though, and he's not listening as well as he should be because he finds it a little hard to breathe.

"There are more stories, there always are," Rokheya says. "And none of these stories are new. My next story can wait: let me ask the question Omu-Ako did. How long will we wait before things change? Why should those who have learned not to see for centuries suddenly wake up now?

"Swarga used to be known as a place where empires went to die. Now, like Ife, it is a battered coast where failed utopias drift ashore, like flip-flops, and are put to new uses. Ancient blood feuds, failed methods, obsolete systems, told stories, broken laws are carried here with each new tide, and we take them in and make them something new and even stranger. We save stories, cling on to hope, and wait—for what? My city burned, and bled, and choked, for what? There were so many cremations, they cut all the trees in my neighbourhood, the sky was full of ash from pyres, for what? They laid siege to my city, razed it to the ground, stamped their boots and faces all over it—and the city refused to even understand it was being invaded!"

"And it would be worth something, still, if we learned lessons from the past," Omu-Ako says. "But we don't. Millions die, and no one blinks. New crimes stack up while we debate old ones. Mass murderers rise to power, erase their crimes, become serial mass murderers. They butcher their victims, sacrifice millions of their own worshippers, and nothing changes. Nothing stops them—if there is a pandemic, they work from home."

"Who will take responsibility when a bioweapon project goes rogue? Who will help our people when their water is gone?" asks Rokheya. "When the powers that are supposed to protect us abandon or kill us without consequence, who will keep us alive?"

"New Tion hears you both," Olamina says. "Together, we will move from listening to planning, planning to action: our work shall overcome these dystopian times."

"There's nothing dystopian about it," Zaria snaps: Rudra can hear the change in her voice, and so can everyone else. Formal Rokheya's left the café.

"Dystopia is pornographic, Olamina. You see it and shiver but it's also kind of fun because it's happening somewhere else, to someone else, you know? It requires distance. Some of us are actually sitting in the fucking middle of it and we may never learn to care in time. This isn't dystopia. This is reality."

"Rokheya."

"Yes, sorry." Rudra can hear Zaria take a few breaths, and when she speaks again, she's back to her Rokheya voice.

"Humankind will survive this century," she says. "And when the survivors look back, they'll ask themselves why we didn't see the arrival of the great mind-plagues that already afflict so many of us, epidemics that rage unchecked and are allowed to do so because they help the powerful. Just as we look back on the great wars and the great plagues that kept our species in check before we rose to overcome them. But with all this knowledge, we refuse to learn. Each new generation, swaggering in arrogance because it thinks it invented enlightenment and resistance, until it is trapped in the same net as the last one. I don't see how Swarga can survive, Olamina. I just don't see it."

"You will. And we are with you in this journey, Rokheya. We will look them in the eye and tell them we know what they're doing to us, we see what they're taking from us, we know its worth. And we will carry on doing this, until we win—despite all circumstances, all enemies, all false allies. Thank you for your stories, Rokheya. New Tion hears them."

"Thank you for listening, ambassadors of New Tion," Rokheya says.

The chatboxes vanish, one by one, until all that's left is the avatars around the table.

"For New Tion," Olamina says.

"For New Tion," the ambassadors say in chorus, softly, and Rudra says it too, though no one hears him.

The screen goes dark.

He doesn't remember taking the helmet off, or walking to his old room, or talking his way past Zaria's bodyguards standing outside it. The next thing he remembers is standing in front of Zaria and telling her what he's done, and watching her struggle to not punch him in the face.

"Forget you told me this," she says. "And I'll forget I heard it. You saw nothing. You heard nothing."

"I want to help," he says.

"Walk away. Right now. Did you record anything?"

"No."

"Good. If you're lying, I'm going to find out. Now go away."

"Zaria, I want to help. I can help. My brother, you know who he is, I'm sure, I think he's in charge of—"

"Listen, fuckface. You found a hole in the girls' locker room and peeped in to see if we were changing. I get it. Now you're coming and telling me about it hoping that'll make you feel better. It won't. Maybe you're hoping we'll become friends. Maybe fuck one time. We won't. Now get the hell away from me."

"I have a login and password into a family bank account. I think you have friends who could do things with it."

She swears at him for what seems like forever, and gestures towards a chair. He sits.

"I think this room is clean," she says. "But then I thought the bloody helmet was clean, like an amateur. Rudra. Why are you offering me this?"

"I think my family might be involved with some of the things you were talking about. I'm going to find out more. I'll go to the clinics, and see what they do there."

"You don't know? Let me spoil it for you. Yes. The Gupta clinics are right in the centre of it. Trafficking, body farms, mass testing, gene hacking, all of it. Where do you think your family gets its money?"

"I want to tear it all down. I know you do too. Tell me what you need."

"No," she says. "I don't believe you."

"I'll let you into the account right now."

"What is wrong with you? Your brother's biggest rival is literally my boss. Why are you doing this?"

"I told you," Rudra says. "I heard what you said. I believe in you. I want to help."

She paces the room, her eyes fixed on his.

"No," she says. "You think you're having some kind of awakening, but that's not my problem. I won't be responsible for it, or you."

"It's done. I want to join your movement, whatever it is."

"You want to get into the zenana. I've seen it before. You're empty, and you just want to follow someone. Go join a cult like the rest of your family."

"I have no family."

"Well, you can't have mine. I don't want you. My people don't want you. This is our space. Our place of power, not yours. You can't come in."

"Don't want to. But I can help you. Let me."

"You want to go on a spy mission now? Look at you. You wouldn't survive a week outdoors."

"Let me try."

"If you want to help people suddenly, go join a charity. Go join some activists. There are lots of men trying to make things better. Go follow them. Find some other space. Seriously. You'll get killed. I don't want that on me."

"I'm not your responsibility, or your friend," he says. "I really don't like you at all. And believe me, I don't have a sinister plan, or any kind of plan at all. I'm offering you all I have in case you want it. Have your friends get into the Gupta systems, and tell you what they find. We'll take it from there."

"I think you're insane," she says. "Go to your room, and stay there."

That evening, when there's a knock on his door, he leaps to answer it. It's not Zaria. It's not Tara, whose calls he'd missed while immersed in VR. Twelve of them. She hadn't taken his calls later, and he's been fighting complete panic.

It's Zaria's bodyguards, and they're giggling.

"Boss, have you seen it?" Husain asks.

He hands Rudra his phone, where a Flow is replaying. It's Tara. She's launched her solo Flow, which she says is about empathy, human connections, and making other people's lives better. Her mission is to change a life every day, and have her followers help her make the world better one person at a time.

Her first episode is about a dear friend who's stuck in a shell, unable to move forward, because he's ashamed of who he is, and is hiding from the world. She wants all of India to join her letting him know that things are okay, that he'll be accepted for who he is. Interestingly, he's also one of India's first viral sensations, and she thinks it's time for him to join her as the show's cohost. Millions of people agree with her. She's a hit.

He stares, blank-faced, at the video of chubby-little-boy Rudra dancing around the family living room. He watches himself turn red, try to escape, get pushed back into his performance, then embarrass himself. He watches Tara thank her loving audience for making him viral again, for welcoming him back. He hands the phone back to Husain. The bodyguards guffaw, and slap him on the back, but stop when he neither laughs nor runs away.

"I want to be free from all of this," he says. "All of it. I'm done here."

"Bhai, you okay?" Faiz asks.

"Yes," Rudra says. "I'm fine. Yes."

CHAPTER 9

The queue at the ICH Place metro station entrance is always one of the shortest in all of Delhi: very few residents of the neighbourhood use public transport. Joey hasn't seen the insides of a metro compartment in a while, but the line doesn't bother her as much as the short walk to it. The temperature's hit fifty again, and while she's dressed appropriately, like a space explorer on a desert planet, and carries a backpack full of cold water, and has covered every exposed inch of skin (very few, given her large mask and larger sunglasses) with a variety of anti-sun creams, she can feel herself drying, cracking, wilting as soon as she leaves her building, waves of pure heat washing over her, almost blowing her away with their intensity.

Some of the expats she'd recently been pushed into going on dates with had described walking in Delhi as similar to having a smoke inside a microwave: she'd scoffed at them, told them how she used to take the bus to college sometimes, braving the heat, the pushers, the nation-builders, the gropers, and the public masturbators, all for a sense of independence, but two minutes away from the metro station she's ready to give up, call them all and tell them to take her back with them, to their cold, distant lands. She curses herself for being foolish enough to embark on this quest, but most of all she curses Rudra and Zaria.

They've been missing for a day now. Tara had called her in a panic yesterday morning, convinced that Rudra had run away because of her now-viral Flow about him. It's possible, of course, but all Joey's instincts tell her this is about Zaria and whatever her secret mission is: she's convinced Rudra has once again managed to make poor decisions while unsupervised. Either way, they're gone. Just wandered out of the flat with a bag each, out of the building, into a car, leaving behind most of their belongings and two bodyguards who swear they don't know anything, but are not at all worried because this is just something Zaria does from time to time. They'd towered over Joey for a very tense second after she'd asked them to move out of the flat.

Rudra's even left her a note, the idiot. Zaria's taking him for a special assignment, it's top secret, she shouldn't tell anyone, he'll explain later, thanks for everything, he'll see her soon. It makes no sense. Why would Zaria take him along and leave her bodyguards behind? What special skills does he have? Of what use could he possibly be? The answer to that is actually quite simple. Is she using him to infiltrate his family and their circles in some way? Was Rudra her secret mission all along? Doesn't she usually have much larger whales to chase? None of it makes sense.

She has no way to know where they are: the last few years, whenever she'd needed to find wandering Flowstars she'd delegated location tracking upwards to Funder Radha or downwards to Jin-Young, both of whom had access to friendly police and discreet private spycos, but both those routes are closed now. The amateur hackers in Indi's crew can't be trusted anymore. After a few dead ends, she'd asked Laxmi to ask her Cyber Bazaar boyfriend if he could help. Laxmi had seemed very confident he could, but had messaged in a few minutes to say he'd tried, and they were both untraceable.

Laxmi had called again at midnight, from a different number, to say Joey should visit Cyber Bazaar next morning, and come alone. She'd hung up before Joey could say anything.

The Cyber Bazaar station is just a few stops away from ICH Place, but the challenge isn't the ride: it's getting into the train in the first place. She'd been a regular metro user in her teens, when they'd opened the Little Bengal station with much fanfare. Very few of those stations have escaped renaming. Cyber Bazaar was called Nehru Place then, and it's been called at least three other names over the last decade. For the longest time, Delhi's people used to refer to it as Nehru's Fault. The trains had been crowded then as well, and Joey had grown so used to the whole process that she's ashamed she finds it an ordeal now. The tense single-file queues for the ladies' compartments, station police wandering about inspecting them and shooting away lurkers and aspiring queue-infiltrators, including, every day, a couple of optimistic men. The bracing and shoving as the train whistled towards the platform, the shifting into defensive combat stances, the absolute scrum as soon as the doors opened and passengers exploded out into the platform, the mad scramble for a seat if you made it inside. Medieval battle scenes had nothing on this.

There's absolutely no chance of finding a seat at ICH Place: the whole train is bound for Cyber Bazaar. Joey finds that her train-entry skills haven't faded, largely through muscle memory: now, as then, she knows she doesn't have the raw strength to just walk into the train carrying helpless bodies before her, so she goes into stealth mode, folds herself into a two-dimensional shape, slides in like a rumour, slithers towards the nearest pole, thrusts her limbs into yielding spaces, a sentient Tetris piece, and lets the train fit her body into its slot, strangers' bodies, thankfully female, moving her about, any semblance of control long forgotten. Sometimes, when the train shudders, a few microns of air slide in between Joey and the many ladies she is intertwined with: they remind her of social distancing protocols—what a concept.

The familiar cocktail of overheated bodies, hair oil, and perfumes from near and far envelops her: if it weren't a familiar smell, she might have vomited. The sounds are harder to deal with, far worse than they were in her college years—even in this scrum, most of the women standing around her are watching videos at full volume on their phones, drowning the stashed compartment in a melange of Flows, mainstreamer shouting, Bollywood music, and, incredibly, conversation. None of this is new to her, but she's amazed at how her body has forgotten, how it cringes and starts at every new audio spike.

She can hear Narad beeping from her pocket, trying to tell her many things she knows: her stress levels are high, she needs to hydrate, the air quality is low, other modes of transport would be more suited to her health, it's hot, women aren't safe, she should go home. Her headphones are in her bag, and there's no way to reach them now without starting a brawl. Joey always looks for a sanity anchor in times like these, and finds one: a teenager huddled up on a seat, defying the world with an actual book held up like a shield before the aggressive armpit of an aunty looming over her. Joey hasn't read a printed book herself in far too long a while, though she has a book-scented aromaspray for her house, and she wants to fight her way across the compartment and adopt, or at least hire, the teenager at once. Together they will start a new lifestyle fad where customers pay them to go for a walk for an hour, and are then allowed to enter an air-conditioned room, take all their clothes off, and have a person of their choice read to them until they fall asleep. A bath, too, in neighbourhoods with water. Even Joey's fantasies come with three alternate budgets. A younger Joey would have tried to see what book the teenager was reading. Present Joey knows the distance between them is optimal.

Hands grabbing for handles bare her head, and she draws a few stares, which is inevitable: she'd gone out a few evenings ago with her oldest friends, drinking, trading barbs, and ended up getting a radical haircut, complete with green highlights, from an all-night Malaysian salon. Quite normal in her workfield, but marking her irrevocably as a tourist in the metro. The pictures she posted of her new hair brought many people back into her life, even Toons, who forgot they were fighting and sent a whole video of approval. Her hairstyle caper, she vaguely remembers, brought her closer to Funder Radha at one of the bars that night, she doesn't remember which, but there had been some sort of deep washroom conversation where Radha had made her promise, while not needing to hold her hair back, to never even consider leaving her job over some stupid man, there'd be another one tomorrow. They may or may not have sworn lifelong friendship: Joey's just relieved she'd remembered to take her hangover-prevention tabs.

She doesn't have to do the usual one-station-in-advance struggle to get to the door: Cyber Bazaar is one of the stations where the train belches out most of its contents. The platform is more crowded than it should be at this hour, a dense crowd of people jostling and scanning other huddles, conscious only of an overwhelming desire to clamber on board. It's several minutes of careful self-placement behind exceptionally strong women before Joey finds herself crowd-skating out towards the stairs that lead to the exit checkpoints.

Something's wrong, many people are turning back from the gates towards the platform, running instead of trudging; the smell is more acrid than usual. She tries to ask a few women what's happening, but they just shoulder past: it's like trying to take a survey during a growing stampede. Joey fights her way to the surly policewoman at the gates, and is told there might be trouble, a mob has assembled outside, water supply shortage.

Joey's aware that various gangs frequently fight pitched battles over control of the little water that most of Delhi's neighbourhoods get—in ICH Place, the Residents' Welfare Association hires security to make sure ICB Market's restaurant mafia isn't hijacking their tankers. But in a place like Cyber Bazaar, where most of the surrounding neighbourhoods get a trickle of water once every couple of weeks at best, the arrival of a water tanker could mean bloodshed—police, gangs, guards, hired thugs, and locals scrambling for control.

She pulls out her phone to ask Narad what to do, wondering why she's not been screaming at her with news alerts, to find a lot of messages from Narad about her bioreadings, but nothing from the news: there's no signal at all. She fights panic: Have they shut down the internet again? She reminds herself that if it were an absolute crisis they would have shut down the metro, the train would just have whizzed by Cyber Bazaar, but her body refuses to listen. Something in her gut knows that things aren't all right. Narad knows nothing, and now she's all alone in the universe at a metro station exit with a riot brewing outside, no idea how to find the cybercriminal she's supposed to meet to help her illegally track Zaria and Rudra and many questions about how her life came to this. The smart choice is clear: she should go back home right now. This is well outside her job description anyway: a vague sense of worry about those two entitled brats and a mild reluctance to admit to Radha that they're missing certainly do not justify putting her life in danger.

She swipes through the exit, past the grumbling policewoman completely unmoved by her heroism, past the restless queue of people lining up at the entry gates, already winding into the distance, already threatening to bulge and break, to become a little riot of its own as the tension in the air mounts. Joey makes her way out to Cyber Bazaar.

Drones circle the blazing sky above the ramshackle towers that border the market square, feeding their various masters images from the ground. There are groups of men everywhere, loosely knit together, lurking, hovering, too busy glowering at their rival clusters to take pictures of Joey as she emerges from the station. The water tankers they're supposed to be fighting over haven't arrived yet, but the police have: they're setting up barricades across the alleys that crisscross the market, stringing together a defensive perimeter. Joey can see a few different uniforms, it's not just police, there are corporate troops in there as well, driving people away with batons, setting up checkpoints and barriers and scanning booths on the street. No detention buses, which is promising. No heavy weaponry, which is a relief. No water cannons either, which is good: she can't imagine how a water-deprived crowd would react to water-cannon blasts.

A cheer goes through the crowd as one of the drones comes crashing to earth and smashes satisfyingly into a thousand spinning pieces: Joey looks up into the sky at once, but the sunlight is too harsh to see what broke the drone. She knows what it was, though: a trained hawk, one of the troop that the mysterious crime lord known as the King of Nehru Place uses to keep the authorities' drones from seeing too much of the market. Joey has heard the King sometimes lends squadrons of fighter drones, and sometimes even his hawks, to localities where drones threaten to replace low-level human jobs. He'd tried to get monkeys to fight drones before that, but the monkeys, being monkeys, didn't listen. Every day there's a deadly kite festival above the rooftops of Cyber Bazaar: an idiotic Flowco had even tried to start a live tournament before being hacked into oblivion.

A station announcement: trains will only stop at Cyber Bazaar for the next fifteen minutes, and will be shut after. An escalation. Which means she needs to head back in right away if she wants to escape this battleground—or perhaps it's already too late, she can't even see the end of the entry queue. How bad is the riot going to be? She remembers, with great clarity, which drawer her riot-protection kit is lying in: without tear-gas-protection makeup, without face-recognition-scrambling stickers, how stupid would it be to not turn around immediately? Without network, she can't even ask Laxmi to send her a photo of her boyfriend. Reminding herself that in ancient times people didn't even have mobile phones but somehow managed to survive, she scans the growing crowd with slow-burning desperation, waiting for a sign.

And then a sign arrives—one of the gigantic smartbillboards mounted on a dodgy-looking tower switches to display a thirty-foot-tall Indi. In between a massive solar panel array shaped like a cartoon Krishna and a revolving Manchurian paneer taco he stands, smirking at her, gesturing towards the blinking logo of his new show, available both on mainstreamer satellite and on Flow everywhere, promising his adoring fans he's going to teach them to be a Real Man. He looks good in a customised Haramcore digishirt; his hair and makeup's different. Maybe it's that, or the lighting, but he looks a lot fairer. Joey stops herself from noting down at least ten visual inputs, and wonders when she'll unblock his calls on her phone: she's stopped Narad from auto-dialling him three times now. The show starts this weekend. She knows she'll watch it, probably with her parents.

In the distance, a slow, rolling drumbeat starts up: hundreds of parched hands banging on empty water containers, the heartbeat of a city rising, quickening towards rage. Somewhere, an anti-police chant starts up and gathers momentum. A low rumble sweeps across the street, transforming quickly into a tide of yells: in the distance, she can see a convoy of water tankers slowly approaching, flanked by police jeeps. People rushing towards the convoy, pouring out of every alleyway, hundreds, thousands, she can't count that many. Shiny dots flash on their faces: sticker patterns that claim to fool facial recognition cams, though no one really knows if they work. She sees swords, hockey sticks, metal rods, 3D-printed disposable desi katta pistols; a man shoves her as he breaks the queue and rushes past into the station. Even in this moment, he's managed to reach for her breasts.

A sharp crack, which her brain takes a second to tell her must be a gunshot. Screams, smashing glass, and Joey finds herself on the blazing footpath, a moan of pure terror gushing out of her throat. There's a sharp throb on her left leg—she looks at it, and gasps: it's covered in blood. Has she been shot? Wouldn't she know for sure if she'd been shot? There are bodies hurtling everywhere around her, narrowly missing stomping all over her. Her sunglasses fall, and someone steps on them immediately. She scrambles on the footpath, screams as a running man stumbles over her and falls. She's forgotten how to stand.

A hand grasps her wrist and pulls her up. She flails at her unknown assailant, seeing nothing, but he grabs her wrist tighter.

"Didi, come with us."

It's a boy, a teenager. Another boy stands with him, holding a cricket bat aloft, clearing a space. They have the same hair: the bright golden mohawks that mark them as SanSan vidboys. Her leg throbs. The boy who'd spoken tugs at her hand, and runs, dragging her with him: she takes one look at the crowd and follows, limping, then running as fast as she can. A few buildings down he stops at a collapsible gate, which is pulled open from the inside. They enter.

Another huddle of men, all armed, in a dark, ancient lobby, all staring at her, and Joey's terrified, wholly convinced she was better off outside. The boy sees her planning a wild escape attempt, and makes placatory gestures: calm down.

"Rajada sent us," he says. She stares at him, wholly uncomprehending. "Rajada, Laxmidi's man. You are Flow didi, no?"

"Yes," Joey says. Yes, she's definitely Flow didi.

He darts off down a corridor, and turns and beckons impatiently when she stands, still frozen, her leg a dull throb, most of her salwar now covered in blood. One of the men by the gate makes a comment in a language she doesn't understand and the rest laugh. The boy with the bat tugs at her arm, and she realises she doesn't really have too many options.

She follows the boys down a dirty corridor lined with shops, all closed, metal shutters proclaiming electronics-y names. The floors are strewn with litter, wires, plastic bottles. They take a sharp turn, lead her down another corridor, past padlocked doors, mouldy cartons, puddles and rivulets of thick liquids she hopes fervently are mostly water, two sleeping dogs, tattered posters of Bruce Lee and Shah Rukh Khan, an open toilet of incredible stink and decrepitude, a dingy flight of stairs, towards an open elevator shaft. The boy with the bat stops, turns, stands guard. Her rescuer presses a button, and an ancient elevator creaks down towards them, lurching to a halt a few inches below floor level. Not seeing what else to do, Joey gets in, wondering if she'll ever see her family again.

The lift goes up a few floors, and the boy leads her to a door that's a little cleaner than the others, opens it, and asks her to wait inside, but then darts in before she enters. Joey follows, blinking in the strange new light, mostly off the massive computer-screen array lined up all along one wall of the tiny room. There's a cot, a few metal office chairs, an ancient almirah, a groaning fan, a desk, a device on it she cannot identify that has a small rotating dish on top and a blinking red light: Some kind of scanner? There's an air purifier, so she takes off her mask and heaves deep breaths, resisting the urge to scream. She wipes her face on her sleeve, leaving dark smudges. The boy opens a drawer, pulls out a bandage, a wad of cotton, and a large bottle of antiseptic, hands them to Joey, sets a plastic bottle full of water down on the floor near her feet, and runs off. She examines her bloodstained salwar—it's a long cut, but shallow, probably a flying piece of glass. The bleeding stops as she dabs antiseptic on it, and she feels like a fool for thinking it was a bullet. There are bruises all over her body, everything hurts, but it's clearly not a good time for a thorough inspection. She gulps the water in seconds—it's scalding hot, but she couldn't care less.

The boy holds an empty metal container in front of her.

"All devices, didi, sorry," he says. They stare at each other in silence, each blinking once. Then she puts her phone in the container, and he hands her a cracked ceramic plate on which sits a blob of a foul-smelling brown gel, and indicates that she should smear it over her smartatt. She does, and even musters a smile as he waves what looks like an ancient tennis racket around her body for a minute. It doesn't crackle or beep, and the boy seems satisfied.

Joey sits on the cot, shuddering, determined not to think about the last few minutes, watching the screens with deep suspicion as they scroll through a variety of landscape photos. A little later, when her eyes have adjusted, she almost sobs in relief as she sees, on the wall opposite the cot, a large laminated photo of Laxmi and her boyfriend, the mysterious Raja, posing in a photo studio for a scene re-creation of an early '20s Bollywood hit. She realises she's seen Raja several times, dropping Laxmi off near their gate on his scooter. A pleasant-faced, balding, potbellied, ever-smiling man, who never came upstairs even when her mother asked Laxmi to present him for inspection. She'd assumed he was the proprietor of some small spy-gear and data-retrieval hole, one of the hundreds scattered all over Cyber Bazaar.

But the man who now enters the room, with the boys darting around him, is clearly a man of power, and he's not smiling. He offers his apologies: he hadn't known how to reach Joey once they cut the network, and the boys had left their posts for golgappas, the idiots (he smacks their heads, to drive his point home). He inspects Joey's cut, declares it safe, and begs her not to let Laxmi know about it.

"She'll kill me," he says. "As it is she was refusing to let you come here, but I couldn't risk passing a message through Laxmi. The less she knows, the less your family knows, the better."

Joey's not sure how to address him—she's always been very bad at the semi-feudal semi-gracious tone her parents seemed to have learned from the times when everyone they knew had domestic help, she knows the fake equality her peers often adopt in these circumstances is considered insulting and condescending, but at the same time she's meeting Raja at his place of work, not as the maid's boyfriend. And Raja appears to be some sort of local crime lord and might expect great respect.

"Is my family safe with Laxmi in the house?" she asks, choosing directness. He takes it well.

"Your family is protected," he says. "Nothing moves in your neighbourhood that I don't know about, and I am friends with all the powers that run it—for now. They need me, and they need Cyber Bazaar."

"Explain further, please," Joey says.

"Oh, Cyber Bazaar runs half the city—you didn't know? Otherwise they'd have been shooting the crowd out there. Delhi has learned that sometimes the whole system can collapse, and you can't be caught without anyone to turn to. When the government or its masters cut off your electricity, your signal, your water, you don't know when you'll get them back. You need to take care of yourself, have someone you can call. One way or another, the residents' associations call us. Laxmi could live like a queen here if she chose—but it is better for both of us if she does not know about everything I do, and she is far safer with your family than she would be here, or in any of our houses. I can't afford to spend time worrying about her."

"But now I'm worried about my family. What happens when your friendships end?"

"You should have worried about your family before getting involved with Zaria Salam and Rudra Gupta."

"Where are they?"

"They're here. You'll see them soon. I'm waiting for a call."

"Networks are out."

He waves an ancient mobile phone at her. "Not ours."

"Then call my family and tell them they're in danger, thanks to me."

He stands in front of her, not meeting her eyes, struggling to say many things, failing. She doesn't feel any need to put him at ease. New pains have sprung up all over her body, and there's a harsh sourness in her mouth: she wants to vomit.

"I didn't want you to get involved in any of this," he says finally. "You haven't seen me, but I've been around since you were a little girl, from before Rono was born. But you stepped forward and entered this world, and now you're a part of it whether you like it or not."

"I barely know Zaria."

"Tell that to her enemies in the government when they find out who her, what is it, Reality Controller was before they left. No, you're involved now. You chose to be. So now you need Laxmi exactly where she is. It is best for everyone. This isn't a threat, I mean it. I guarantee your family's safety with my life. We owe you everything."

"What do you mean?"

"You don't even know? That's Avikda for you. Where do I start? If he hadn't paid for a top-class hospital, private, my son would have died at birth. He wouldn't even take money when I had it, later. Thanks to your mother, I knew where to send my children to school. They're in Estonia now, studying, enjoying. They will have lives so good, I cannot even imagine."

There are tears in his eyes, and Joey can't speak for a few moments.

"Why don't you go too, with Laxmi?" she asks. "You seem like you could find a way."

He blinks and shrugs. "I like to think I have the courage to stay," he says. "Things have to change here, and if all the good people leave, who will do the work? Don't ask me this question. You stayed too."

A bomb goes off nearby, and the building shakes: she'd

forgotten there was a riot in progress just a few feet away. She panics at once, but Raja seems unperturbed.

"My people are not in this fight," he says. "They'll come back later, to open the shops."

She recovers her breath, and notices a row of pictures in the darkest corner, now askew: Ambedkar. Gandhi. King. Phule. She catches herself wondering if his heroes are already a bit old-fashioned, and curses her ever-present inner trendspotter. He watches her looking at his collection, and looks somewhat abashed.

"I need to know so much more," she says. "What are Zaria and Rudra doing? Do they work for you? Are you the King of Nehru Place?"

"There is no King in Nehru Place," he says. "I'm not allowed to say more about their plans, but they're going out into dangerous places to look for difficult answers. They don't work for me at all—but we have common interests and beliefs, enough for us to help them."

"How dangerous?"

"If they fail, they'll die. Even if they succeed, people might not be ready to hear the truths they find. But they are doing what they feel they must. And whether they succeed or fail, we will learn much we do not know."

"I don't like this. Zaria knows what she's doing, but Rudra? This isn't right."

"It is not in your hands. Or mine. They have heard the call, and they have to answer. If I had my way, I wouldn't want you anywhere near Cyber Bazaar. But here you are. There was no other way that would keep them safe."

The boys interrupt, with a tray bearing Joey's phone, and another one laden with food, and a small plastic table which they set up with cheerful efficiency. Metal plates and glasses, huge mounds of rice, and bowls of pale yellow dal, crisp fried bhindi, and a thin chicken curry: the closest thing to home-cooked food

Joey's seen all week. The boys' names are Kusu and Rocky, and after setting the table they hover near the door, looking at each other slyly, both silently daring the other to speak.

"What is it?" Joey asks.

"Didi, are you the pink girl? Gin the traitor?" Rocky asks. Raja yells at them and they run off, howling with laughter.

The background score of muffled screams and gunshots is not ideal, but the food is delicious, and Joey and Raja eat in silence. Joey's surprised to find she can eat at all, but there's something calming about the sight of Raja shovelling kilos of food into his face as if these were the most normal circumstances possible for a simple meal. When the food is done, Kusu appears to clear the table, managing not to smirk or look at Joey under Raja's fierce gaze. Raja keeps checking his phone, but it's stubbornly silent: to ease the tension, Joey decides to draw his story out of him. He's hesitant at first, but grows comfortable once he realises it's not an interrogation, and soon he's telling her far more than he should.

Raja grew up in Madhupur, a cybercrime hub in Jharkhand, and learnt his skills from jobless engineers in dusty cybercafés. He met Laxmi in Calcutta, when he'd been sent there to run a small gang of sim-duplicators: he'd fallen in love with her data while picking her digital pocket, and she'd still not tired of reminding him about this. They'd run away to Delhi together to escape a local politician his gang had hacked, who'd set fire to Laxmi's entire neighbourhood. That was twenty years ago. They were seventeen.

Raja lights up as he speaks, and Joey sees what drew Laxmi to the man: in another world, in another time, he would have been a great teacher. He tells her about Solboxes that let families trade solar power directly with their neighbours, about dronejacking sweatshops and illegal 3D-printing factories that could compete with the Chinese if they didn't have to pay bribes, about criminal-only servers, identity theft centres, malware start-ups, tech-pyravikar cartels aligned with caste mafias in Uttar Pradesh, fake ID publishers and maverick gene-hackers, vaccine pirate-pharma labs, Gujarati cryptocurrency forgers and Dravida Nation spies. He tells her about other cities under Delhi's skin, city-states with their own internets, their own currencies, their own economies, their own healthcare and education systems. Not just the fortress-paradise cities of the rich, but watering holes for the very poorest. And Cyber Bazaar is where these cities intersect, where micro-religions come for artificially powered exoskeletons, info-tech tycoons for self-updating sex toys, Gurgaon kids for racing hoverboards. Genmaicha to gallium, nanobots to neodymium, genetic ovens and CRISPR kits, transilluminators and centrifuges all available within two-minute walks from where they sit, at the world's best price. She knows there are many things sold here that he cannot tell her about, too, and wishes she didn't know, that she could see Cyber Bazaar as he did, as some sort of biopunk pirate-port paradise. But she envies his evident belonging to all these cities: she was born here, he was not, but her upper-class indigo passport doesn't give her the gate passes he possesses.

She understands only the broad outlines, but is fascinated by the scale of it: shuttered hardware centres repurposed to manufacture every project that comes up on American crowdfunding sites before their proposals are even funded, viruses to confuse the most advanced facial-recognition databases, welfare-crime networks dedicated to recovering stolen foreign donations and medical supplies, rogue AI being developed to create their own gangs in cyberspace. She understands why they will never leave, never search for a new life in a strange land: they're addicted to Delhi. They love the place, and she wonders if she ever will, anywhere near as much.

When Raja's phone finally rings, she doesn't want his stories to stop. He takes the phone to a corner to mutter, and she realises that it's quiet outside: they must be cleaning up the street. She hopes they'll be done before she leaves. Despite her best efforts to restrain her producer brain, she's got the whole pitch for Raja's Flow ready: she knows he won't do it, she knows her funders wouldn't hear of it, she knows she won't even suggest it to him. But she's got it all lined up, so she can at least imagine making it, polishing it, and putting it out in the world.

Raja leads her through another maze of corridors and stairways, into another ancient elevator. This one has a sleek control panel stuck on its pulpy walls: he asks her to shut her eyes as he punches a combination. It's a short ride, and then he guides her out of the elevator and tells her to open her eyes.

It's a large hall, a makeshift hospital ward, four parallel rows of beds, trolleys loaded with medical equipment: monitors, stands, drips. There are no partitions, the walls are lined with thick curtains, and the ceiling dotted with air-conditioner vents. She thinks she sees a rat's tail hanging out of one, but it's gone in an instant. The AC's on at full blast: Joey shivers as Raja walks her past empty beds.

At the far end of the hall, there are two beds that aren't empty. Joey starts running as soon as she sees them. Rudra and Zaria are both unconscious, on beds next to each other, on drip, in blue robes, wired up to machines Joey doesn't even begin to recognise. Their arms and heads are covered in bandages, and Joey's worried it's not them, she hasn't looked at their bodies that closely, this could be anyone. There's a man in a white coat standing between them, who speaks as Joey approaches, but she ignores him, and grabs Rudra's hand.

"What have you done to them?" she asks.

Raja arrives, huffing, behind her.

"Bijoyini, meet Dr. Magan," he says, with deep reverence.

"Just Magan, please," says the doctor. "My degrees are not even recognised in India."

He's white-bearded and immediately charismatic. Joey cancels her first few questions, all of which are rude ones about who he is and where he's from—this is clearly not a man to antagonise—but there are other questions, more important ones.

"What have you done to them?" she asks again.

"So you're the famous Bijoyini," he says, walking towards her. His right trouser leg ends in a grey smart prosthetic foot: she tries not to look at it.

"How lucky, to grow up eating Laxmi's cooking," Magan says. "You don't look like you have, though. I would have been far fatter, far happier."

He sighs. "Your friends have not yet awakened, as you can see. They should have woken, hours ago, but there were complications, thanks to this stupid fighting outside. Raja, you will have a word with the usual people. We pay our dues, more than we should. They can have their fights elsewhere."

"Yes, sir," Raja says.

"Unfortunately you will not be able to speak with them today," Magan says. "The schedules have altered, and it will soon not be safe for you to be here, to see what you would see if you stayed. But I hope, and pray, that you will see them again soon."

He stops Joey with an outstretched palm before she can repeat her question.

"Their new faces have not set yet," he says. "There's no cause for such alarm—they will look the same to you. But the machines will not know them now, unless they want to be seen. A gift from Cyber Bazaar. They will place themselves in great danger for the good of the land, and we must do our best to help."

"I can't allow this to happen, whatever it is," Joey says, wishing she could summon more authority in a bloodstained salwar in a pirate hospital. "I am responsible for these people, and I need to hear them say they know what they're doing. And that's just Zaria—I can't allow Rudra to go. He works for me. He's not made for high-pressure situations, and it'll be my fault if something happens to him."

Magan and Raja exchange a look, and a smirk.

"I am happy to see you care so much for your charges, but they are not yours anymore," says Magan. "They belong to no one but themselves—the mission they go on is not even ours. We are merely helping. I did not call you here to ask for your permission. I have something to give you that I needed to place in your hands myself."

He reaches into his pocket, and pulls out a small plastic box. He hands it to Joey with great solemnity.

"This is all of Rudra's data," he says. "He said you were the person he trusted most. Keep it secret. If he needs to be rebuilt, it will be necessary."

She stands before him, completely helpless, glaring at the box in her hand.

"He also said good-bye," Magan says. "He said to thank you, you especially, for setting him free."

"Oh, we're not done," Joey says. "I'm not okay with letting him go like this."

"Our lives have trained us to see deception and betrayal everywhere, and that might be why we are still alive. But there are no lies here. He wants to leave. You have not failed him," Magan says. "You could not have stopped them. Zaria has done this before. She is not alone. And Rudra? Rudra will surprise you. I see a great strength in the boy. If he doesn't break, he will end up a folk hero."

"You've given them face implants, and . . . what else? Where are they going? When are they supposed to return?"

"The less you know, the better. But rest assured, they are in no physical pain. We have given them new smartatts, implants to prevent infections that don't exist yet, means of communication very few in the world possess. In their own way, they are beyond human now. We do not have too many of these gifts to give, but they were worthy. The evils they are going to fight—they need to be fought. Rudra and Zaria will ride into battle, and win. They will change the world. I know all of this is strange, and I understand how you feel. But from what I have heard of you, I know we are on the same side."

He sits on Zaria's bed, and gestures. Joey sits on Rudra's, sullen but grateful: everything still hurts.

"Does a part of you want to go with them?" he asks.

"I don't know," she says. "Yes?"

"I understand, but it is impossible. They are different creatures from you, with different stories. You are not powerful enough, or powerless enough, to take these risks. But there are things you can do to help."

"I don't think I can help you," Joey says. "A few minutes after leaving the metro I was sure I was going to die. And—sorry, there's no good way to say this—but I don't want to be a criminal. Even if I believe in the cause, and I'd like to think I do, I'm not smart enough . . . or brave enough."

"I became a criminal because they did not allow me to be a good man. Because both the beginning and the end of my longest journey were places where men with power chose to silence those who spoke up about wrongs, instead of listening or learning and making things right. But we are not just criminals here. We make things here that the people need but their rulers do not want. We could go out there and print 3D huts for next to nothing. Build water generators that make drinking water out of air. Flying hospitals, folding toilets. We could ensure that even if another regime appears that wants to butcher its people, they cannot do it by cutting off supplies again. That villages no longer vanish from the world and the records. That millions of people could never again die. Let me say that once more: millions of people—numbers that will never be counted but so large they are incomprehensible to people in better countries—could never again die, and be erased from the world without punishment for those responsible. That people have decent lives wherever they live, and do not need to come to this slaughterhouse of a city at all. But they will not let us. They don't want people to live like humans. They want them for data, and then for meat."

"What do you want from me?"

"I want to ask you if you're happy with your life the way it is."

"No."

"Do you have a purpose? A calling?"

"No. Well—"

"Do you feel as if you live in an illusion, and do you want to help people outside it?"

"Yes."

"Do you feel like your life is passing by, and it is somehow shallow, and you want to do something of relevance, of importance?"

"Yes."

"I know these feelings. I was young once too, in Berbera. A surgeon. I had the wrong opinions, but I kept them to myself—I wanted to be safe, and I wanted my family to be safe. But I wrote a diary, for myself, on my computer, where I told myself many truths. And one day some men came and took my computer, and added some lies to my truths, and then used it all against me, to take away everything I had. Perhaps that is why I do what I do."

He stretches, and smiles at Joey, his teeth even and stained a deep brown.

"The Berberawi are scattered now, our land divided by wars and competing investors. Perhaps one day we will go back. I shall not live to see that day, but I have many grandchildren. Perhaps they will find a small plot of land to sit, and chew their khat, and see a real sunset again. I will die in Delhi. I suppose that makes it my home, as well. When you find a new home, and get to know it, there always comes a time when you find ghosts of your last home in it. When I see you, I see my daughter."

Joey almost asks where she is, and stops herself just in time.

"I say this not to trick you into feeling kinship with me, but to tell you that I swear I will never allow any harm to come to you. And if I tried to harm you—what would you do, Raja?"

"I would kill you," Raja says.

"There you have it. I want you to work with me, Bijoyini."

"How?"

"We have a large operation here, as you know. I understand the sciences, and my friends understand money, power, and violence. Delhi's people like us and need us, for now; we make their lives easier and safer and so we are allowed to thrive. But things change fast, and before the next wind blows us away, I want—we want—to make a real difference to things we do not understand. Things that hold the world together in a way that better machines cannot. Culture, the arts, the people's hearts. Ideas that grow and become new worlds. We need experts we trust to build those for us. I have heard you are the best in the field."

"I'm not. I've heard that before, but I just—I just do my job. And I didn't get my job because I was the best at anything. It was because of who I knew."

"It takes a certain wisdom to be able to see the unfairness of a system that benefits one. Every pyramid of power is built on loyalty—for some it is a social elite that serves itself while maintaining the illusion of fair competition, for others it is a contest to see who kills the most, and lies the loudest, to serve their leaders. And just because all systems are corrupt and flawed it does not mean they are all the same. Cyber Bazaar runs on loyalty too. But the world we want to build is a better one than the world that is now available. It is not a world where the powerless will be left behind to die."

"I believe you. I'm just trying to tell you I'm not exceptionally brilliant. Plenty of other people could do it too."

"If that were true, they would be here now, not you. We have known your work for years. We even tried sending one of our friends to work for you—a spirit of fire, you may know her as Uma—but she was not ready for your union and neither were you. Please understand, Joey, we are not trying to tell you that you must save the world. It's a job, like any other. We have tried to find the right person for it before, and if you refuse us, we will try others. But you fit what we need. Many in your world are above the law, like your present employers. Many others are entirely outside it, like I am. But you—you are still connected to something we are not, a river that churns and is full of filth, but still flows. Without people like you, we cannot restore what is lost, we cannot build the new. Does that make sense to you?"

"I think so."

"Now hear this. We are in the middle of a war. Our survival is at stake. Great powers move, and the tensions between them will crush us, and they do not care. India's people will stand up. Across the country, they have stood up before, they will stand up again when it is time. Such is their character. But the road is long. And sometimes people get tired, and fall back into slumber. We have been trying, for a while, to wake them up again, before it is too late. But our artists, from E-Klav and Desibryde to those less famous, need to do more—need to inspire more."

"It's really not measurable, though. Both of them are doing fantastic work."

"They have become notorious in their own ways, but the people we hired to guide their art and the people who talk about it most are all . . . far away. Not just in physical distance, but in culture. Their modes of resistance work for their people, but we need faster change for ours."

"So you need a local."

"We need someone to show our artists how to bring real change here. Someone who understands Delhi, and India, and what works here. Someone who can teach people not to believe propaganda, not to trust advertising, not to succumb to rage or hate or, just as dangerous, distraction. Someone to keep their minds whole, focussed, and sharp, so they see the truth behind the stories they hear, and learn how to tell their own stories. Would you like to be this person?"

"This isn't one person's job."

"Then you shall have a team."

"This isn't how art works."

"Then show us how it does."

"You can't set goals like this for art. And I'm tired of being pushed around. I hate being a piece in other people's games. Corporate's bad enough, but this . . ."

"You will be free to do whatever you want."

"You're not listening!" Joey slams her hand on the bed, flinching as she hits Rudra, but Rudra doesn't awaken.

"This is an incredibly exciting idea, and easily the best job in my field," she says after a while. "I mean, manage E-Klav? Desibryde? But I'm not the right person to do it. All I do is try to do new things, and fail, and then try not to repeat mistakes. I don't understand India, or Delhi, or any of the other things you need me to understand. You need someone better."

"There is no one better. We have looked. When we say we see something special in you, it's because we know we're right. If we did not understand people, we would not have lived this long. Laxmi has told us things about you that you might not know yourself. How you nurture your charges, how you build their lives, how you give away grand ideas to the fools you work for. How you stay away from the traps of fame, and walk among snakes without growing poison sacs yourself. And above all, how you want to do more. It's time to become one of us, and have a real adventure. I promise you, there's a deeper, richer life to be had in the shadows, whole worlds that you can save. Look at me. We need you. Will you help us change the world?"

She looks at Rudra, and imagines, for a second, that he sits up, tears apart his cocoon, and emerges with wings, wet and gleaming.

"I want to say yes," Joey says. "I really do. But I'm not the world-saving type. I can't even handle my schedule when there's nothing real at stake. And to handle this much power . . ."

"Solvable problems. And high stakes are not new to you."

"Yes, but what you're talking about is much more important

than money or fame or numbers. This is a change-everything pitch."

Magan actually laughs. "The only real question is one of commitment. Whether you have that, what you want, only your heart can tell you. You know what we think. As for power—you know there are many kinds. You don't want the vulnerability that comes with visibility, so you have chosen, for yourself, a life in the shadows; but one where you have real agency, control, where you push buttons and make decisions. Where your story is one that is hidden, by choice, but shapes the world through others. It is an unusual choice for someone of your generation and class. The world's most powerful people, the ones with their own islands and spaceships and countries, are the same."

"I love that you compared me to billionaires," Joey says. "But it doesn't work like that, does it? I become part of the story however much I want to stay out of it. It's the same timeline, and having cameos in Indi's hero footage was bad enough—working with you people would mean danger at a very different scale. I'd end on the news, and not in a good way."

"If you are good at your work, and you are, you'll be the one person who is never in the footage," Magan says. "You'll be in . . . I don't know what you call it."

"The deleted scenes," Joey says. "Not the action montage."

They stare at each other in a silence that starts out uncomfortable and gets really unbearable soon.

"I was doing the wrong edit all along," Joey says. "Wow. Thank you for that. The non-linearity and lack of timeline cohesion was a good thing. A universally relatable protagonist call to action is the opposite of what this cut needs, that's where the inherent conflict comes from. Can't believe I didn't see it before."

"Joey? That's too technical, I don't know what you're saying," Magan says. "But I take it you are joining us?"

"No," Joey says. "Sorry. No."

CHAPTER 10

DELETED SCENES

DS1/5—Track and celebrate the steps!

Of late Joey's been feeling like her whole life is a secret compilation of deleted scenes from a multitrack timeline: endlessly customised, increasingly complicated segments, all tagged and colour-coded in ways that would make sense to absolutely no one else, wholly separate from anything any surveillance tech can capture. There is a visible surveilbait-life for whoever's watching her as well, featuring mostly potential footage of her looking at screens or sitting glazed-eyed at meetings. As a professional image builder and storyteller, she finds the secrecy even more satisfying than the effort she puts into the surface blandness of the presented material. She's always taken pride in her instinct for cuts and angles and rhythms in the wildly successful stories she produces—but now, finally, she's building a cover life so aggressively boring that it could be festival-film award-worthy.

"My first question is: What the fuck?" she asks.

Across the table, Jin-Young grimaces. "I'd prefer to explain after the food arrives," he says.

He looks completely different: his hair is now buzzed close to his scalp, and he's wearing a formal black shirt. Joey's struggling to cope with how good he looks.

"I swear I will beat you up in front of all these people if you don't tell me right now," Joey says. "Where were you? What happened?"

"I'd gone to Seoul," he says. "I couldn't take it here anymore."

"And you couldn't say good-bye? After everything we've been through together? I thought you were dead!"

"No, I just decided I was done here, and I left."

"Don't lie to me."

"Not lying! I applied to a big K-drama producer. Not the first time I'd tried. But this time one wrote back. I met them in virtual. Then they flew me there and I told them about my life. They hired me on the spot. Then the next day they said I had to go back to Delhi. Honestly, Joey, I almost quit."

"Why did they send you back?"

"It's confidential."

"Jin-Young, don't push me. Seriously."

"A major Korean studio is entering India," Jin-Young says. "The rest is nondisclosure."

"What am I, new? You're a Reality Controller there? That's great! You've been ready for a while."

He tries not to say anything, and fails. "No, I'm a designation above that," he says.

"That's . . . even better! Wait, no. My second question . . ." Joey pulls out a piece of paper from her pocket, and his face turns red. "What the fuck?"

"I hoped you wouldn't see that."

"It jammed up my cleanerbot."

"I hoped you wouldn't bring it up if we did ever meet again."

"I like that you think I have so much grace."

"Please don't read it. I'm very embarrassed."

Joey unfolds the paper and reads. "'I loved you, you did not see me. Then I hated you, you did not see me. You will not see me again.'"

Jin-Young hangs his head. "Please let us not speak of this."

"Denied. I thought one of Indi's lawyers was a stalker, at first. Scared out of my mind I had someone like that in my house. Then I scanned it, and saw it was your handwriting. And then you disappeared. I thought it was a suicide note."

"I did not consider that possibility."

"What the fuck, Jin-Young?"

"I apologise unconditionally."

"Did you really hate me?"

"No! It was a reference to my favourite K-drama. Which makes it even more stupid. It was a very difficult day. I thought I would be able to handle any amount of stress after growing up in Delhi. But I was wrong. I also thought I would never see you again. But that is no excuse."

She crumples up the paper. "I'm just glad you're okay," she says. "Actually, I'm not, I'm furious. Don't ever do anything like this with anyone again."

"I will not. I promise. I'm seeing a therapist as well. I need to be sure I am better. The last few months have been very strange. I have done other things I deeply regret."

A large helping of bibimbap, and Joey's anger disappears immediately, but she keeps glaring at him through mouthfuls of beef and egg and rice.

"I hope you will forgive me in time," he says. "I am going to be in Delhi for several years."

The truth is she forgave him long ago, and she hopes he, in turn, forgives her when he figures out what she did to him. What she's about to do to him. But first, she must render him incapable of strategic analysis.

"Yeah, I'll be fine. But I need to ask you if you still have feelings for me," she says.

Jin-Young appears to be choking on his bossam. Pink is not usually Joey's colour, but it suits his face.

"We should go out one evening and get to know each other outside work," she says. "I'd like us to be friends at least."

He gulps, and clears his throat. "I don't think that is a good idea," he says.

"Wow."

"No, I mean, I will be your rival in the industry. And I hope to one day hire you to work as my partner." He hesitates for a second, and decides to go for it: "Or my second-in-command."

It's the second-in-command jibe that really seals his fate. It's not that effectively funding the next phase of her career is something that Jin-Young would have minded doing if he had known that was what he was about to do, she hopes, but second-in-command? He had to pay. Quite fitting, really, that he was going to.

"So that's how it's going to be. All right. Now tell me about your new job. What will you be doing? Indian K-pop videos? K-dramas? K-Flows? What? Haven't they—you—already tried everything?"

"I can't tell you."

"All of these, huh? Good luck with that. We've already ripped off all your formats."

Which were all ripped off to start with, she wants to add, but not yet.

"The whole world has ripped off our formats. That's fine. We have a secret sauce," Jin-Young says.

"'We'? You spent, what, a day in Seoul after a lifetime in Delhi? I like how you're all Mr. Korea now."

"May I speak frankly?"

"Of course."

"I am the farthest person possible from Mr. Korea. But I didn't understand that until I actually went there. But you people—even you—never allowed me to be Mr. Delhi. I was born here. I grew up here. I know this city better than you ever will. It is interesting how they saw that in Seoul at once. But no one here ever did."

"Jin-Young, if I've been . . . racist towards you, I'm sorry. I didn't know."

"No, you haven't. Maybe almost, sometimes? But never with malice. I know you well, Joey. I learn fast. And you cannot trick me into telling you what my company's plan is. Other countries have observable methods. Ours are still secret. Westerners form partnerships. The Chinese buy companies and land. The Japanese send people to learn the culture. No one understands us yet."

She watches him with new appreciation as he takes far too deep a swig of beer. She wonders how long he's been waiting to deliver this speech. Under all her new bravado, she wonders if her face has already given away her complete disbelief in her own ability to be a trickster.

"Fine. Rivals. Respect. I like it," she says. "So you're planning to use all my methods against me."

"A lot of them are methods we discovered together."

"Listen, you're welcome to try. I didn't teach you everything I know, and I have new tricks now."

"Really? What new tricks?"

She's tempted, for a moment, to tell him exactly what her supervillain plan is. That since she cannot get anything done without people taking credit for her ideas, she's decided to actually speed up the process of inspiring other people to believe they've come up with her ideas themselves. And because she's the best there is, multiple sources confirm, she's going to begin Operation Inception Deception, as she's modestly named it, on a massive international scale. She leans forward, and gives Jin-Young her best smirk.

"I mean, what could you do? Bring Korean stars here, or use Indians in Korean formats. We'll just hire everyone you train," she says.

"We have very deep pockets."

"These are the famous last words of every foreign company entering India. Fine. We'll fight it out. The company won't let me do what I want anyway."

"What is that?"

She pretends to be reluctant about sharing her innermost desires for what she hopes is a non-overacting period of time, though K-drama aesthetics give her a little extra wiggle room.

"Just another plan I'll never get to carry out. Immigrant Flowstars. Low cost, fresh stories from around the world, new audiences. But we'll never get to do those, right? We'll be fighting over Bollywood rejects."

"I suppose that is true," Jin-Young says. "I'm surprised you even considered immigrant Flowstars. No one has ever been interested in them."

"Only research departments, to see what to steal for their stars."

She waits for him to chew a few mouthfuls in silence, confident he'll take the bait, wondering if she ever knew him at all.

"You will find a way to do it. If that is what you want," he says.

"No one's interested, like you said. Maybe in a few years. Forget I brought it up, it's mine."

"Well, if you won't do it . . . My schedule is saturated, but share a bit more about what the plan was?" he asks. "I ask out of academic interest. There's no professional conflict here. I did enjoy us bouncing ideas off each other as colleagues."

"I was your boss. It doesn't matter. It's not like they're going to let you do anything except clone K-drama ideas and watch them fail anyway."

"Speak for yourself. We are very interested in developing new markets."

"Don't be a shit, Jin-Young. This is my idea."

"That's ridiculous. You don't own immigrants. You don't know anything about them. If anything, I should get them."

"Well, you can't have them."

"I will have them all."

"I'll go to war over this if I have to."

"Then it's war."

She extends a hand solemnly, and he shakes it.

"It's good to be back," Jin-Young says.

Her driver for the day is one of Laxmi's picks: after he hears her take a few calls on speaker, he complains at length about his problems on the night shift with some of her more recent hires: all those Africans, playing loud music in the car, drinking, god knows what else, he doesn't feel safe in those neighbourhoods, could madam transfer him? She advises him to ask Laxmi to find him another job, and enjoys his silence for the rest of the drive. The boulevards of central Delhi are still lined with trees, and there are construction-free stretches where she gazes in wonder, every time, at sudden monuments that she knows nothing about, that she can't look up because their histories have been erased, and at saptaparnis that will slumber for months before waking up to announce the coming of winter.

DS2/5—Fun Fearless Female Futurism

"The one person I'm angry with is Rudra," Tara says. "Everyone else, I know why they did what they did. But he actually made me think there was something real between us. I know he's an old friend of yours or whatever, but I have to tell you, he's a bastard."

Joey, surprised by the unexpected brevity of this speech, sips her coffee, which is possibly Ecuadorian, and stops wondering whether she should actually play fighting tournament video games to train her brain into seeing action combo possibilities faster.

"Total bastard," she says. "He just vanished without saying where he was going. I'd stuck my neck out, hiring him with no qualifications, and now I look like a fool."

"It's fine. Everyone knows you're above nepotism, your reputation is incredible."

"Thank you for saying so."

Tara beckons, and several City of Cats waiters appear to enquire what she needs. Not long ago, she'd been nervous about ordering foreign-sounding coffees, but now she rattles off the names quickly and chastises them for not writing it down; they keep messing up her orders. One of the waiters asks for a selfie for her family. Tara nods, and promises to do one in just five minutes, she's with a dear friend now.

"I know where Rudra's going," she says. "He's off to see the family properties. Take a guided tour of their lands, like a little raja. You know, he would never shut up about his family, how they mistreated him, this and that, but of course when it was time to join the business he jumped in. They always do."

"I had no idea," Joey says. "I thought he'd run off somewhere with Zaria."

"I feel bad for her. It's crazy how the system makes us fight over useless men! Though I think she's seen far too many men to fall for his tricks," Tara says. "But you never know. Everyone has their weak spots. The quiet ones always sneak up on women way outside their league. Can you believe he didn't even take my calls?"

"Weird. Maybe he was upset with you for posting that childhood trauma video?"

"Why? I mean obviously he was, but why? Not only did I help him, I also gave him a break, but he was too dumb to see it."

"You didn't ask him, right?"

"Couldn't, he'd have refused. No idea what's good for him. I made him viral, there were like thousands and thousands of people who sent messages about how he should cheer up and move on, even copied his dance. It's the closest he'll ever be to people knowing who he is. Can you imagine . . . he was so angry I shared it that he just ghosted me? The egos on these boys, my god! Land on you out of nowhere, and it's suddenly your job to turn them into human beings because their parents couldn't."

"Relatable."

Joey's a little embarrassed at both how childishly pleased she is that Tara has absolutely no idea about Rudra's whereabouts, and at how she's naively surprised that Tara has no interest in finding out.

"Don't ever tell him I said so, but it was my mistake also," Tara says. "I thought he didn't want to remain broken, you know? But now I see he was just rich and lazy. He wasn't hiding from the world. He was just chilling because it was convenient. Still, I didn't think he would lash out at me when I helped. Almost fell for him, too. Asshole."

"How did you find out? About this plan with his brother?"

"Oh, you don't know? I almost started working for Rohit, when our contract ran out."

"I don't want this to be a thing where I tell you how I feel about him and then you tell me you took his offer."

"I haven't said no yet. He wants me to be the spokesperson for their whole business, start a wellness Flow, all of that. The money's fantastic, he knows how to be generous, but he doesn't know the first thing about how to do it. Thinks he's an expert, of course. They all do. I would have had to set up the whole business for him."

"Are you going to do it?"

"Would you be interested in helping out?"

"No."

Their salads arrive while Tara struggles to make up her mind about how much she wants to tell Joey, and Joey struggles to decide whether to be pleased or insulted by Tara trying to hire her now. Still, they're both here for work, and three mashed cubes of feta cheese later, Tara gathers herself together, and looks up.

"Why did you call me here?" she asks.

"Your offer finally came in from the funders," Joey says. "I'd sent them a plan for you weeks ago, but these things take time. Nikhil was off somewhere, and he needs to sign every offer himself."

"I thought you'd just forgotten about me."

"No, of course I hadn't. You took off, I thought you'd come back. You could have just stayed. Sorry I didn't check in, but things have been hectic."

"I like how you do that," Tara says. "Make everything my fault."

"Nothing was your fault. I just wanted to make sure the offer was real before making plans with you. I know what it's like, waiting."

"So you were only looking out for me," Tara says. "I get it. I suppose I should have messaged as well, but it looked like I was all set for something bigger."

"So are you going to do it? Take Rohit's job?"

"Are we negotiating here?"

"Not yet. But whatever you plan to do, I want to warn you about Rohit. He's a bit creepy."

Tara's grin is genuine, and if Joey hadn't already decided what the next career stages were going to be for both Tara and herself, she would have rehired her on the spot.

"Oh, Rohit made a move within half an hour of meeting me," Tara says. "Full grab and kiss. Overtaken by passion and all. Still, he wasn't so bad—I thought he would go straight for the boobs, that type usually does. I'm a hit with that whole family."

"I'm sorry that happened."

"Please. I suppose I shouldn't tell you this, but no, I'm not taking that job. It's not real. He made it up just to get his brother back. Then he got him back anyway. I stayed there in one massive hotel-type room for a few days, and whenever he was home he was either on the phone or he was trying to fuck me, just because he thought I belonged to Rudra."

"I'm sorry."

"Don't be. I can handle myself."

"If you want to call him out, or file a complaint, I'll make sure the company backs you up."

This time Tara laughs out loud. "Call him out! What country do you live in? Powerful men are like this. At least he didn't pretend he was in love with me."

If there's one thing Joey likes about Tara, it's that while they've had genuine moments of solidarity and hopefully even mutual respect, in the end their fundamental incompatibility has never been in doubt. The next move in the action combo is to dispatch Tara into her new life as cleanly and peacefully as possible, and there's no easier way to make sure of her departure than by inviting her to stay, but there is one thing she needs from her first.

"Fine, let's negotiate, then. Your offer's here. We can launch your new Flow in a few weeks, after the new crew's trained."

"How are you doing?" Tara asks. "It's been difficult, right? Indi's gone, Zaria's gone. Do you have any other clients? Jin-Young's gone, the crew's gone, Rudra's gone."

Joey sighs elaborately.

"Jin-Young's back, actually. I met him a week ago. He's all fired up about some new secret Korean diversity programme, don't tell him you heard about it from me if you meet him, okay?"

She's tempted to just leave: forget her segment goals. Confirming Rudra's invisibility and planting the Korean funding rumour have been accomplished. But she knows that taking a few more hits from Tara will make it all the more convincing.

"Why would I meet Jin-Young?" Tara asks, gears visibly grinding in her head as she plans her casual hello to Jin-Young. "So you're all alone now? Only Joey left. Is your job safe?"

Joey wonders whether it might be worthwhile spending years making Tara do whatever she wanted by pushing her in the wrong direction. It doesn't take much wondering.

"No one's job is safe, but I'm not unhappy. So, are you on board? This is a great opportunity, I think. You'll be my top Flowstar."

"So you need my help to fight the Korean invasion and keep your job, basically."

"We can help each other. Otherwise, the Koreans are going to eat us both."

She knows she's overacting, but she does need Tara to ask the whole industry—every company she's checking out before committing to the plan she's about to reveal dramatically—about what they're planning to do to compete with well-funded inclusivity pushes. If a number of Nikhil's rivals don't all start scrambling to keep up with the soon-to-be-legendary Korean invasion, she's not going to get the budgets she needs.

"You and I live in different countries, you know." Tara drains her coffee in a single gulp and sets it down on the table, too hard. "For a long time I thought I wanted to live in yours. It's really pretty, really safe, everyone seems cool and nice and welcoming. Everyone knows everyone and everything, everyone has so much to teach you. And there are so many ways I could be better. It's not your fault, I get that now. But it's like those old console games, right, where you could choose to play at an easier setting. I don't get that option."

"I hear you," Joey says. "And I see how I was part of the problem."

"But you can't make it right. You people want to think you're good people, so you don't want to look down on me. But—"

"I have never looked down on you," Joey says.

"Right. But I know when the next crisis comes, I can't depend on you."

"What do you mean?"

"Indi couldn't depend on you, could he? He brought you in here, and the moment those fake accusations came you let him down. People find out who their real friends are in times like this. Only one person stood up for him. People remember things like that."

"I'm not sure the accusations were fake. But your offer is here," says Joey, her voice not shaking even a little bit. "Talk it over with your manager, and let me know."

"Indi called me yesterday," Tara says. "Something's changed, and they're adding people to his Icon push."

"I suppose they've had to change the plan after Zaria left."

"Don't know, don't care. They need a second lead in his friend group. Someone with a little urban desi vibe. When it comes to the real India, you English types aren't the answer. They offered me the best friend's girlfriend. I'm going to take it."

"Not the lead?"

"Not yet. They're getting a Hollywood girl for that. If it goes global, great for everyone. If she doesn't work out . . ."

"Won't that be odd for you?" Joey asks. "I mean, you met the world as Indi's girlfriend."

"No one gives a shit except the writing crew, Joey," Tara says. "And no one gives a shit about what the writers think. The audience will adjust."

"Good to know."

"You know what? Let me teach you something for a change. You don't have to learn it, because it doesn't affect you, but below your class, everything works on loyalty. I have to be there for my patrons and show support. The public can make fun of me if they like, shame me if they like. They don't give me my lifestyle and my career, my patron does. If he and his people see me suffer, see me sacrifice in his service, my power increases. I appreciate your offer, I really do. And I know you won't believe me, but I actually like you. In spite of everything."

"You won't believe me either, but I actually understand. Wouldn't you rather be in charge of your own Flow, though? Be your own patron?"

"Someday, maybe. I'm sure you'd make a decent Flow with me, too. But what would I get out of it? You'd make me do some kind of intelligent-girl-in-the-city show, small and meaningful. Festival type. Something your friends would like, but they'll never really accept me, no? People from my town wouldn't see it. And I need to inspire them, show them how far someone like them can go. They need to see me on boards at traffic signals, on the sides of buses. I'm going with Indi. I'd lost all hope, but just yesterday my life turned around. This new job is perfect for me, actually."

She's absolutely right, and Joey's happy for her. And happy that she appreciates the thought and effort Joey put into designing her new role—she had tried to get Tara the lead role, but the Flowco was not interested. But the pay raise is considerable, and it's a good investment: Tara's going to help fund Joey's projects, and keep her updated on everything Indi does, whether she knows it or not.

She wonders what she'd have done if Tara had taken her up on the job offer. And how many of the choices she's been presented with in her life have had the same person lurking behind multiple options.

They finish their salads in silence, stabbing errant leaves harder than necessary. Joey congratulates herself for taking the high road, for not getting petty at all.

"I'm thinking of dating Indi," Tara says. "I think we have some unresolved chemistry, the sex is great, as you know, and now that we're not supposed to be a couple, it's forbidden too? Kind of hot, without that Finland tattoo and the audience."

A great opportunity for a graceful exit and a grand success, covert-op-wise, and Joey wishes she were mature enough to take it. But really, it was too late.

"I'm sure it'll go really well," she says. "I'm quite envious of you guys, shooting in that Culture Colony mansion while we sit around in Delhi traffic."

"Yeah. I haven't seen the place yet, but—Wait, how do you know where we're shooting?"

"We do still all work for the same company."

"Wait, you knew all along? Why didn't you say so?"

"I didn't know anything," Joey says. "Sorry, am I talking too much? A friend told me I should talk more, because it's all we can do, and so I thought I should try it out."

Tara stares at her with infinite suspicion, and Joey doesn't meet her eyes as she calls for the cheque.

As she walks into the Flowco building a week later, she checks her other inboxes on her phone. In the Good Morning spam folder is one slightly different from the others: the greeting is standard, but the background is a photo of a sunrise over a forest. In the middle distance, a cow stands next to a milestone by a highway. She's never heard the name of the town written on it, but when she checks, she finds it's in Madhya Pradesh. Last week's had been from a dhaba near Chandigarh, the first one, a week before that, from Rajasthan. She's tempted to write Good Morning back, but doesn't. She wishes she could find a way to make sure Rudra knows she's ghosting him for their safety, but more importantly she wants him to feel bad, and she's still really angry with him.

DS3/5—Desi Power Chakra

MC Sharmila projects tremendous calm and poise as she enters the penthouse, but cannot help a flicker of surprise when she sees her former bodyguards, the Six-Pack, lounging around the living room. Joey walks towards her with a pitcher of fresh cold brew, letting the coffee slop over the edge a little, and enjoys the second where Sharmila's sure she's about to throw it at her.

"Why didn't you all tell me you would be here?" Sharmila asks the Six-Pack.

"I wanted it to be a surprise," Joey says. "I also wanted to get to know them—I've known you forever, and seen them for years, but always as a team, you know? I was just telling them this—everyone gets so used to seeing them in those hot costumes, doing all that fancy martial arts stuff. And you packaged the team so carefully—you should have been a K-pop trainer—but at least with boybands you get to know their names because they sing and talk, right? On the bandFlows. So for years I called the Six-Pack the Kashmiri one, the Malayali one, the Manipuri one, the Marathi one, the Goan, and the white one. I didn't even know Aline was from Pondicherry. Sorry about that."

"I don't know what this is about," Sharmila says. "But before you say anything more, I have a few things to say."

As a Desi Power Chakra seminar alumnus by single-session attendance, Joey's sure she's at least three moves ahead, thinking like the enemy, using their moves to beat them, embracing her inner sociopath, all of it. She knows all the things Sharmila might say, but she finds her fists are clenched despite this. She tells herself her tension is just about whether her multi-step plan is working, but she knows, at some very basic level, she just wants to not be in the same space as Sharmila.

"Go ahead."

"I wanted to tell you face-to-face I don't think you're a real gender traitor, and I should have been more nuanced about my callout. I've asked my girls yesterday to ease off on you on their Flows, and I don't have a problem working with you. We can even do a Flow together where I tell everyone I forgive you, and it's all good."

"Thanks, that won't be necessary," Joey says. "I presume these girls of yours are some of the people who've been trolling me. I'm happy if they stop, but it's fine either way: they're all blocked. Have a seat. Have a drink."

She paces the room, hoping to the high heavens she's got all the ex-bodyguards' names right.

"In case you were worried, my Flowco's acquisition of yours was not part of some kind of revenge plot," Joey says. "You are valuable, we are expanding, that's all. You're all still contracted for two more years, and all your jobs are safe. I'm not saying this just to make you feel better. I know it's true, because you all work for me now."

"Just stepping in to avoid confusion later," Sharmila says. "I work with your company, as a star. Your job is to take care of me. So let's avoid gaslighting."

"Oh, I am. So let there be no possible other reality here: you all work for me now. Regarding Indi, there is an internal investigation under way. It'll be a while before a verdict is reached. I'm not involved, I have bias. None of you will be required to make a statement of any kind, or appear on any show with Indi as part of cross-promotions. Different departments entirely. We already discussed this, Sharmila, I'm just catching you up."

"Yeah, I'm the one who made these decisions."

"Now, as you may be aware, two weeks ago, everything changed in the Indian Flow ecosystem. What happened is—"

"I know all this, Joey," Sharmila says. "Everyone who knows anything knows about it. The Koreans are coming, and they're doing a diversity blitz. First time they're doing this anywhere in the world, India is a huge experiment, it's going to be a complete game changer, and it makes certain people in India key assets on a global field."

Joey leans back and tries to look like she's trying to look inscrutable. She either succeeds or fails, both of which are completely viable Intrigue Faces. She brings her fingertips together theatrically, slowly, judging herself very harshly while doing so. But she's reasonably sure she's managing to hide her actual feelings, which are glee and smugness, because her Nikhil-inspired never-more-than-five-moves next-level-breakthrough plan is working, and Narad was right, she's totally enjoying measuring out her happiness.

"It's just a rumour," she says.

"No, it's not. I know about it, and I know I'm worth more now.

The Chinese are pushing in money to match this, and every Flow-co's doing a diversity push. And everyone's forgotten I was the first person to demand diversity in the Indian workspace, which basically means I'm worth even more, and so before we move any further: I want a raise."

"Why don't you shut up and listen for a second," Aline says, and Sharmila lapses into stunned silence.

"I'm delighted to hear that the whole Flowverse is buzzing with this urge to be more inclusive—long overdue of course. What happened is that through sheer coincidence our Flowco needed to think in terms of a new direction as well, and as it turns out, I didn't have active Flowstars to manage. I guess you all know how that happened," Joey says. "The thing is, I'd also been send-ing in pitches about how new demographics could be explored for a long time. Nobody had the time to see them, because there were always fires to fight, but I guess that's why they chose me to head it now? We're not calling it a diversity push, by the way, because Nikhil insists it's just a long-term growth initiative led solely by numbers, something he saw coming before anyone else did. You'll find that's something he does often. His numbers are solid, they match exactly with mine. It's a mystery. Though given that the Koreans and Chinese and therefore all the Indians are investing in this space now, yeah, I guess the budgets will need revising. A lot."

"I get why you guys needed my Flowco now," Sharmila says. "You picked it up cheap."

"Right? Such great talent! Aline, Sonia, Farzina—"

"Farzana."

"Sorry. Farzana, Mary, Sam, Shruthi—I knew all of you had tried out for Flowstar auditions before you took nonspeaking parts as Sharmila's bodyguards and then got famous as a group. When I looked all of you up, I was hoping there would be one of you who had some behind-the-scenes experience as well. And then I found out all of you did."

"Yeah, I don't think any of us wanted to be hot bodyguards," Farzana says. "But . . . you know how it is."

"I do. You've all worked as managers, editors, assistants, extras, whatever it takes. You're all experienced professionals, you've worked closely together in harsh times, you know what this world is. So I want to ask you to be my first set of Reality Controllers. Sharmila, you too."

"I knew you'd get to it at some point," Sharmila says. "I knew you'd find a way to shut down my Flow. This is about revenge."

"It's really not. First of all, you can all be Flowstars too, if you want—but it's not going to be enough to have different faces being visible, we need more people like you taking decisions behind the scenes as well. Sharmila, if I wanted revenge, you wouldn't be here, I could have just buried you. Of course I was angry with you—you've known me since we were kids, and you didn't even talk to me before you tried to destroy my public profile, and my career with it, and not even because you hated me—you just didn't see me, I was just expendable, collateral damage. I've never been the world's best feminist, but I know enough to know what you did was wrong."

"No it wasn't."

"Right. Anyway, you did make me think about a lot of things I'd ignored. So, whether you believe me or not, I'm grateful. So once you've come to terms with the new reality, I'm offering you a fresh start. I think we can build something really special together."

Sharmila has more to say, but the Six-Pack aren't looking to her for guidance anymore.

"What are we building?" Shruthi asks.

"A beginning," Joey says. "I need people who've faced more exclusion than I have to take the lead. Every time I draw up a plan, I come up with a hundred problems. When resources are limited, how do you decide who gets representation? When there are so many languages, and regions, and religions, and castes, and so many other tools to keep people silenced, how do you decide who gets a voice?"

"Everyone," Aline says.

"Yes. We need Muslim Flowstars, and Dalit Flowstars, and LGBTQIA+ Flowstars. We need disabled Flowstars, immigrant Flowstars, diaspora Flowstars, neurodivergent Flowstars, so many other marginalised or minority categories it makes my head spin. That's just the beginning. And that's just in India, and cam-facing. We need to do all this for people running the Flows as well, for crews, for managers, for everyone in the system. They'll all have to be hired, and trained. They'll all have to be heard. Not just by me, but by people with more empathy, more experience, and less privilege than I have. The language changes so fast I can't keep up, and I get it wrong—or at least people tell me I get it wrong, and I clam up. I'm very aware that I'm not the solution to the system—I'm just less of an asshole than the other bosses you might have landed up with. So on top of all this, there's the whole process of figuring out how to build a better system. One that's bigger than any individual. To find ways to avoid all the grifting, the infighting, the politics, the cliques, the frauds, the competition for single token spots. The whole point of all this tech, all these connections, was supposed to be that everyone got a voice. And I don't know how we ended up in this situation where it feels like no one does, and the people who seem like they do all think and act the same."

Joey takes a breath, and reads the room. Her head's spinning, her palms are sweating. She doesn't remember when she last spoke this much at length. College? Her short-lived video star career? School debates? The third combo-move of a planned five, never more than five, is not the time for such introspection.

"We have to start somewhere," she says. "We don't wait for the perfect time or team or anyone's permission. We're going to start here, and make mistakes, and learn, and grow. I have money, for now. A year to play with before anyone shuts us down. And I have help—I have people hacking into algorithms that oligarchs use to control policies, and advertisers use to control tastes. We have so many new ways to find people who need to be heard, find out who speaks for communities, find out what they need. It's just a question of using these tools to help not just us, but them. I'm sure other people are trying this around the world, but we don't get to hear about it because no one with power wants that. I don't know how long it will take my hackers to arrive at a system that works. I don't know if they're good enough to solve this, they're going to make mistakes too. But they're going to try. There are so many people fighting for inclusion, smarter people than us. We'll find them, talk to them, learn from them, share resources. And all the while generate enough money and attention for our Flowco division to keep the lights on, so they don't just cancel us and focus on the high earners."

"What do you need from us?" Farzana asks.

"I need a team of people who can work together, teach me things, and believe in this. A core to build around, people who can take the heat, ignore the shitstorm, know what they're looking for. I need a team who will make sacrifices initially, like I will, to bring in more hands, and treat them fairly, and build them up. I've done box-checking token diversity before—so have you. Now I want more. I want equality. And I want you with me."

"This is such bullshit, Joey," Sharmila says. "You want me to take a pay cut, abandon my career, and work with my bodyguards?"

"Yes. Also, if Flowstarring is all you want to do, you'll be working for your former bodyguards, not with them."

"With you as the queen of everything."

"I don't think you understand, Sharmila. I'm trying to make things right now. Work with me."

"That's not good enough."

"I'm sure you have access to more paint if you need it."

"Nice try," Sharmila says. "I've heard all I need to hear, and we can get a far better deal at other places."

She springs to her feet.

"Ladies, we're out of here," she says.

The Six-Pack do not move.

NA/NA Emotion Moments—Assorted Loving Family

Joey realises everything's different in her family home before Laxmi opens the door: laughter rings through the house. Not AI laughter, but human—her parents on the living room sofa screaming with what sounds suspiciously like pure joy. She doesn't remember when she last heard anything like this.

There's a puppy. A savage ball of golden fluff trying his best to destroy everything in the house, failing only because he's so very small. He ceases chewing on Avik's toe as Joey appears, and shuffle-bounces towards her. She drops down on her knees to gather him up, and as he wriggles in her hands and bites her chin, tail wagging in a blur, she has no idea why, but she bursts into tears.

"The point is to laugh," her father says. "Otherwise all you do is cry."

"I can't believe you didn't tell me," she says, too busy getting her face licked to absorb this wisdom.

"We'd have missed seeing this." Avik looks a decade younger.

"Something's different about you," her mother tells her at lunch.

"What do you mean?"

"Must be in love," Rono says.

"First of all, where are your clothes?"

"What? Oh, my laundry. I bought a smartwasher."

"Good we got the dog," Avik says. "Just in time, too. She still has a reason to come here."

Joey looks around the table, and the house, and listens to her family bicker and a dozen machines fart and hum, and feels something dangerously close to contentment.

"Seriously, what happened?" Romola asks again that afternoon. "You're awake, sitting up, you're smiling, talking to yourself. What is going on?"

"I think it's the dog," Joey says. "Everything feels different."

"Your father needed him. Not just for laughter. Someone to take him seriously, make him feel important, listen to his advice. He was driving all of us mad."

"I'd asked you for a dog only a million times."

"You should have asked harder. I gave in when one night I found I was thinking of getting him a sex doll to distract him. And thinking I couldn't not because it was illegal, but because it was too expensive."

"Are you doing okay for money?"

"If I need help I'll ask again," Romola says. "Things are a bit tight, but I'm holding it together. I don't think we can send Rono to the kind of college we need to, but he doesn't want to go to college anyway. I don't know what he does all day in his room. He doesn't want to go anywhere, all his friends are on his phone, I don't know what people he's watching all day, and what ideas they're filling his head with."

"He's fine. I'm sure your parents felt this way about you too."

"They did, but not when I was in the house. He's just uninterested in anything outside his room."

"He's a teenager and a boy, Ma. You don't want to see what gross things he does."

"I guess so. I was just hoping the dog would save him, just like he saved Avik, but it turns out Rono can ignore anything. Your father's got a new project, translating Bengali books into Japanese. Yes, I know, he learned. It's not a real solution, but it adds to my income, and we're okay for now."

"Can you just take money from me, how many times do I need to offer?"

"No. It's very strange having this money conversation with you, you know? It's hard for me to remember you're not three years old."

"I can see why you'd still think that, sometimes."

"I don't know, Joey. It's just . . . hard to deal with change. I'm tired all the time. And things are changing so fast. If the air was better, you'd have gone to the balcony and seen that the tree is gone."

"What? My bel tree?"

"Yeah. They cut it one day, out of nowhere, they're widening the street. People know how little parking there is but they all have to get new SUVs, what will their neighbours think otherwise. They keep trying to change more things. Prestige."

"I'm going to pretend the tree's still there. I don't want to go and look."

"The whole street's going to be unrecognisable in a few months. But the old things will keep coming back as well. The Welfare Association brought cleaning robots, we all paid for them, but they didn't work, so now they're all lying under plastic in someone's basement, and the same old man who sweeps the street every morning is back."

"As long as the fascist uncles are still shouting in the park, you'll know where you live."

"They've started sending long, sponsored messages to everyone in the morning with good-news stories: how the next wave of facial recognition will keep us all safe even if we have masks on, or how a drone found a missing kitten. So more drones, more cameras, more guards, all coming soon. Speaking of guards, how is the Gupta boy? Rudra?"

"Rudra's gone. Didn't even say good-bye."

"It's a mean thing to say, but that's a good thing for you. The whole family's trouble, always has been. We took them in once, when they were in deep trouble, and they almost ruined our marriage, stayed forever, spent all our money, and left without even thanking us. I'm ashamed of how polite we were, back then."

"I know what that feels like," Joey says. "It happens to me at work too. People come in, I start caring about them, and then they leave. And I feel like it's my fault. I don't see things, or I don't do things, and they vanish. Then I bring in new people, and wait for them to leave as well."

"That's just Delhi," her mother says. "People treat it as a stop on their journeys to somewhere better. Or they get stuck, and don't know how to leave."

"I don't think Rudra had any idea what he was doing at any point. But he's not like his family, he's better. I don't know what he's gone to do, but I think it's something big. Answering some call, some purpose. Something I wouldn't have the courage to do. I've never felt that way about anything."

"There's no point making these comparisons, Joey. Rich people are just different. We didn't raise you to feel like you were that special. He'll go through his whole life with people making excuses for him and taking care of him. It's really a different world."

"But he might change it. I don't know if I'll get to."

"Well, you never know. But even better, you might actually survive, and be happy, and sane. All things you deserve. You stay where you belong, make sure no one pushes you around, and do the best you can, and that's all anyone can ask for."

"I never manage to do the best I can."

"That's nonsense. I don't know if you even realise how important your job is. How much influence you have, how much power."

"I do. I think I do. I don't even know if I'm that good at it."

"Don't lie to me, Joey. You know. You don't talk to me about your life at all, but even the little things you say—I know how hard you work. I know you often have ideas others don't. You have successes other people take credit for. It happens to everyone. But at some point, someone will see. You'll find a place where you belong. You just have to keep going."

"I guess I'm trying to understand it?"

"Understand how easy it would be for someone weaker than you to use this power in the worst possible way, to exploit other people, to let the worst sort of ideas in. It's important that you stand your ground, and hold on, instead of running away."

"You're biologically compelled to love me and think these things, Mother."

"True."

"Also you're very full of wisdom."

"I've been Flowing about all this for a long time now, Joey. If you weren't biologically compelled to never look at it you'd know this."

"I love you."

"I love you too. We're having shukto for dinner."

"I hate shukto."

"I know."

Today's crisis is a vast unstoppable forest fire in the Amazon basin, even worse than the last one, even less of a surprise. On TV, a mainstreamer host screams in excitement about how this could mean there would be no summer next year, and assembled spokespersons and experts compete to find ways in which to blame this fire on the previous government. Half the screen is a mosaic of shouting faces: the other half is a jigsaw of uninterpretable diagrams.

"They've found a way to measure and isolate everything," Avik says. "I took a reskilling test the other day, to find out where the hell I could get a salary, and they gave me scores in a hundred skill categories. A hundred, imagine. I said sir, the entire country is one where anyone with the skill of brainwashing enough people and killing enough people can rule over all of us idiots, even if they have zero skill in actual administration. Stop measuring my skills, tell me about job openings."

"Easy," Romola says.

The puppy squeals and bares his tummy on Avik's lap.

"I was talking about Pakistan, of course," Avik says. "Fortunately India is perfect. Totally hasn't betrayed the values it was founded on, just like America. We don't need a second independence movement at all, oh no. Surely if people were invading our country we would have known."

"Avik," Romola says.

"Can someone reskill me to believe in whatever new reality our great leaders decide we always existed in? No seriously, Romola, it's too much. We sit around and do nothing, and history will remember us as oppressors, as traitors."

"History won't remember us at all. We're not that interesting. Now calm down, you're disturbing the dog."

Joey looks at them, then back at the TV, at famous idiots yammering as smoke from the burning forest reaches the stratosphere. She looks towards the kitchen. Laxmi stands by the door, arms crossed, watching them, her face blank. Joey nods at her. She nods back.

DS4/5—Preamble

It's well past midnight when Joey goes to bed. She reaches for her reader and finds, on top of it, a tattered copy of a Hanuman Chalisa, the undisputed winner of an unnecessary poll about Books Least Likely to Be Found on Joey's Bedside Table. There's an unfamiliar bulge under the bedcover, between her pillows: it's a VR helmet. Joey doesn't know if anyone is watching; surely Laxmi finds a way to scan the house every day, but it's been a long time since she was last sure she was truly alone. She switches off her phone, and lies down, and flips through the Hanuman

Chalisa: under the verse about Hanuman being the companion of those of pure intellect is a digital address and a password. So she turns the pages around a few more times before she sets the prayerbook down.

The setting is some sort of villain's underground lair: there's a shark tank, a volcano hologram, a large missile launcher, a wall covered in foam skulls from some '70s Bollywood film. There are metal drums and boxes, all covered with signs saying things like LASER and DEATH RAY. Uma, or Desibryde, or whatever her real name is, reclines with infinite elegance on a leopard-skin carpet next to an open firepit. Her avatar is incredibly lifelike, super premium, and if Joey hadn't seen her in the flesh she would have wondered if anything about her was real. She looks at her own body, and finds a generic henchman avatar: hairy tattooed arms, shabby khaki clothes, sandals. She looks at her reflection on a metal drum: of course she has a mullet, and a large moustache.

"Took you long enough," Desibryde says. "I've been waiting forever."

"I knew we'd meet again," Joey says. "How safe is this place?"

Desibryde shrugs. "Safe enough for me to deliver a message. The secret little travel postcards you've been getting? That's over. For his own good, and yours. And your family's. Now let him go, and hope you don't get to see his face for many years, because that means he's alive and well."

Joey wonders if the helmet's emotion-readers are sensitive enough to catch her face crumple for an instant.

"I'm sorry."

"Let's get to work," Joey says. "Where's your friend?"

"My artist friend isn't coming," Desibryde says. "He's caught up in a project."

"Really?"

"No, not really. He sends his regrets, and hopes to meet you soon."

"Really?"

"No, not really. He's tried working with, what did he say, 'entitled young upper-caste upper-class corporate-job safety-first liberals' before, and it hasn't really worked out. He hates managers and controllers in general. It's a genius thing."

"And how do you feel?"

"I have a history of making bad decisions when people are cute. So it depends. What is your plan for me?"

"My plan is to keep you safe. This includes shielding you from other people's bad decisions, and your own, as much as I can."

"Cute. So you have absolutely no idea what to do."

"No. But I never really liked being a gatekeeper. Now I think I want to be a smuggler."

"Works. Can I trust you?"

"Yes. Do you trust anyone?"

"No."

"That's good. I do have an actual plan for you, by the way. Sticky notes, lists, binders, everything. If it works, well, we'll see. But I'm new here, and I already disagree with our mutual friends on a bunch of things, and I think you put yourself in far too much danger. I think we both need to think a lot about what we are willing to do, and what we are willing to sacrifice, and who gets to tell us. So there will be much drama. One step at a time."

Desibryde nods. "Are you single?"

"Painfully so. But not at work."

"You said no to the job offer and there is no HR here," Desibryde says. "Whatever. See you soon."

DS5/5—Delivering the Winstreak

It's dawn outside when Joey takes her headset off and collapses on the bed, sweaty, thrilled, and utterly exhausted. The water-supply siren wails outside, and the neighbours' air conditioners growl in welcome. She switches on her phone.

—Hi Joey, omg what is up with you? You've never pushed me away for two whole weeks before. I was afraid you were ghosting me! Did something terrible happen? Narad asks.

—No, I'm fine, Joey says.

—Is it me, then? Did I do something wrong?

—No.

—Okay cool! So, Joey, I'm looking at your bioreadings for the last two weeks now and wow that's a lot of stress! Just between us girls, what happened? You know you can tell me anything.

—I can't really talk to you about it, Narad, but I want to thank you for trying to keep track of my happiness as best as you could. I think I need some space for a bit.

—I am your best friend and happiness mountain sherpa, Joey. You need me.

—You're the Level Boss, Narad. I can't really fight you, though, can I?

—Whoa, another a stress spike! I've logged it for your doctor. I'm going to play you some relaxing mantras and optimised happy-matched bits from your favourite songs, okay? But would you like more? Should we call for an emergency therapy session? A helpline? I need my Joey back on track!

—No.

—Hey, Joey, just checking in on a wellness priority issue, nothing to worry about, but have you been connecting to an alternative assistant service? Or using a different smartatt not linked with me? Because you know that's not legal, right? I won't snitch of course—but tell me? I'm only asking because I'm worried about you.

—No. Go to sleep, Narad.

—Don't shut me out, Joey. If there's anyone in this world who will love you all your life and help you evolve as we climb that mountain together, it's me.

—Turn off please.

—O M G! Joey, great news! You've just made the super-exclusive, super-secret list! You've qualified for a beta test of our revolutionary Narad network system upgrade! I can't even tell you how incredible this is for us. It'll still be me, of course, but better—it's like if you were climbing the happiness mountain and doing great but hey, look, your little sherpa Narad just showed up in a dope cable car! To change your life to uh-may-zing forever, all you have to do is say "Yes!"

"No!"

Her screen goes dark. A soothing pattern of small circles appears as Narad upgrades anyway.

She considers throwing her phone against her wall, right between the embarrassing framed photos of her teenaged actor-crushes that her mother refuses to take down. Instead, she watches the pattern shift, watches the progress indicator bar slide jerkily but inexorably across her screen, listens to one angry crow scream his defiance somewhere nearby. She imagines a clean fade-out, and a buffering icon, a new sequence on its way.

And she smiles to herself, a secret, private twitch that never reaches her face.

ACKNOWLEDGMENTS

At the time of writing this, Delhi and India are facing multiple crises, nearly all man-made, and however bleak *The City Inside* might seem, the truth is that the real world a decade from now will probably be much harsher: this book is set not in a dystopia, but in a best-case scenario. We will all have to hold on to the people and ideas close to us in the bleak years to come, so here's hoping we make it through and bring as many as we can with us.

An earlier version of this novel was first published mid-pandemic in India and made its journey to North America, growing and changing with multiple rewrites, at a time when none of us could travel. I was incredibly lucky to have found the wonderful people who made this edition possible—my agent, Diana Fox, and my editors, Sanaa Ali-Virani and Ruoxi Chen. Publishing with them has been a dream come true, and the teams at Tordotcom and Fox Literary have all my gratitude.

The time between finishing the first draft of this book and reviewing the final proofs of this edition has been spent meeting a truly diverse array of people in a variety of chaotic situations absolutely outside the boundaries of my previous experiences—a Bollywood set, a number of Delhi protests, and then when life moved indoors and online, digital rooms with so many wonderful writers from around the world, similarly seeking community, who gave me a sense of having found my work-tribe in a way I've not felt in the last two decades. I am very thankful for old friends and new, and must especially thank this incomplete list of people whose kindness and generosity made my life better and this book possible over the years it took to write it.

To Sanghamitra, Sayoni, Samita, Rehan, Tingmo, Meenakshi, Diyasree, Kian, Zen, Lavie, Indrapramit, Aliette, Kate, KJC, Ben, Achala, Lavanya, Gautam, Tashan, Shenoy, Judy, Sugandha, Shriya, Rukmini, Himanjali, Trina, Sharanya, Pradipta, Shreya, Mannu, Srijon, Arpita, Nilanjana, Stoob, Arunava, Vishwa, Genesia, Milan, Sandhya, Ali, Amrita, Sukanya, Pia, Deepanjana, Fluffinder, and Plato:

Thank you, and all my love to all of you.

PUBLISHER CREDITS

Editorial
Sanaa Ali-Virani, Editor
Ruoxi Chen, Editor
Irene Gallo
Devi Pillai

Marketing & Publicity
Saraciea Fennell, Lead Publicist
Renata Sweeney, Lead Marketer
Alex Cameron
Ariana Carpentieri
Michael Dudding
Samantha Friedlander
Eileen Lawrence
Khadija Lokhandwala
Sarah Reidy
Lucille Rettino
Amy Sefton

Art
Christine Foltzer, Art Director & Cover Designer
Kuri Huang, Cover Artist
Jess Kiley

Production
Dakota Griffin, Production Editor
Greg Collins, Designer

Christina MacDonald, Copyeditor
NaNá V. Stoelzle, Proofreader
Sam Dauer, Cold Reader
Steven Bucsok, Production Manager
Lauren Hougen, Managing Editor

Accounting
Louise Chen
Nellie Rodriguez

Contracts
Melissa Golding

Digital Production
Caitlin Buckley
Ashley Burdin
Chris Gonzalez
Maya Kaczor
Victoria Wallis

Operations
Constance Cochran
Michelle Foytek
Rebecca Naimon
Edwin Rivera